C000132458

THOSE YOU TRUST

BERNIE STEADMAN

BLOODHOUND
— BOOKS —

Copyright © 2020 Bernie Steadman
The right of Bernie Steadman to be identified as the Author of the Work has
been asserted by her in accordance to the Copyright, Designs and Patents Act
1988.
First published in 2020 by Bloodhound Books
Apart from any use permitted under UK copyright law, this publication may
only be reproduced, stored, or transmitted, in any form, or by any means, with
prior permission in writing of the publisher or, in the case of reprographic
production, in accordance with the terms of licences issued by the Copyright
Licensing Agency.
All characters in this publication are fictitious and any resemblance to real
persons, living or dead, is purely coincidental.
www.bloodhoundbooks.com

Print ISBN 978-1-913942-09-0

ALSO BY BERNIE STEADMAN

PROLOGUE

HOW IT BEGAN...

However much we think our lives are under control, planned out and set on a certain course, sometimes life offers us a choice. The road ahead forks unexpectedly and we get to choose which way we will go. Take one path and all will stay the same. Take the other, and our lives will change forever. I took the other.

A letter was the catalyst. I was eating breakfast in my cavernous kitchen at the start of another ordinary working day. It was early, and I could hear Will getting ready upstairs so I opened the letter quickly and skimmed the contents. Postmarked Crete, it was short and to the point. I had inherited a house and a sum of money from my deceased grandmother, Nyssa Georgiou. It was in the seaside town of Kissamos in Crete. The keys and the cash would be available to me as soon as I was able to verify my identity, or the legacy could be sold and the profits transferred to a bank if I preferred.

I read it twice more. I'd inherited a house from a grandmother who I thought was called Cybele, but who was called Nyssa. I hadn't been to Crete in almost thirty years despite being the only child of Greek immigrants, and yet she had left me her house. Surprised doesn't cover it. My heart did a funny little flip and just for a second, I allowed myself to think of sunshine, sea, sand, food, escape. For some reason I wasn't able to articulate at that instant, I hid the letter in my bag, washed my plate and mug, dried them, put them away and cleaned down the worktop. It was better to leave it like that than face disapproval so early in the morning.

Will thundered down the stairs and stood impatiently at the kitchen door. He was immaculate in a charcoal-grey suit and open-necked white shirt. 'Ready at last?' he asked, his eyes running over my hair and choice of clothes. No comment was good. He could never understand my need to eat in the mornings though. I think he saw it as a weakness, a digestive slacking. I knew that if I didn't eat I'd have a pounding headache by ten o'clock so I usually got up before him and had eggs and spinach or something similar with no carbs in it, naturally.

We drove into Alderley Edge towards our smart new office. Hunter Design was picked out in burnished steel on the polished concrete wall. If Will noticed I was quiet he didn't say anything. It was then that I realised I was quiet nearly all the time these days. I glanced across at him and saw a stranger, a man driven by work and success. Not my Will anymore. I wasn't his Anna anymore either. What on earth had I been doing for the last ten years? Living a life I hated. I clutched my bag close to my chest, like it was something precious. It was.

Hunter Design consisted of Will, the architect, and me, the interior designer. We also had several staff members who managed everything else. It was a tight little business, well-respected for quality and we had begun to attract major design projects in Manchester and as far away as London. Hunter Design was going places. It was what Will had always wanted.

That morning Will had a meeting and I had a pile of paperwork to sign off, so I shut the door and got straight onto Google Maps where I scanned the town of Kissamos, looking for the house and dredging up ancient childhood memories of walking up from the beach, along a narrow road to a pair of old houses. I was delighted to find it. It was a semi-detached house, built prewar, I guessed. It had a tiny front garden with a tatty old bench under the window, and a larger back garden enclosed by a stone wall, behind which a lane ran parallel to the road into town. There wasn't much else to see, but I wasted another half hour prowling the streets and alleyways, zooming along the beaches, trying to remember the places I had visited when I was a child. I'd spent several holidays on the island with my mother visiting her relatives and enjoying the sun and sand and sea. Dad never came, as he said someone always had to mind the restaurant, and he never talked about Crete, or his family. Neither did Mum, well, not about his family. Then the holidays had suddenly stopped, and I'd never been back.

I hovered the mouse over the house roof. It was this little house we had stayed in, though, on my holidays. I remembered it well, even if I had no recollection of my grandmother's face. And no photos, of course, because of Dad's refusal to discuss or be reminded of his past. He and Mum ran a Greek restaurant in South Manchester, and had done for thirty years. They worked hard and had bought it as soon as they were able to. It was their whole life, and I didn't think Dad had ever forgiven me for not making it mine. Well, I thought, excitement and hope welling up in me, I might just be able to make somewhere else mine. Properly mine. Hope bubbled so close to the surface. I closed the site down, erased the search from the computer, and wrote back to the solicitor in Kissamos accepting the house.

~

And that was the start of the end. The end of my marriage, the start of divorce proceedings. The end of my involvement in Hunter Design, the start of me finding my own clients. The end of living in that awful, empty designer house, the start of me growing my hair and wearing red. It was a hard, painfully fought two years, especially the bit where I had to move back in with my parents because Will had cancelled all my access to our money.

There was nobody except my parents that I even wanted to say goodbye to. What did that say about my fabulous life? To say I had hurt Will would be fair, but what I had really hurt was his sense of himself as a family man, a man with a wife. He had never played the role well, but he liked the look of normality, and I'd presumed to take it away from him. He was in disbelief for the first four months, hassled me for the next four and fought me for every penny of the business until we finally reached a settlement that would give me enough money to support myself until I sorted out what I wanted to do with my freedom. By the time I held the decree nisi in my hand, I knew exactly what I wanted to do. The money would pay to make the little house in Crete my home, and give me time to make a new life.

And after all that pain and upset, there I was. In Crete. In Crete at the beginning of March though. Hold any ideas of sun-drenched beaches. I couldn't wait any longer to get away from my parents, once all the court business was over, and I wanted to have my own little house sorted out and finished before summer came. Why have work done when it was hot if I could get it done early in the year? And there was nothing to hold me back, was there?

Stepping out of the taxi in front of my new home, I stood and breathed in the cool air of Crete. Early flowers, orange blossom, I think, and the smell of the sea which was only a few hundred metres away, welcomed me. I stared at the house that I'd devoured online, my heart tapping out a staccato rhythm. The taxi driver hauled both large suitcases from the boot and disappeared in a squeal of tyres. I was here. *O Lefkos Oikos*, The White House, stood at the foot of the White Mountains and they stood quietly behind the town, like the ridged spine of an enormous creature.

A woman waited in the doorway, smiling. She had come from the solicitor's office and spoke good English apparently, which would help as my Greek was unpractised and slow. 'Welcome to Kissamos,' she said and handed me a bunch of keys. 'This is your house. Please come to the office tomorrow and we will give you the papers that you need.' She gave a shy smile. 'I have arranged for the water and electricity to be switched on, and the telephone will work, I think, as the engineer fitted the internet connection yesterday.'

'That's wonderful, thank you,' I said. She really had saved me lots of work. The solicitor had been so helpful, too. It was a good sign, I thought, that this was where I was meant to be.

'It is dusty inside. You will have to work hard to clean it, but it will be a lovely home. Good luck!' And with that, she headed off in the direction of town. Leaving me standing in front of my house. I felt properly alone for the first time in my life.

I left the cases on the doorstep and went inside. The back door was wide open, allowing a breeze to stir the dust. Everywhere I looked was evidence of the grandmother I couldn't remember. Traditional pottery covered the old dresser, photographs of people I didn't recognise hung from the walls.

Every chair had a lace cover over it. I picked one up. Hand-sewn lace. The old fireplace still had ashes in the grate. It smelt musty as, I supposed, it would after two years unoccupied.

The kitchen had a well-used range cooker, a battered table and chairs, an old pot sink and several cupboards piled full of china. Through the kitchen door I could see the potential for a garden between the weeds and the rubbish piled up. Somebody had been in after my grandmother had died and emptied the fridge and food cupboard, but there was a lot of her personality still there, waiting. I hoped she was pleased that I was here.

I climbed the narrow stairs and found two bedrooms and a bathroom. The bedding was still on the main bed, and it gave me a little shiver that it hadn't been touched since my grandmother had died in it. I couldn't sleep in that room, not until I'd given everything a good spring clean. The back room was better as a bare mattress lay on an old metal frame, and it had been where Mum and I had slept when I was a child. I could manage that. I just had to do one day at a time, of course. I had the rest of my life to get it straight.

I pulled my suitcases over the threshold, opened them on the living room floor, took out the bedding I had brought with me, and made up a bed. I would use grandmother's beautiful woollen blankets once I'd aired them. I ventured outside and hung the blankets on the old line, then into the kitchen and rattled around, finding a pan with a lip, cups and plates. I turned on the water, and ran it for a while to clear the pipes, then put the pan on to heat a little water for tea. The second suitcase was full of essentials, including tea bags and an electric kettle.

I sat on a kitchen chair and surveyed my little kingdom. It was charming. Filthy and in need of hard work, but charming. There was a lot to do just to make it habitable, and I was on my own, with rusty Greek and not knowing a soul. I battled down sudden feelings of panic. What the hell was I doing? Really? Running away. I had run away. Then I gave myself a good talking to. This was the start of my adventure. I had to make it work, or go home like a fool.

I got to work.

1

I worked on the house flat out for two weeks; emptying, airing, repainting, and spending a small fortune on things I needed, like new mattresses and a decent fridge and hob. I loved doing it and collapsed exhausted into bed each night. I'd found a couple of local builders, too, which helped hugely.

Then I realised that apart from workmen, shopkeepers and the local taverna owner, I hadn't spoken to many people at all. My circle was very small; too small. I'd been a little nervous speaking Greek to native speakers when I'd first arrived on the island and knew my Greek needed improvement, and that something had to be done. Then I met Cathy Sinclair in the taverna, and my life changed.

The expat society, run by Cathy, a Scottish woman, was offering Greek conversation classes on a Thursday, in a room in the town hall. On the first day of the course, only four weeks ago, I'd arrived early. Half a dozen chairs sat in a circle in the middle of a large space, so I'd loitered at the door, pretending to study my phone. I'd picked up a working knowledge of the language from my parents who still spoke Greek at home, but they had been keen for me to be a good English girl, and I grew rusty as I got older, especially after I left home and didn't need Greek anymore. Now, I needed to be able to talk to the builders, the plumber, the bank, and the annoying man at the town hall who hadn't yet processed my application for a work permit. I thought Greek conversation might loosen me up a little and broaden my vocabulary.

Cathy had trotted in a few minutes later. 'Ah, Anna, isn't it? Welcome, do come in and sit down.' She was a tiny woman with a refined Edinburgh accent and a head of short-cropped grey hair. She was wrapped up well in a wool poncho and jeans. I put her in her sixties, but she was hard to place. Some people just stop dyeing their hair early.

'Cold today, isn't it? Have you been here long?' she asked.

Cold? I'd say eighteen degrees at the beginning of April was miraculous. I dropped onto a hard chair. 'Not long, only a few weeks in fact. I've been busy doing up my grandmother's house. She left it to me. It's a lot of work, and I realised I needed to speak to some humans rather than just talking to the wall. And I must improve my Greek, so I came along.'

She'd smiled at me, encouragingly. Ex-teacher, definitely. 'So sorry to hear of your loss,' she said. 'Were you close to your maternal grandmother?'

'No. I don't recall ever meeting her. The legacy came as a surprise, but it came at exactly the right time.' I hadn't wanted to say more, and was saved by the inrush of four other people. There were two teenagers, Syrian refugees I soon discovered, who had been offered asylum, and two men. One who looked Greek, like me, and one who looked the opposite.

'Leo Arakis, pleased to meet you,' said the Greek-looking one. He had a warm, firm handshake, a very white grin and a strong American accent. He wore chinos and a Ralph Lauren polo shirt, which looked a lot like he was trying too hard. A businessman working over here? The leisurewear look didn't fit him as comfortably as a suit would. He gave me a good looking over, and I looked back; he was a very attractive man.

The other guy, Alex, was Swedish, and the antithesis of Leo. Also tall, but with a long, lean body and the weathered brown skin of someone who worked outside. He had the most wonderful pale-blue eyes and strong, workman's hands. Sailor?

I'd looked around while we waited for the teacher and listened to Cathy grilling the other newcomers. I'd wondered what they were all thinking about me. Probably nothing. I can't stop myself from trying to work out who people are and what they might do before they even speak. It's my favourite game and used to drive my ex-husband crazy. I like to observe people; it's what makes me good at my job. If I'm designing the interiors of their house, I can tell a huge amount from the clothes they wear, the way they talk and their aspirations.

Finally, in came our teacher, Cassia Papadikis, a young, pale Greek woman with a different accent from the islanders. Athens-born I guessed. She took over and we began.

An hour and a half later, I was hot, sweaty and way out of my comfort zone. Cassia had made us tell each other our backgrounds, and I'd been able to explain that I was a designer, but I'd had to keep asking for help with words such as architecture (architektoniki) and interior design (esoteriki diakosmisi). I'd scribbled notes like a madwoman, and was delighted when we finished and the American, Leo, had suggested we walk down the road to the beach for an early evening drink before we went home.

The two Syrian boys had disappeared quickly. As I had suspected, they were attending lessons because they had to, although one of them had shown a good grasp of the language.

The rest of us had strolled down to the promenade and I'd taken them to Maria's Taverna. I knew very few people on the island as yet, and Maria, if not her sullen husband, Spiros, had become a friend.

We'd sat outside to watch the sky slowly deepening and the sea, so dark it was navy blue, shimmering under a low rising moon. Maria had bustled out to take our order. She knew Cathy and me, of course. It was at the taverna that I'd met Cathy and she told me about the classes. 'Anna, Cathy, it is so good to see you. Welcome to my taverna.' She'd grinned at the two men accompanying us and gave me a wink. She knew I hadn't spoken to a man other than for business reasons for weeks, and I knew she wouldn't give me a break from now on.

'Kalispera, Maria,' said Leo, and he'd ordered local wine and some small plates of feta, stuffed vine leaves and olives for all of us. Mr 'I'm in charge'. I wondered if that would annoy Alex. But he was fine about it, in fact he gave me a little smile as Leo ordered. I liked that he didn't feel threatened by the American's brashness.

'So, Anna,' Leo had said, pouring me a glass of red wine and blocking out the others, 'what's your story?'

I hadn't wanted to say that I had just escaped from a messy divorce to a difficult man, so I left that bit out and talked about my business.

I didn't get much chance to talk to Cathy or Alex for the next hour as Leo took centre stage that first night, charming us with tales of his life in America and his plans for a restaurant and casino business in Crete. He patted the top pocket of his shirt whenever somebody asked him about permissions and licences. Was he indicating that he had cash to bribe the officials? Blimey. I didn't much fancy his chances if that was the plan.

I drank wine and nibbled cheese and felt more at home than

I had since I arrived. At last I'd started to meet people and make friends.

I had no idea then how much that little group of people would change my life over the next few weeks.

Nikos Kokorakis stirred sugar into his breakfast coffee and gazed out across the plain towards the sea. Behind him, he could hear Delphine moving around in the bedroom, getting ready to go out again, no doubt. The balcony was cool in the early morning sun, and he liked it best this way, before the burning heat of summer came. He tapped the spoon against his teeth. The arrival of this English girl, Anna Georgiou, what did it mean? How could his mother have left her house to a stranger? It was upsetting, and took him straight back to the day forty years ago, when his family had split forever. Could Anna Georgiou be a Kokorakis? Theo's daughter, perhaps? He'd gone to England. All his brother would have to have done was to change his name, and who could blame him for that? Theo's wife was related to the old woman who lived next door to his mother. Had his mother kept such a secret from him? Had she been seeing Galena and Theo all along, and did they have a child that he knew nothing about?

Delphine came out and placed a cool hand on his shoulder. 'It's too chilly out here for me, I don't know how you stand it. I'm meeting a friend for coffee and going shopping in Chania. The spring collections will be in all the shops.' He didn't respond. She kissed the top of his greying head, sighed, and flopped down into the chair next to his. 'What? What is it? You've been moping around for days.'

He raised bloodshot eyes, the legacy of too many late nights and too much work, and gave her a sad smile. 'It's nothing, nothing,' he said.

She growled at him, 'Just tell me. How bad can it be? Have you shot someone?'

He gave another little smile. 'I cannot...'

'For goodness' sake, Niko, you are like a bear with a headache. It's impossible for me, and for the staff. We can't say anything right anymore. Please, just tell me. It will be okay, I promise. Share the burden. I am your wife after all.'

Kokorakis let out a huge sigh. 'I will tell you, but you won't want to hear it. I will understand if...' He stopped and cleared his throat.

Delphine sat up straighter in her chair. 'I'm listening.'

'I have never told you about my brothers, Delphie.' He took her hand and rubbed the palm with his thumb. 'I will tell you now, if you will listen. It is time.'

Delphine's eyes widened. 'You have brothers? But...'

'Just listen. We were three sons of Andreas, not one, as I have always pretended. But my father, always a cold man as you know, wanted no trouble when it came time to take over the family business. So...' He hesitated, face turned away.

'It's okay, Niko, you need to tell me,' said his wife. 'It will be good to get this out at last. It's been burning you up.'

He rubbed his hand across his eyes. 'It's hard to tell it though. I'm ashamed.' He huffed out a sigh. 'I was twenty-one, Theo was eighteen and Stephanos only sixteen. Father stood us in front of the old oak table and said I was to inherit everything, and the other two had to leave the island and go abroad, never to return, on pain of death for them and their families.'

Delphine gasped. 'He couldn't do that, surely?'

'He could. You could make that threat after the war, when everybody owned guns. It is traditional for the eldest son to inherit.' He shrugged. 'Delphie, there are so many bodies buried in these mountains that nobody has ever found, and anyway, we believed his threat. We were terrified of him. He drank and was vicious to our mother and hard on us. There was little love in the family from him, it was our mother who kept us together. He gave my brothers money to set up their new lives abroad and three days to get out.' He looked up at his wife. 'He took their family, their home, their friends and their mother away from them forever. It was so terrible, I have never been able to talk about it until now.' He wiped his eyes. 'Mother sat behind father, crying out "You're breaking my heart, Andreas, breaking my heart" but he would not relent. To him it made perfect sense. There would be no messy family stuff to interrupt business. And the worst thing is, Delphie, I stood with that evil old brute, and let him destroy my family. That is the kind of man I am. It's why I'm ashamed.'

Delphine clasped a hand across her mouth and stared at her husband.

Into the silence that followed, Nikos wiped his eyes with one meaty fist. 'They cried, they yelled, but it made no difference. Theo went to England, Stephie to America. I have never heard from them since. My mother left that night, too, and went to live in the little house in the village next to her friend. She never spoke to my father or me again.'

Delphine gripped her hands in her lap. 'Niko, that's awful, to have never heard from your brothers again. And your poor, poor mother. No wonder she left her home. I could never blame her for leaving your father, odious man, but I never knew about the rift in the family...' Tentatively, she placed her hand on his knee and squeezed. 'I'm glad you told me. It's okay.'

'It's not okay, Delphie.' He raised his voice, anguish spilling over into rushed words. 'I should have said no to him. All three of us could have refused to do what he said and fought him. *We* could have killed *him* and buried him in the mountains. Or we could all have walked away, and left him with nobody.' He gulped down air. 'But I didn't. I'm weak, and you know I am. We were so scared of him.'

He wiped his eyes again and calmed himself with deep breaths. 'Don't do that shushing thing with your hands. Yes, I run a profitable business, and I have respect, but did I ever contact my brothers and make amends, invite them back to share in all this? No, I let it be. I got rich.' Tears rolled down his face, unchecked this time. 'And now, what does it mean that the girl is here? What does it mean, Delphie? Can I ask for forgiveness now?'

Delphine found tissues in her pocket and passed them to her husband, but she didn't speak. Instead, she looked out over the tops of the houses towards the sea, dark and endless blue.

'See, you can't even look at me, and why would you? I am cursed. You know that is true. That is why we could not have children of our own.' He looked at her again. 'It was never you, my darling girl, even though I pretended it was. It made me feel better to blame you. God cursed me for my cowardice, and soon enough he will take all this away from me, as I have no family to leave it to. Unless...'

Delphine latched onto the tiny thread of hope. 'Unless you can make the girl your heir? If she is your niece, you mean.' She pursed her lips. 'Let me find out a little more about her.' Slowly, she rose and turned away. 'I need to think about what you have said. I'll be back later.' She straightened her shoulders and tugged down the hem of her dress. 'You should clean yourself up, Niko, you have a meeting at noon.'

∿

Delphine cancelled coffee with her friend, drove the car down to the seafront and sat outside Maria's Taverna with the engine running. The spring rain pelted down. Nikos might have admitted his weakness to her, but to him, face was everything. There was no way he could be seen to show weakness in front of the people he employed. She'd known in her heart for years that he was infertile, not her, and still she'd stayed until it was too late. She'd been seduced by the life of a rich man's wife, and had to pay the price. Everything had a price.

Maybe, if this girl was his niece, then all the worry about succession would be answered, and she might get back a little of the Nikos she used to know. Maybe.

She peered into the taverna, trying to see through the steamed-up windows. She had asked Spiros to text her next time the English girl went in and he had, a few minutes before. Unfortunately, she couldn't see much. She growled in frustration. Well, she could either go in, or go away. If she went in it would cause huge amounts of gossip and chat – why would Delphine Kokorakis be in a cheap little taverna down at the beach? She couldn't exactly travel anonymously here; everyone knew who she was.

No, she thought, accelerating away, she needed to find a way to bump into Anna Georgiou. She had assumed the girl was related to Nikos' mother's side of the family because of the family name, but she could well be Theo's daughter. There was no law to say he couldn't change his name. Why would he want to keep it? His mother hadn't. And that could mean that old

Nyssa had kept in touch with her sons after all. Or at least with one of them. Interesting.

Delphine was not a woman given to flights of fancy, but a small flutter in the pit of her stomach told her that this arrival could be something good. If Nikos faced up to his fears and met with his brothers, that would surely end a long and bitter separation, and this girl could be the catalyst for that change. In the meantime, she would enjoy having a husband who had lost his usual swagger and was being honest for the first time in thirty years. There may be other children too, perhaps born to the other brother, who could also inherit all that Nikos had worked for.

The priest was next on her list for a visit; he was a Georgiou. She turned towards the centre of the town, and the church at its heart.

Father Georgiou looked up in amazement as Delphine Kokorakis slipped into his small office behind the church and closed the door behind her. He pushed back his chair and stood, shaking the table and rocking the pile of papers he'd been studying. 'Please, Mrs Kokorakis, take a seat. I never expected you to come to me; you know I will always come out to the house if you have a problem...'

Delphine perched on a wooden chair that creaked even under her tiny weight. She stayed on the edge; ready to leap to her feet should it prove unsafe. 'I have a question for you, Father,' she said. 'I wondered if you have had the time to speak to the young woman who has set up home in the house of my husband's mother?'

Georgiou's face adopted a familiar puzzled frown and Delphine sighed. 'Do you even know who I'm talking about?' she asked.

'Of course, but she is English, and not a member of the church, so why would I go to see her?'

'Because she is a Georgiou, Father. She's Greek. She could be related to you, couldn't she?'

Georgiou pulled at his beard. 'I see what you mean. But can I ask why she is interesting you?'

'Oh, it's nothing. I wondered if she had family on the island, that is all. Do let me know if you go and see her, won't you? I'd be keen to know if she has relatives here in Kissamos, and very grateful to the church.' She gave him a tight smile, and pulled a fifty-euro note from her purse. 'For the collection,' she murmured, dropping it onto the desk. 'I'll see myself out. Thank you, Father.'

Father Georgiou watched her slip out through the door and rubbed his beard. Of course he knew about Anna being on the island, but he wasn't at all sure he wanted to tell the Kokorakises anything about her. He shifted his bulk out from behind the desk, pocketed the note, grabbed his hat and walking stick and went to see his mother.

3

I stretched out on the sunlounger in my walled back garden and listened to birds finding a mate, and cars driving up the road, and the chatter of two women as they carried home their shopping, and relaxed. A few weeks into my new life, and I was working physically harder than I ever had, but in my head all was calm for the first time in ages. In fact, I didn't think I'd actually relaxed properly for years. My legs poked out from under my cropped jeans and, although I do take a tan really well, at this time of the year they were that peculiar shade of pale blue that afflicts most Brits in winter. Ah well, that would soon be remedied when the sun did its job.

I scraped paint out from the underside of my fingernails with the tip of a screwdriver. The house was coming along beautifully. I'd kept the old dresser and highly-carved cupboard with all of Grandmother's china and precious things in, and the scrubbed pine kitchen table scratched with many years' worth of knife marks, but much of the other stuff, all her old bed linens and clothes had had to go. I'd put papers and other personal objects I'd found into an old wooden box that had always lived in the cupboard at the top of the stairs. I would go through it when I had time and find out more about my grandmother.

I stopped what I was doing and stared off towards the trees. Sometimes the smallest thing can take me back to my life in my designer house with Will. It was the screwdriver. In the ten years we were together, I never saw him use a tool. He paid for everything to be done. Manual work was beneath him, apparently. Now, I was relishing getting my hands extremely dirty in my own little house.

A loud banging on the front door brought me out of my reflections. I ran through the kitchen and living room to greet Mr Andreiou at the door.

'At last, I thought you weren't coming,' I said.

Mr Andreiou's bushy brows rose and fell, in an imitation of sadness. He reached out and clipped his apprentice behind the ear. 'Pah, late, always late. Sorry, Miss. We're here now, so...' He gestured towards the little staircase, and I stood back, swallowing my irritation. Getting a modern shower into the bathroom was my number one priority. It took forever to fill the ancient cast-iron bath, even though it was the most luxurious thing to sink into when a bath was needed. I led them upstairs, closed off the bedroom doors and stood back. The pair had sorted out the electrics downstairs, putting in a modern electric hob, washing machine and fridge. Their work was good. They were just late. Always.

Once the demolition was finally underway, I took a glance around my beautiful, plain-white living room, with its dark oak furniture, comfy sofas, throws and bright cushions. It was perfect. I knew I could be happy here. But not just yet, I thought, as the hammering began right above my head. Time for a walk and a visit to the taverna for lunch.

∾

Kissamos Bay is over in the western corner of Crete. It's a deep bay, with long arms on either side stretching out into the sea, protecting boats and sailors once they are inside its reach. At this time of the year, I had the beach of narrow, shingly sand almost to myself. I passed an elderly woman slapping a squid repeatedly onto a rock, rinsing it in seawater, then slapping it again until she deemed it tender enough to cook. She grinned at me toothlessly and waved as I shouted, 'Kalimera!'

Striding out, I spotted dark clouds moving in swiftly from the west over the White Mountains and remembered I didn't have a coat with me. I gauged the distance to the taverna, realised I wouldn't make it, and broke into a run anyway.

Drenched and shivering, I staggered up the steps, shoved open the taverna door and slammed it behind me. The place was heaving; every window was steamed up and there was nowhere to sit. Market day. Maria waved me over to the bar, where she shoved her husband off a stool and sat me down.

'Spiro, run upstairs and bring Anna the shawl on the back of the bedroom door.'

Spiros gave her a look meant to pierce steel, but did as he was told.

'Thanks, Spiros,' I said, then corrected myself, 'sorry, Spiro.' I was going to have to get to grips with using colloquial language properly, and leaving the 's' off men's names when talking to them was only the start of a minefield of difference.

Maria rubbed my cold arms with her warm hands. 'You need to be ready for rain in the spring, Anna!'

'I know. I used to live in Manchester – it rains all the time there. Should have known better.'

Minutes later, wrapped in Maria's wool shawl, hands warming around a mug of her mother's recipe mountain tea, I felt human again. 'Thank you so much, Maria, it's so cosy, and I love this tea.' I had come to enjoy the savoury flavour of sage and other herbs taken straight off the mountainside, dried and made into a herbal tea that was reputed to cure anything.

'Good. Drink. It will warm you up.' She gave me a sly look and hugged herself. 'Of course, what you really need to warm you up is one of those very handsome men you brought here...'

'Yeah, chance would be a fine thing,' I muttered, 'but, you know, I'm happy to be single right now, Maria. Escaping the last one was bad enough.'

Maria gave me a knowing smile and disappeared into the kitchen. I glanced round at the other people sheltering from the rain. There were many locals, all men, sitting and playing card games or dominoes, and a few early season tourists studying maps and eating pastries. In the corner was Cathy drinking coffee, buried in the local English language newspaper. I waved at her, but stayed where I was, drying out.

Through the window I could just make out a flashy red sports car, parked up but with the engine running, disgorging exhaust fumes into the wet air. It didn't stay long. Behind it rolled in a new-looking black SUV, and out of it climbed Leo Arakis, from my Greek class. Small world, I thought as he hustled through the door and shook his head to clear the rain off. Several of the older folk got up from their tables and shuffled past him, and he held the door open for them.

'Anna,' he said, spotting me, 'nice to see you again, and not in class, so we can talk in English!' He also waved at Cathy sitting in the corner. Turning back to face the bar, so that he came and stood next to me, I played with my almost empty mug of mountain tea.

'Can't say I'm into that local herbal stuff,' he said, dropping a large bag onto the floor between his feet and leaning on the counter. 'Do you actually like it?'

'I do, it's soothing.' I twirled the dregs around in the bottom of the mug. 'I was about to order some lunch,' I said. 'Would you like to join me?'

'Our first date,' he said, grinning at me. 'That would be great, I'm starving.'

I actually blushed as I led him to a vacant table. It was quite different meeting him here, rather than having a quick drink after class.

When Maria appeared with the menus, her eyes were huge, as was her grin. She put the menus in front of us, then looked more closely at Leo's face. 'Forgive me, Leo,' she said to him, 'but what is your family name? You remind me of someone here on the island. Do you have family here?'

Leo shrugged. 'I'm Leonidas Arakis, so I guess there must be relatives here somewhere on Crete. I'm planning on looking them up when I get a minute. Fava bean stew for me please,' he said.

'And for me, it's the best on the island,' I added.

Maria stood quietly for a moment and I could see her scrolling through her memory banks. 'Okay, maybe I don't know you then. But you do look familiar.'

Leo laughed loudly. 'I'm a dark-haired, dark-eyed man on an island full of them. I guess I look familiar to everyone.'

But I watched his eyes, and he knew exactly what she was getting at. It would be interesting if we both had family on the island. I'd been expecting mine to pop up as soon as I opened up the house, but so far, no luck. It was possible that my grand-mother didn't have anybody here on the island left alive, I suppose. And I would get little information from my parents, that was for sure.

Lunch took a while to arrive, so he had a coffee, which gave me time to quiz Leo about his restaurant-cum-casino plans. 'Have you found a site yet?' He'd been looking for weeks.

'I think so. I went to look at it first thing. It's on the far western end of the bay. An old run-down house on half an acre of land going right to the sea.' He reached into the holdall at his side and brought out a much-folded map of the area.

I love maps. There's something about the lines and the way they tell the story of the landscape that I find fascinating, and this was one of the whole of the western side of the island. I smoothed out the creases and waited while Leo weighted down the corners with the salt and pepper pots. His hands were square-palmed, and long-fingered. They didn't look anything like Will's pale, slender hands. The hands of an artist, Will would always tell me, with a self-conscious smirk that said, 'I think it's silly, of course, but what can you do?'

I dragged myself away from thinking about Will. I have a tendency to wallow, and there had been plenty of times recently where I'd wallowed way too much. Instead, I focused on Leo's finger tracing the road round the bay and ending on the far side.

'There's not much there,' he said, 'a few houses and the beach. It's the main route to the far west and down to Elafonisi and Paleochora, though, so I hope it gets lots of summer traffic.' He paused and finished his coffee while I studied the map, wondering why there were areas ringed in red that were nowhere near the sea. Other possible sites, I guessed.

'You know, I will need a designer for the casino and restaurant, if I ever get the permission to build,' Leo said. 'Do you have a portfolio I could look at sometime?'

Did I? Wow. 'I certainly do. Have a look on my website, and get back to me. I'd be delighted to help if I can.' That was a pleasant surprise. It would be my first job on the island if I got it. I jotted my website address onto the corner of the map for him.

'That's great, I'll let you know. I'm sure we can work together.' He grinned and went back to studying the map, tapping his fingers against his chin as he did so.

I saw that under that vast smile his confidence was all bluster. He was nervous about this venture, but trying to hide it. And so he should be nervous, had he any idea about how things work on these island communities? He wouldn't be able to just blather his way in and step on local toes and it would all be fine. I didn't envy him. 'It's a brave move, setting up over here. Did you have a restaurant in America?'

He turned caramel eyes towards me. 'I didn't own one, but I worked for my father after leaving college, and he has a chain of Greek restaurants along the East Coast.'

'God, it's such a small world! That's what my parents do in Manchester. Although they only have the one restaurant. Not an ambitious bone in his body, my dad. So, you decided to set up on your own over here, then? Back to the family roots.'

'I guess you could say that, in one way.'

I was wondering what exactly that meant when two shallow bowls of steaming fava bean stew arrived, accompanied by soft bread. Maria waited until the map had been cleared away and placed the bowls on the table. 'Enjoy,' she said, and winked at me, again.

It was, of course, hot and delicious, and I was pleased that Leo stopped talking and gave the food his full attention. It meant I could too. After years of constantly being told I was too fat, and counting every calorie, it was a delight to tuck in and enjoy good food without the nagging.

I wiped up the last of the stew with a crust of bread and grinned sideways at him. 'Said she could cook. Was I wrong?'

Leo patted his mouth and grinned back. 'Your assessment was spot on, Miss Georgiou. Coffee?'

Maria swooped in and collected the bowls. 'Two Greek coffees coming up,' she said. 'Everything okay with the food?'

I let Leo praise her extravagantly while she poured coffee. It gave me a moment to take stock. So far, over the past few weeks, Leo appeared to be a friendly man who had practically offered me a job. Could he be more? I didn't know. He didn't give a lot away about himself. I was terrified of getting involved with another man after Will, and Leo gave off the same superficially confident charm vibe. It was just his type I was attracted to, and look where that had got me. Divorce court and living back with my parents for months.

'Penny for them,' Leo said.

I hadn't realised that I'd been looking through the window onto a slowly brightening sky. I've been doing that a lot recently, drifting away into my own world. It used to be my self-defence, but now it was because I had the time to do it. 'Oh, nothing special, just dreaming.' I sipped the coffee. It was too strong and sweet for me, really, but it gave me a sudden pang for home and Mum and Dad and normality. 'Thinking about home.'

Leo gave a little chuckle. 'Well, you won't get me feeling homesick. This is where I want to be, doing what I want to do.'

'So you've left your past behind as well.'

'I guess. But I'm bringing everything I've learned with me, so it's all kind of coming with me, if you know what I mean.'

'Are you married, Leo? Kids?'

'Straight to the point, eh?' He lost the smile and began to tap at his chin with his fingers. 'Yes, Anna, I am married, but we haven't lived together for two years, and she is filing for divorce. I hope. I have two kids at high school, and I video message them every day. I have a clean driving licence and no known communicable diseases and I love my mother. Is that a satisfactory résumé for you?' He took a sip of coffee, jaw working.

I could feel the blush starting in my chest. Could have started in my toes. There you go, Georgiou, open your big mouth, put your foot in it, just like Will is always telling you. Better get out. 'Please,' I stammered, 'as you bought food for the language group again last week, let me pay for lunch. Then I have to go and check on my builders. They're demolishing my bathroom, and I'm hoping it's not the whole house.' Babbling? Oh, yes.

I pushed back my chair and fished around in my jeans pocket, finding twenty euros to pass to a surprised Maria, and her warm shawl went over the counter too. 'I really enjoyed lunch, Leo. Do let me know if you want me to go ahead with some designs for you, as soon as you have planning permission, of course.' I gave him a bright smile, waved at Maria and practically ran out of the bar.

4

I scurried off up the road, head down. What had happened there? One minute we were enjoying lunch, the next he goes all tight-lipped and moody on me. It was ridiculous but I felt upset. Like I'd ruined the start of what could have been a romance, or at least a friendship. And boy, did I need more friends. I hadn't been rude, had I? I replayed the scene, but I couldn't get to the bottom of why he would be so angry at a question about his home. Unless, of course, he was going through a divorce even worse than mine had been. For once, the mountains, usually solid and protective, loomed hard above me.

The sound of hammering echoing down the street cheered me up a bit. 'Ah well, at least I'm getting a shower,' I muttered. Who understands men, anyway? Not me. Ten years with a control freak had left me confused about practically everything to do with relationships.

I had a sudden revelation as I reached the house. During ten years with Will, the only men I ever spoke to alone were either clients or the husbands of friends. The more I thought on my marriage, the more disappointed I became with myself. How could I not see what was happening?

'Kalispera!'

I jumped. I didn't realise I'd been standing outside the house looking at the front door. Mrs Pantelides, the next-door neighbour, had returned from a visit to her daughter in Heraklion. We hadn't really talked much as she'd been gone for two weeks.

'Sorry,' I said in Greek. 'I was dreaming. Good evening to you.'

Mrs Pantelides said, surprising me, 'Do you need help? You were so far away,' in very good English.

'Sorry, I was thinking about something. My Greek is still a bit slow, I'm afraid.'

'Your Greek is good,' she said and smiled at me. She pointed at my front door. 'So much noise.'

'New bathroom,' I said, 'with a shower.'

'Ah.' She tapped the side of her nose. 'You make sure they charge you fair. I will come in when they have finished and check the work.' She gave me a look that went all the way up and down. 'I can see your grandmother, and perhaps, your grandfather. Around the eyes and the chin.'

'Did you know them, Mrs Pantelides?' I didn't remember her from my childhood visits, but she may have known them. I had some memories of the woman who lived next door, but nothing concrete like a name or a face. Kindness, I remembered. I felt a surge of excitement. Perhaps I could find out something about my family here on the island after all.

'I knew Nyssa and Andreas when they were young, many years ago.' Mrs Pantelides leaned hard against the low wall that fronted her house. 'Excuse me, I am very tired now. After the journey on the bus.' She chuckled and reverted to Greek. 'Ah, what it is to be an old woman.' She turned and struggled up the path to her door.

'Can we talk again?' I asked, desperate not to lose her before we'd had a chance to get to know each other.

She waved and closed the door behind her.

I sat on the little wall outside the front door and wondered exactly how old my neighbour was. Eighty if she was a day. My grandmother had been over ninety when she died. The only thing was, my grandmother and grandfather on Mum's side were called Alexandros and Cybele Georgiou. I knew so little about my father's parents, only that my grandmother, whose surname appeared to also be Georgiou, had left me the house. Why she had done that, I had no idea and nobody could tell me, especially not my parents. There was a mystery here I had to solve, not least the issue of whether my parents were both from a long line of people called the same name. Which, in a such a religious country, struck me as a bit peculiar.

I'd temporarily forgotten about the builders and indeed Leo the Oversensitive, and it was the sudden ceasing of noise that brought me back into the present. Cautiously, I opened the front door and almost cried. I did cry, a bit. There was dust and dirt everywhere. The air hung thick with it. 'Mr Andreiou! What's happened?'

A big head, mouth covered in a handkerchief, appeared at the top of the stairs.

'Ah, Miss,' he said. 'Plaster is very old. It all came off in one go. Very messy.' He spoke in pidgin, slow Greek, which suited me just fine.

'I know it's messy, I can see that.' I coughed and held my hand across my mouth. 'What are you doing about it?' I shouted from the doorway. My lovely house, it was filthy. I couldn't walk any further inside without protection – it was toxic.

'Not to worry. All the old plaster has gone now. Tonight, we replaster. Next week, when the plaster is dry, we do electrics for the shower and everything will be good, yes?' He rubbed his hand across his eyes, properly taking in the mess for the first time. 'I didn't know it would be so bad. Maybe you stay at hotel tonight?'

Vasilis, the assistant builder, bustled into the living room from the back of the house lugging a huge empty straw basket, which he carried up the narrow stairs on his head, banging into the wall as he did so and squeezing past his boss.

'Where has the old plaster gone, Mr Andreiou?' I asked, dreading the response.

'No worries, Miss. In the back garden, we will move it tomorrow also. Okay? Then we wait for plaster to dry, and we tile the wall, and put in shower. No worries. I will put some water on for you tonight. Okay?' He grinned at me.

Wasn't much I could do except agree, was there?

I closed the door behind me and sat back down on the wall outside. My laptop. My books. My beautiful old dresser with all my precious things on it. My drawings for the design job that I had almost finished for a UK client. Everything would have to come out, be cleaned down and put back again. It would set me back weeks. For a moment, I heard the voice of Will, calm and kind as he always was when he was directing my life. 'Think about what you're doing, Anna. You're not cut out for all this. You should let me handle it.' I bit down hard on my hand. No more of that. The one thing my marriage taught me more than anything else was helplessness. Of course I could manage, and I would. But I didn't know if that was actually true then.

Above my head, the sound of sweeping made me grateful that at least they had finished taking the plaster off. I hadn't given a thought to the state of the plaster when I commissioned the new bathroom. It was an old house and probably hadn't been touched since the original bathroom went in years ago. I should have known that. But there was no point sitting and berating myself. The builders were just getting on with it, so I would too.

Plucking up courage, I walked around to the back gate and surveyed the garden over the wall. The corner that I'd imagined would become a small vegetable patch was heaped with pinky-white lumps of plaster. A thin layer of dust sat all over the garden. A big tub of new plaster squatted in the middle of the path.

I tramped through it all and went into the kitchen, where every surface was also covered, apart from some cat-size footprints that followed a path across the top of the furniture to a small space behind the sofa. I sighed. She'd been trying to get in for days. 'Come out, puss,' I said, and the thinnest cat – a young, grey female tabby – slunk out from where she was hiding.

'What on earth are you doing in here?' I asked her, and picked her up. She started to purr immediately, and I realised she was just what I needed. Something warm and alive, and let's face it – grateful – to cuddle. 'I'm having a helluva day, puss,' I murmured into her fur, feeling some of the tension seeping away. She purred more and padded on my sleeve. She was very young. 'Shall I see what's in the fridge?' I gave her yogurt and the piece of leftover fried fish I had been planning on having for dinner. They were gone in seconds. She looked up at me, miaowed, and sauntered back out the door. Cat, one; Anna, nil.

I stood there feeling like there must be something I could do, but there was little point in hanging around. It was only just gone three so I expected the men to work for at least another few hours to get a coat of plaster on the walls. I rescued the laptop and filled a bag with essentials for a night away. At least I had closed the bedroom doors before they started work so those rooms were fine, and the bathroom had been emptied ready for the work to begin.

I rang the local hotel and booked in. It was the only place open so early in the year, and that was mainly for business people. I could have asked Maria if I could stay at the taverna, but I didn't want to answer her questions about Leo. I couldn't work out what went wrong myself, and I wasn't ready to share it with her anyway; she was way too interested in my lack of love life. I'd rather sort it out in my own head when I was settled into the hotel with a large gin and tonic and the promise of a good meal ahead.

Mr Andreiou agreed to lock the front and back doors when he left, so I lugged bag and laptop back down the road and along the deserted promenade to the other end of the main street, where there were lights on already in the hotel, and a couple of men were drinking at the bar. I put my stuff in the pleasant corner room they gave me, had a long hot shower and changed into my mustard cashmere jumper and black jeans. The nights were cold so early in the year, and the threat of rain hung in the air. I wrapped the beautiful hand-knitted woollen shawl I had found in grandmother's cupboard around my shoulders and took the laptop down to the bar, where the wifi connection was good. There was a free table in the window. I could watch the sunset and get on with some work.

I was feeling pretty low as I set out my laptop and folders, lower than I'd been since arriving in the town. I was trying so hard with my little house, and now it was in a terrible mess. The thing with Leo had upset me more than it should. Maybe I just wasn't cut out for this life, after all. Maybe Will... I pulled myself up short. I recognised that voice. That man in my ear again. Deep breaths the therapist had said; breathe him out and away. So I did the breathing, and I did feel calmer after a few minutes. I looked out at the darkening sky, and watched thunderclouds build to the north.

I do know that it's sometimes necessary for you to be taken completely out of your comfort zone to realise what a spoilt, privileged life you've led. And I understood that lesson all too clearly sitting on my own in a bar in a foreign country that I couldn't yet call my own. I was so used to having everything managed for me that I panicked at the slightest obstacle – it was only a bit of plaster dust, after all. It would clean up. I had to get a grip. After all, this was a real adventure I was on, and it was the rest of my life, happening now.

Cheered, I ordered a gin and tonic and dived into the final design changes to meet my latest client's brief. My restaurant design was well underway for a Scottish hotel and I'd really had fun with the tartan and leather brief – very gentleman's club. Funnily enough, I could manage all that stuff when it was for business; the delays, builders not turning up, clients changing their minds at the last minute. It was my private life I'd struggled with. Was still struggling with.

The waiter brought nuts and olives with the drink, and they were good. I nibbled and sipped and became so involved in the work I didn't see the black SUV draw up and a familiar figure get out. It was only when he stood at the bar and ordered a drink that I realised it was Leo. Of course, where else would he stay? With my new spirit of not being a wimp, I slammed the laptop lid down and stood up. I'd apologise for running off and being nosy and then it was up to him.

He turned as I approached him and gave a half-smile.

'I'm sorry about this afternoon,' I said. 'I didn't mean to be rude.'

Leo shrugged. 'It was nothing. I'm a little raw about my wife, is all. Can I get you a drink?' He crinkled his eyes at me.

I ordered another gin.

It seemed pointless to carry on trying to work, so I took it all back to the bedroom, checked myself out in the mirror and decided to see what the night might bring. But whatever happened, I wasn't going to let him mention his wife, and I wasn't going to talk about Will either.

The night brought far more than I expected.

Leo was charming and invited me to eat with him as I'd bought lunch, so I could hardly refuse, could I? We chatted and drank a little and I relaxed. There was something a little off, a little guarded about Leo, but he was good company; I don't think I'd laughed so much for years. The low mood evaporated, and I allowed myself a few little fantasies involving Leo Arakis.

After two gins and lamb moussaka, half a bottle of wine and the obligatory free carafe of raki, which we foolishly finished so that it was immediately topped up again, I was drunk. Giggly drunk.

The dining room emptied sometime after ten o'clock so we moved back to the bar, where we ordered coffee and sank into a sofa.

'Thank you for this evening, Anna,' said Leo, his hand over mine. 'I was hurting earlier today.' His eyes shifted away from mine. 'I agreed with my wife that we would ask for a divorce on the grounds of my adultery, but...' – he grabbed hold of the other hand too – 'I have never been unfaithful to her, never. I want you to believe me.'

He was staring hard at me, his eyes darting all over my face. I wasn't quite sure what he wanted. 'Err... that's fine, Leo,' I said, feeling a bit uncomfortable at the confession. 'You know I don't really care why you've split up, it's not my business. If you say you're separated, you're separated.' I took my hands back. The bloke was intense. It cooled me off a little. I mean, I fancied him like mad, and my body was giving him, and me, all the right signals. It was just that I knew I could never be involved with Leo, he was too intense for me, and I had been there, done that. So what exactly did I think I was doing?

His eyes fixed on mine and I had a wobble. So much for

never wanting to be involved. It didn't have to be too serious, did it? We could have some fun without me making a life commitment. After all, I was a free woman. I sat up a little straighter and looked at him properly. As if I might divine his intentions from his face. It's never worked for me before. Think about this, girl, before you do anything rash, I told myself, but I was already lost.

'Are you okay?' Leo asked. 'You look a little cold.' He took off his jacket and arranged it around my shoulders. He left one arm around my neck, and was so close I could smell Paco Rabanne. Gently, he pulled my head towards him and kissed me on the mouth. 'I can think of a way to keep us warm,' he murmured, doing his looking-deep-into-my-eyes thing again. Hypnotising me.

It was working. I laughed a little, unsure of where this was going, until a long-stifled need to be loved, held, and desired shot up and out of me like a tsunami. No point in resisting. I grabbed hold of his face with both hands and kissed him hard. It was suddenly urgent, a need to get skin on skin, to lose myself for a while. Urgent and exciting.

I woke in the early dawn, feeling pretty pleased with myself, but also a bit scared. Leo was facing me and breathing evenly, one arm stretched out towards me. Dark eyelashes, a stubble of dark beard, hair curling around his face. Nice. I didn't want a relationship with Leo, but the sex had been delicious, and maybe he felt the same way? I rolled over and wriggled backwards until I was snuggled against him and waited for him to wake up. It didn't take long.

5

Maria opened the taverna early. It was usually Spiros' job, as the only customers were fishermen wanting coffee and raki to see them out onto their boats. It gave her a couple of hours to do the other jobs that had to be done to keep the place afloat; kneading bread dough, baking cakes, cooking meals, cleaning. Her work began when it was still dark, but it was usually after nine when tourists and locals rolled down to start their day with a coffee.

She checked the clock again. It was gone seven. Spiros had been called away by Nikos Kokorakis last night, and she had heard nothing from him. She worried that Spiros was out of his depth with that monster. But what could she do? Everything they had was because of Kokorakis. It was hard to deny him anything.

Maria sorted food in the cupboards and checked the fridge. She banged the fridge door shut. So typical that Kokorakis had only to snap his fingers and Spiros went running, even though he had the taverna to open. Who was going to feed her chickens, collect the eggs, plant the seeds for summer salad? Buy the vegetables and meat, cook all the food? She banged about a bit more, heating a pot of bitumen-strong coffee and arranging cups, plates and glasses on the counter.

She served the regulars with bad grace as they sloped in, hardly responding to their idle chat. They soon drank up and shuffled out to catch the morning tide.

Spiros returned an hour later. She could smell the alcohol on him, and something else. Smoke? 'Well?' she demanded. 'I have been here doing your work, and you just disappear off to do your master's bidding without a thought as to how we will manage when I can't even get to the market.'

Spiros pulled a hand from his pocket. It was stuffed with bank notes. He grinned at her, swaying slightly.

Maria's eyes bulged. 'How much is that?'

Spiros dropped the cash onto the counter and began to count. 'Five hundred euros, Maria Angeliki. For one night's work.'

'That must have been some job,' she replied, taking the pile of cash and pushing it deep into her apron pocket. 'Some job.' She eyed her husband. He was a little drunk, but the look behind his smiling eyes told her a different story. 'What did he make you do? Tell me, you know I won't rest until I know.'

She sat him on a stool and poured him coffee, adding too much sugar. 'Drink it.'

Spiros scrubbed his hands across his face. Behind the smile his eyes were red. 'We went over to the south coast. Some trouble with a young guy down there not paying his rent.' He glanced at his wife's face. 'Don't worry, I just had to rough him up a little.'

'And then what? He paid up and you are all good friends?'

Spiros shook his head and rubbed sore eyes with both hands. 'No, then we burnt down his bar.' He drank the coffee in one long draught and peered into the distance. 'The house next door caught fire as well, but the people are safe. Safe enough.'

She shook her head slowly. It all figured. 'So you and your friends destroyed a young man's business because he got behind with his rent? This is what you have come to?'

Spiros pushed her away and looked longingly at the raki bottle on its shelf. 'No, it was an accident.'

'Accident? How do you set a business on fire in an accident?' She tutted in disgust. 'You were all drunk, weren't you?'

He shrugged. 'You know that if we hadn't paid our rent on time all these years, we would have had the same treatment. It's always the same on the island, you know this, always has been. So less of your complaining and let me get a bit of sleep before the day starts.' He ducked behind the counter and dragged himself up the narrow stairs.

'The day started two hours ago!'

Maria stood in the empty taverna, holding a damp cloth, feeling hollow. Spiros had been a good man once, but now look at him. The pawn of a rich man. She surveyed her taverna; it represented all that she had accomplished and achieved in the forty-five years she had been alive, and she felt sick that it all belonged to Kokorakis. A shudder ran through her. Even she had belonged to him once, before she had grown too old for his tastes. She attacked the clean tables, scrubbing at them until the sweat poured from her.

Maria was relieved to see the spritely Scottish lady, Cathy, heading for the door, clutching her daily English newspaper. She was always good company.

'Kalimera, dear,' said Cathy and sat in her usual corner so she could see who came and went. 'You're working hard.'

'Kalimera, Cathy. You're early this morning.'

Cathy smiled. 'It's language class, we've had to change to mornings because of Cassia's work and I needed a coffee and a chance to swot up on my homework.' She took out an old-fashioned exercise book and pen and placed them side by side on the table. 'I'm not as quick at this as I used to be, I'm afraid.'

'Your Greek is very good, don't worry. And Cassia is a very nice teacher. Coffee?'

'Ooh, yes, please, and a pastry if you have any.'

It was as Cathy sipped her coffee and studied her notes, and Maria helped her with her pronunciation, that they saw Anna walking back towards her house escorted by Leo Arakis, who was carrying an overnight bag.

Cathy's mouth dropped open. 'Well,' she said, through a mouth full of crumbs, 'that girl is a fast worker, I must say. She's only known him a few weeks!'

Maria laughed for the first time that day. 'She certainly is, and who can blame her, Cathy? He's very handsome.'

6

I allowed Leo to walk me back to the house, but then I sent him packing as there was no way I wanted him to see my dusty disaster. He kissed me out on the street, and I got a sudden pang of embarrassment. All the old ladies, including Mrs Pantelides, would be peeking through their windows. They didn't have much else to do. And I wasn't sure I wanted to be seen as part of a couple already. Still, it was a very nice kiss, and a very warm hug, and he promised to see me later, so I decided to stop panicking like a fool and enjoy the feeling. It had been a long time. And I was a single woman, after all. These people knew nothing of my history.

It was coming up towards nine and I needed to tidy the place, and myself, before language class. Thursdays came around far too regularly in my opinion, and I preferred a late afternoon option, but there you go, we had to have a teacher. Gingerly, I opened the front door. The dust had settled into a white layer covering every surface, but nothing could have put me in a bad mood that morning. It may as well sit there until the builders had finished clearing away and then I could tackle it properly.

I ran upstairs and put my stuff away safely in the bedroom, deciding on jeans and a cotton jumper for the day. Then I dared the bathroom. It was transformed. The walls were the soft pink of new plaster. They glowed in the morning sun streaming through the tiny window. I was definitely keeping that colour. The roll-topped bath stood away from the wall now that the old plaster was no longer there, and it looked good. I could see how the shower would fit in the corner now that an old cupboard had been removed. It was going to be okay, wasn't it? I really needed to stop catastrophising everything.

I balanced the mirror on the window ledge and gave myself a good looking at. It could just have been the walls glowing, of course. Would people know what I'd been up to? I always think you can tell when people have had good sex, there's a softness to them. The face in the mirror certainly told a different story from the stressed-out old hag of the day before. Funny what a night of passion and an attentive male would do for a girl. I grinned and wondered what on earth I'd done with my language folder, and had a moment of guilt that I'd done very little actual Greek speaking over the week.

I finally found the folder under the bed and had to run to the town hall to get there on time. I pounded up the steps and made a noisier entrance than I'd have wanted, only to find the class in absolute silence, including Cassia, the teacher. 'Sorry I'm late,' I blurted, but I wasn't, it hadn't struck ten o'clock yet. 'Have I missed something?' I asked, worried that Leo had told them about the night before.

Cassia's eyes were swollen and red. She'd been crying, hard. 'What is it, Cassia?' I looked to the others for some help. What the hell had happened?

Cathy spoke first. 'There was a fire last night, in Paleochora, on the south of the island.'

'Was it her home?'

'No, not Cassia's house, but that of her brother, Constantinos. The fire has destroyed his home and his business, I'm afraid.'

'Oh no, was it an electrical fault?' I'd seen the state of some of the wiring on Crete, and it was dangerous. I knelt down next to Cassia and put my hand on her knee.

Leo cleared his throat. 'Not exactly, they beat her brother up before they torched his business.'

'Local hoodlums?' asked Alex, a frown settling between his eyebrows. 'Though why would they pick on a restaurant owner?'

'No,' said Cassia. 'My brother got behind with his rent. I didn't know how bad it had become, but he ignored the warnings, and...'

'The owner wouldn't listen?' said Alex.

She shook her head. 'Tino is a wonderful human being, but he's not good at handling the money side of the business. He's a cook first and foremost. I do the books for him usually. But he's had a bad winter. It happens sometimes, but I never thought it would come to this. It is barbaric.'

Leo interrupted, anger giving an edge to his voice. 'Why didn't he pay his rent, Cassia? How did he expect to get away with it? Surely he knows how these things work?'

I looked at Leo in a new light. What did I really know about him? I wondered if what he had been patting in his top pocket when we first met really had been a wad of cash to line the pockets of the people who actually ran the town.

'Tino is idealistic,' whispered Cassia. 'He thought they would give him more time because he has started a community café to give work to some of the unemployed young people in the town. All profits go to helping local people. He's not making money from this except for wages. Some of the people he helps may well be the children of the men who burnt down his house, but...' She shuddered out a long sigh and wiped her eyes.

Cathy put her arm around Cassia's shoulders and pulled her to her feet. 'I think we should cancel the class today, and go and get a coffee. Perhaps there is something we can do to help?'

Cassia shook her head. 'No, but thank you for being so kind. There is nothing to do. My brother will go back to our parents in Athens when he is better, and that is that. He will stay with me until then. It is such a shame for his neighbours, who have nothing to do with this. They have lost their home as well. They are elderly people.' She burst into a fresh bout of sobbing, over-whelmed.

I was still being a bit dim. 'But why set fire to the place?'

'They were drunk, Tino said. I doubt they did it on purpose.'

'Same result though,' said Alex. 'Local thugs for hire.'

'Well, there is one thing I can do,' said Leo, rising to his feet and dangling his car keys. 'I can drive you over the mountain to collect your brother.'

Cassia glanced up at him. 'But I can't ask you to do that.'

'You didn't ask,' he said. 'I offered, and I'd like to help.' He turned to me. 'Come with us, Anna?'

'Of course,' I said, 'but let's get a drink first, and give Cassia time to freshen up. Shall we go to Maria's?' I saw the look on Cassia's face, she wanted to go straight away, but a few moments to herself would be better than jumping straight into the car. There wasn't really a rush anymore, was there? 'We won't stay long, Cassia. It will give Leo time to collect the car.'

She nodded, gathered up her bag and jacket and stood there, staring at the floor. It was sad to see.

It was a subdued walk down to the quayside. The rain had stopped and watery sun was breaking through clouds. There was only a gentle wind and no one hiding from the rain in the cafés. It was sparkling, with the clean air that only a heavy overnight downpour can bring. The sea was a paler blue today but still topped with white caps which chased each other up onto the sand as we rounded the corner. Leo brushed my hand with his fingers as we walked and I felt a pleasurable twinge, low in the groin. I smiled at him. Later, Romeo.

I took a deep breath to calm down before the five of us trooped into the taverna and stood in a huddle until Maria pushed two tables together in the window. I knew I needed to think about what had happened to Cassia's brother, and to figure out a bit more about Leo's business plans, but there was time for that later.

Maria came back out from the kitchen with a tray of freshly-baked cheese pies balanced in one hand. She glanced at the clock. 'Short lesson today? Are they so good they don't need you anymore, Cassia?' She stopped short when she saw Cassia's face and spoke in rapid Greek to our teacher, who responded equally quickly. I caught most of it.

Then Maria just dropped the tray on the counter, shouted to Spiros up the stairs and they disappeared into the kitchen when he staggered down. He looked like he hadn't slept. Maria had looked like she was about to explode while she waited for him at the foot of the stairs and she did, all over him once they were shut in the kitchen. Pity I couldn't hear it, but the intent was clear. It was low and vicious on both sides. I'd heard my parents arguing like this when I was a kid, and I hadn't understood it then either.

'What just happened, Cassia?' I asked.

Cassia dropped her heavy bag on the floor and sank into a chair. She shrugged. 'I told her who did it.' She got back up and went to the ladies' bathroom.

'She knows? Can't we call the police?' I looked to Leo but he was focused on the door where Spiros had disappeared into the kitchen, and was tapping his chin with his fingers. I felt a cold shiver on that warm day. Surely that could not be true? Not Spiros. But Leo met my gaze, and there was no humour in his eyes. He shook his head at me, so I didn't say anything.

Alex took my elbow. 'Here, sit down and we can order when one of them returns. Cathy, take a seat.' He too, looked grim.

I sat, Leo pulling his chair close to mine. I could smell the cheese pies, an aroma that would normally have me salivating, but I felt a bit numb. I'd found out far more this morning than I wanted to know about this island and some of the people on it.

Maria bustled out of the kitchen, took our orders without a comment or a sly glance in my direction. She served us quickly and disappeared back into the kitchen. Something was definitely wrong.

The cheese pies were, of course, delicious, and even Cassia cheered up when Cathy suggested taking a couple for her brother. We were quick, and Maria wouldn't accept any money for the food and drinks, she simply ushered us out of the taverna. I'd seen some of her black moods over the past few weeks, but this was different, she looked furious.

'Cassia, why was Maria so angry with Spiros?'

Cassia dipped her head. 'I cannot say, Anna. I cannot say.' She checked her phone for messages to avoid talking to me.

That wasn't the same as 'I don't know', was it? Not remotely the same.

7

As a child on holiday I had travelled all over the island with my mother and grandmother on buses. I'd had no idea who they were gossiping about, or who we were going to visit, so I would stare out of the window at the wild scenery of the central island. There is no such thing as a straight road here. As soon as you get off the main coast road, terrain determines direction. The mountains are steep and the granite rock so hard that roads can't go through them; instead they go over and round, in a mad zigzag which offers stunning views, and an upset stomach if you happen to be travelling in the back of a car.

Returning as an adult, I saw it all with very different eyes. The fields and farms, rock walls and canyons told of a tough, hard past, where the people hacked their living from the stone. Now, goats grazed along the paths and up the sides of the hills, fields were tamed, with fruit and olive trees supplementing their income. Tiny spring flowers, white and yellow, pushed their way through snow as we reached the top of the mountain road. Old broken-down huts, once the winter homes of shepherds, stood empty and neglected, slowly going back into the land. 'It's so cold up here.'

Cassia said, 'There is snow in the mountains until May or even June sometimes. You will learn that Crete has its own climate, Anna. I would not get caught out in the mountains without suitable clothing. Many tourists get into trouble up here.'

'I'll remember that. It is beautiful, though, isn't it?'

'It is, and a very different place to the towns. It is, in a way, the real Crete, away from the tourists. Town law does not apply in the mountains.'

'It doesn't apply in the towns much either,' said Leo, and I sank back into my seat.

I couldn't help noticing that the road signs had gunshot holes in them. Evidence of teenage overexcitement, I hoped, rather than the mountain people taking the law into their own hands. There weren't many cultures, I guessed, that gave their sons a gun on their fifteenth birthday.

Leo didn't speak much after that; he had to concentrate to stay on the road. Neither did Cassia, which was understandable. So I had time to think about setting up businesses on the island. It wasn't just Leo's problem, was it? I had sort of set up a business, too. I had been working only the night before. But if I took on a contract from Leo, I would then be a legitimate business owner on the island. I had to get back and hassle the man at the town hall as I was working illegally at the moment. I didn't have to pay rent, like Cassia's brother, but I didn't want to upset anyone, either. Not if it went as badly as this. The thought drifted through that I could keep quiet, do my work online and tell nobody. But that wouldn't work. I have no 'stop and think' filters – as soon as someone asked me what I did for a living I'd be all over them with detail – how could that stay secret for long? No, for me, the right way was the only way, otherwise I couldn't sleep at night.

I wasn't looking forward to seeing what those thugs had

done to Constantinos' business, and I couldn't help worrying about the elderly neighbours, who had possibly lost everything.

'Are you from Athens, originally, Cassia?' I asked, trying to take my mind off the fire.

She turned slightly in her seat. 'Yes, we came over together a few years ago, after university. We are twins, as you will see.' She sniffed and wiped her nose again. 'My training is as a human rights lawyer, and I wanted to set up practice here, but, in the current climate, that is very difficult, so I have been teaching to give me some income, and volunteering at a law practice in Chania.'

Leo said, 'That way your face becomes known and you might be able to get a paid job.'

'Yes, you understand. It is the way things are done here. My difficulty is that I want to help refugees with their claims for asylum, and they are very unpopular in Greece.'

'Not just in Greece,' I said. 'So your job is likely to upset the local business people?'

'No, it is the opposite. Much of the crime here is committed by people coming across the water to make a killing. They are not asylum seekers, they are drug runners and people smugglers. They are the people I want to fight, and Mr K is with me on that. That is why I am so upset about what he did to Tino.'

'You know who the guy behind all this is?' I may have squealed that last word. 'Have you told the police? And who is he?'

Cassia and Leo shared a look. I hate it when people do that. 'What? What am I missing?' I pulled myself forward between the front seats.

'Can we have this conversation when I'm not driving round ridiculous bends in a hire car, please?' he asked, and glanced at me in the rear-view mirror.

I subsided back into my seat. I didn't like the way this was going at all. Not one bit. What had I got myself tangled up in?

I suddenly remembered the look on my father's face as I told him I was going to accept Grandmother's house and move to Crete. He glared at Mum in a way I'd never seen him look at anyone, and spat out 'See? See what you have done?' I couldn't make sense of it then; it was only a house and I was able to fly home anytime. But maybe I was beginning to understand why Dad had moved away never to return. If he wouldn't co-operate with someone like 'Mr K' all those years ago, then perhaps he had no choice. I had a pang of homesickness to go with my car sickness.

Paleochora is called the jewel of the south coast, and it really is beautiful even early in the season. It was a rocky approach down through the mountains, and then the low white houses ranged back up the road towards us and a small town filled the flat land between mountain and sea. Flowers spilled from containers and baskets and scented the roads. Young trees were bursting with buds, ready to flower. It was beautiful, and peaceful. We drove along the main road, with the sea lapping against the shore on our left and I looked longingly at the sheltered cafés along the beach. Couldn't we just stop there, and not go to see the ruin of Constantinos' place?

Leo followed Cassia's directions towards the end of the long beach and up a small side street where he parked the car and I staggered out, gulping in fresh air and trying not to throw up. I've never been good in the back of cars, but that journey had been a killer.

I smelt the smoke immediately, and not just from the cigarette Leo had lit as soon as he stepped out of the car. Ahead, in a small public square lined with trees and benches in the middle, a fire engine finished its work and police directed people away from the two burnt-out buildings.

Cassia ran ahead, scanning for her brother, but I saw him first. It was hard to miss him. The same slight, willowy figure as his sister, but with an arm in plaster and a face already coming up blue and black. 'He's over there,' I said, tugging at her arm.

Constantinos was sitting on a bench directly opposite the wreck of his café and home. Cassia ran to him and touched his face. He hardly responded.

Next to him sat an elderly couple dressed in black. The wife openly weeping, the husband coughing out hard sighs.

'These people brought me to get you, Tino,' Cassia said to her brother.

He looked at her and gave a sad little smile. 'Well, I have nowhere else left to go.'

I found Leo's hand. It was desperate. We watched the end of the clean-up and got out of the way when the police and fire engine drove past us back down the road. The café was ruined, as was the little house that was attached to it. Only rafters remained to show that they had once been dwellings. The designer in me wanted to start planning a rebuild, to help them make it better, but I knew it was a futile effort to help to put things right in a place where they could never be right.

I could feel Leo's anger radiating from him; he was crushing my fingers. 'Ow,' I said and he turned to me. But he couldn't see me, he'd gone somewhere else. Imagining what might happen to his own dreams if he couldn't pay up, no doubt.

I extricated myself and squatted down next to Cassia and her brother. I marvelled at the close resemblance between them. 'I'm so sorry, Constantino,' I said. Maybe I should have come up with something better, but I was, really was. It was a disaster. I couldn't bear to look at the old couple, but I did, and patted the weeping woman on the hand. She smiled her thanks, but I felt totally wretched.

'Tino,' he replied. 'Tino is fine.'

'I'd like to help if I can,' I said, but it was difficult to see how. Wouldn't stop me trying though.

'Thanks for bringing me over the mountain,' said Cassia to Leo, who loomed above us.

Leo still wasn't really present, but he shook Tinos' hand and muttered a few words at him. The burning had shaken him more than I expected. He always seemed so self-assured, with that clean-cut American gloss about him. Did Mr K have something to do with him, too? Perhaps my American fling wasn't quite the man he tried to portray.

'Coffee is needed,' I said, standing up on knees that creaked a bit. 'Will you both come with us?'

'Could I have an hour or so with my brother,' asked Cassia, 'and then maybe we could have lunch before we go back? We have a few things to sort out.' She took his good hand and squeezed it. 'I have brought pies from Maria, you should eat something.' She opened the paper bag and placed it on his lap but he didn't look at them.

Quietly, Cassia passed the pies to the elderly couple. The woman nodded her thanks, and said in Greek, 'We have nothing left.'

'No family?' I asked, horrified that they would be alone to face this ruin.

'Oh, yes,' she said, 'my sister will help, but for now we stay at the taverna.' She gestured behind. 'We are not ready to go yet.'

It was time for us to go, though. I felt we were intruding by hanging around offering pointless platitudes. We arranged to meet at a restaurant nearby and I walked Leo back to the seafront and a café that promised good European coffee. Don't get me wrong, I love almost everything Cretan, but I wanted a proper cappuccino, with froth, and one that wasn't too bitter, or too sweet. Not easy to come by. The best coffee I'd had so far was near the bus station in Heraklion, which, at more than a hundred miles away, was a bit far to travel for a morning cuppa. Besides, I wanted to take my mind off the sadness and find out about this Mr K character.

'Right, Leo Arakis, tell me what you know,' I said as soon as the waiter had moved away. 'Spare me nothing. I already feel like a total dimwit, so enlighten me. Who is "Mr K", for a start?'

Leo sipped at his coffee and gave a little nod of approval. 'There was no reason for you to know about him, that's all. He's a landlord, and a landowner and owner of several other major businesses in the area. Quite the big man in these parts.' Leo took another sip, drew hard on his cigarette, then blew smoke straight at me. 'His name is Nikos Kokorakis, and he lives in Kissamos, not far from you. I know about him because he is the owner of the house and land I want to buy. But I don't like his tactics much.'

'He lives in my town? Wow. But his name is almost the same as yours. Are you *related* to him?'

'No! Are you related to everyone called Georgiou? Listen, Anna, when the Turks occupied Crete, they gave all the residents the surname "Akis". It means "small". It was a way of subjugating them, I think. So there are lots of people in Crete whose names end that way. It's your family name that is from elsewhere in Greece.' He calmed down a bit. 'Yes, I agree, my family are definitely from this island, so who knows who I'm related to?'

'So you do have connections on the island despite what you told Maria at the taverna? That's quite exciting!'

He shifted on the hard chair. 'I don't *know* if I have anybody still here. My father embraced America and we holidayed in Florida, and never came back over here. It's a long, long way. Dad's not the sort of guy who would keep in touch for old times' sake. And then we grew up, and my eldest brother took over the running of the restaurant chain, and my youngest brother trained as a chef, and I...' He shrugged.

'You felt that you didn't fit into the mould that had been prepared for you?'

'Exactly. I was involved in acquiring land and setting up new restaurants, but there was nothing in it for me except a wage. I want to be in charge of my own project, Anna. I want to deliver for myself, and not work my butt off so all that I have achieved goes to my older brother when my father dies.'

'That's a bit eighteenth century, isn't it? Shouldn't you share the business with your brothers when your father dies?'

'You'd think, wouldn't you?' His mouth twisted into a tight grimace. 'You know what they say; you can take the boy out of Crete, but you can't get Crete out of the boy. And that is so true of my father. Me and my younger brother would get money, but not the business. "It's how it has always been", he said. So, I asked for the money straight away, and decided to come back to somewhere where I might have some roots, and try to start a new life while I'm young enough to do it.'

'And was your dad happy with that?'

Leo guffawed. 'Oh Christ, no! It was horrendous. I felt most sorry for Mom, who was caught in the middle. He did give me my share, but he refused to allow me to come to Crete, and then cut me off because I came anyway.' He stared directly into my eyes. 'Anna, I'm thirty-two years old; he doesn't get to answer for me anymore.'

'And now you find that a guy who will burn down your house if you default on the rent is the owner of the land you want to buy? No wonder you're upset.' I took his hand. He really had burnt all his bridges, hadn't he? Seeing what Kokorakis had done to Tinos must have been a shock. 'I'm so sorry, Leo. But, you know, there's no reason why you won't succeed here. You have a great concept in the restaurant with a casino. Kissamos needs something a bit more upmarket. You'll have to charm Mr K.' He didn't respond.

I gave his hand a shake. 'Come on, snap out of it. You can do this!'

I was wasting my breath.

Cassia arrived towing her brother by the arm, and we walked into town for lunch. It was fine, I chatted away and made small talk with Cassia, and we both pretended that the men with us weren't lost in different thoughts entirely. It was pleasant to be in such a beautiful place without the usual thousands of tourists cluttering the place up with hire cars and bikes, but I was glad to set off for home as the afternoon wore on.

Tinos came back over the mountain with us, carrying a small bag of possessions he had rescued. There was nothing left for him in Paleochora.

Leo dropped them both at Cassia's flat in the old town, and then he drove up to my place. I hadn't given the workmen a thought while we had been away. In fact, I felt like I'd been away for several days rather than one.

As we drew up, my front door flew open and Mrs Pantelides, of all people, came out wearing a huge flowery apron and waving a duster at me.

'What's going on?' I asked her, jumping from the car.

'Ah, Anna, I have made sure those lazy boys finish the job, like I said I would. Come, come.'

She gestured at me and led me into my own living room, like a visitor. I could hardly speak. The place was transformed. Vasilis was in there polishing the top of the old dresser, and all the old china I had kept was surrounding a bowl of hot water on the kitchen table, being washed, I presumed, by Mrs P.

'Wow,' I said, 'this is fantastic. Thank you so much.' I kissed her on her cheek, and she took my hand and proudly led me into the kitchen, and that looked good too. It was as if nothing had happened to cause all the mess. Stupidly, I felt tears starting. To receive such kindness after witnessing the cruel end to a young man's dreams was sobering. What a contradiction this island was.

Leo followed us, his head almost scraping the ceiling. 'Fabulous place, Anna,' he said.

I introduced Mrs P, who fawned over him until I couldn't stand it anymore and had to go out into the back garden, where Mr Andreiou was shovelling plaster into sacks and piling them into a wheelbarrow.

'Ah, you are back. Almost done. We were here at dawn today. Long day.' He waggled bushy eyebrows. 'Mrs Pantelides: she-devil.' He laughed, making little pinching movements with his hands, like a crab. 'Checking, checking...'

I laughed with him. She was turning out to be quite a formidable ally in her own way.

'Upstairs? Go upstairs and see the bathroom, please.' He looked anxious. Mrs P really had sorted him out.

I went upstairs and yes, there was a clean, well-prepared bathroom, ready for the shower to go in and the tiles to go on. There would be none of this trendy wet room nonsense for me, I wanted dry floors and well-tiled walls. I couldn't wait for it to be ready. I tried the tap, and, just as he had promised, out came hot water. Water heated by a boiler. I wasn't going to rely on solar in the winter months. It was going to be great.

Leo squashed into the bathroom behind me. He'd relaxed a bit on the journey back and pushed both arms around my middle. 'This is a great little place,' he said into my neck, 'and I assume the bedroom is through that door?' He pulled me round so I was facing the bedroom door, but what I saw was Mrs Pantelides' headscarf coming for us up the stairs. I opened the bedroom door and shuffled us into the space. There was not a great deal of room for three people to stand on the landing of my house.

Mrs P stood panting, an expectant smile on her face.

'It's wonderful, Mrs Pantelides, you really got them working hard. It's so nice to come back to a clean house, and the bathroom is going to be lovely.'

The old lady smiled. 'You are welcome. We all need help sometimes, especially when we are new and don't understand how things are done here. I'm tired now, Anna. I'll go home.' She held tightly onto the banister and trod heavily on the stairs to go back down.

I couldn't help wondering how she got up and down the stairs in her own house. And then wondered if she lived entirely downstairs. I'd have to look out for her in future.

By six o'clock they had all gone. I sat Leo on the sofa with a beer and curled up next to him, hugging a glass of red. What a day it had been. 'Are you okay?'

He put the beer on the side table and held me in both arms, burying his head in my neck. 'No, and yes,' he said.

Only the cat had dinner that night. We had too much red wine, but Leo needed me, and I needed something too, and it was different this time. Not so frantic, more watching each other and trying to please, and we were both looking for release. Later, I slept like a child, probably for the first time since I'd arrived on Crete.

8

Delphine slammed open the door to her husband's office and stood there, holding onto a newspaper, nostrils flaring, until Nikos sent his managers away to start their day and sat back in his chair.

'You need to speak to me?' he asked mildly.

'Look what your donkeys did,' she spat, and unfolded the newspaper. She flattened it onto the desk and pointed at the elderly couple sitting forlornly on the bench. 'Look. Look at them. I hope you are proud that you have left them with nothing.'

Nikos went to interrupt.

'No. And look at this boy, this angel of mercy. He was giving jobs to the unemployed, giving a community back its self-respect, but you, you had to make a point, didn't you?'

'Delphie...'

'No. You have gone too far. You must fix this now. Now, Niko.' Delphine glared at her husband until he shook his head in resignation, reached into the drawer and drew out his chequebook. 'How much?'

She stood very still and calculated. 'They need a new house, clothes, furniture... Give me one hundred and fifty thousand euros.'

Nikos sighed and wrote the cheque. 'It wasn't supposed to happen like that, Delphie. You know I would never...'

'Don't,' she said. 'They work for you, and you know that Spiros is a drunken idiot. You are now responsible for this family and this boy. You almost killed them. An elderly couple who have never done wrong in their lives.'

He passed over the cheque. 'And the young man? You know he can't be allowed to get away with not paying his rent on time; nobody can. If I let him get away with it, everybody will try.'

Delphine growled. 'You could have overlooked it this one time, for a boy trying to help our people. You have forgotten yourself, husband. You have lost your heart. And your head, you old fool.' She pursed her lips, trying to work out what would be appropriate. The old couple would take the money without question but Constantinos Papadikis wouldn't. His sister was a lawyer and so were his parents. She would have to think about the best way to smooth this over.

'I'll try to sort out Constantinos, but they are not fools, the Papadikises. They are a major family in Athens. There may be repercussions.'

Nikos looked astounded. 'They cannot hurt me. Who are they? Athens elite, so what? They are nothing here. Stop worrying, Delphie. You sort out the old couple and find something for the boy to do. Keep him occupied and out of our hair. It will be fine, you will see.'

Delphine picked up the cheque and stalked from the room, slamming the door to finish her point.

Nikos pushed back his chair and stretched. The view across the bay never failed to soothe him. It had seemed wise not to argue with Delphie. It usually was. She had such a soft heart under that chill exterior.

It was all going to hell, wasn't it? He had asked the boys to warn young Papadikis that he would have to pay up at last. He'd waited three months. He said maybe a few broken chairs, a punch or two. Normally they would follow orders, but Spiros was becoming a liability because of the drink, loyal servant that he was. And now it had cost Nikos all his profit for the last two months to help out an old couple who were simply collateral damage, and a boy who would certainly have learnt his lesson.

Nikos pulled open a drawer and took out a folder. Inside were the deeds to Spiros' and Maria's taverna, and for as long as he had those, both Maria and Spiros were his. But perhaps the time had come to let them go. He could sell the taverna for fifty thousand, he was sure. He allowed himself a smirk as old memories of Maria as a young woman in his bed, grateful and pliant and so beautiful, surfaced. Good old days, when things worked as they should.

He poured himself an early brandy and stood at the picture window that overlooked the town and the bay. His old family home stood at the end of the drive, empty now. He had wanted to demolish it, but something had made him keep it, even after his father had died. Delphie had wanted a modern, light-filled house, and he had indulged her and built the grandest house in town. Nowadays, however, it just felt empty with no children and no grandchildren to fill it. His thoughts returned to his brothers, as they had over these last few weeks. He wondered what their lives were like in their new countries, and whether they had ever wanted to return. Whether he had many nieces and nephews who knew nothing about him.

And then his thoughts jumped to Anna Georgiou. He hadn't tried to find out anything about her yet, although he had Spiros keeping an eye on her movements, and he was almost sure she was Theo's daughter despite the name change. Now she seemed to have a lover, another foreigner with a local name; Leonidas Arakis. Who was he?

Whatever was happening, it was going to be bad for him; he knew that. He took another sip, but the brandy tasted sickly and he longed for the simple foods and drinks of his childhood and youth, when the raki was rough and potent. And so was he.

Delphine drove over the mountain roads without seeing the scenery. She had unloosed a deep anger that kept threatening to overwhelm her. It had all gone too far, this 'Mr K' business. It was a different world now, and it was about time Nikos accepted that he couldn't carry on the way he was. No policeman would come knocking, she knew that, not when Nikos would make reparation, but the idiot had allowed things to go too far. The authorities couldn't ignore him, now he'd overstepped a boundary. 'Look at Al Capone,' she yelled at the mountains, 'he wasn't shot or stabbed, the tax people got him. The lawyers got him.' Nikos was old too. In his sixties now, and with no heir the other major families would be lining up their eager sons ready for a takeover. Without a strong succession plan, it could get very messy indeed. It was time for her to act.

She pulled in close to the burnt-out houses in Paleochora and got out of the car. What a mess. An unnecessary mess that yet again she had to clear up. You couldn't, mustn't, hurt the poor people. Nikos knew that, and so did that brute Spiros. Hadn't he been one of them not so long ago? She clicked the lock on the car and noticed several people staring at her. More than once she wondered at her need to own a red sports car which marked her out more surely than any sign over her head.

Delphine rapped on the door of the taverna on the square and asked to speak to the elderly couple who were staying there.

The owner backed away respectfully and ushered her into the dining room.

Delphine wasn't long inside. She felt deep shame at the grateful tears of the couple as they pocketed enough euros to buy clothes and necessities. Now she had to choose them a house in the village. They would need everything, and they were overwhelmed that Delphine Kokorakis wanted to help even though it was her husband who had ruined their lives.

Clambering back into her car for the hour-long journey home, Delphine thought hard about what had to be done, and decided she could kill two birds with one stone, and get the girl, Anna Georgiou, to help decorate and design the new house. She smiled and stepped on the accelerator. Excellent plan; the girl would not be able to resist helping, and Delphine would be able to find out more about her intentions.

9

L eo went back to the hotel early the following morning, saying he had to travel to Chania for business, and I was glad to have some time on my own. The cat was waiting, balanced on the narrow windowsill in the kitchen and miaowing to get in. I really did not want a cat, but she was hard to ignore. I gave her neck a good scrub with my nails and planned my day.

I needed to shop, and do domestic stuff. I was quite looking forward to a normal day. I made herbal tea and sank onto the sofa in my lovely clean house and fell into a minor wallow in the past, thinking about how different life might have been had I never met Will Hunter.

I was only eighteen and new at university, and there was Will, cool and handsome and distant in the pub with his friends around him. I smiled at him; he was very attractive. He'd glared at me, through me it felt like, and didn't smile back, so I hid my embarrassment and turned back to the gang I was with. If he wanted to play it that way, then that was fair enough. He must have singled me out for further study at that point, although it was months before we actually had a date.

Once we were together, that was it for both of us. We really were inseparable, and in that awful way that girls have, I gave up all my friends and fun nights out, and chats about makeup and clothes, and worries about getting assignments completed on time. I grew up overnight, and suddenly we were living together, much to my dad's horror, and I was already behaving like a wife, learning to cook and keep a flat tidy, and pay the bills because Will never could remember to do it. And that is how we continued through our first degrees, and afterwards I worked as a designer, and supported Will through his master's degree, and then we set up our business.

I'd had exactly two boyfriends in my short life. Three, now. Until I ran away to Crete, I had never been free to do anything on my own. I couldn't believe how ground down I had been. I know I was complicit in it. I know that. What an idiot.

I could feel the tears starting so I scrubbed them away, and sent Will back to where he came from. He'd groomed me to be his mother and I'd let him. But I didn't have to hang onto him anymore. And, a warning voice in my head said, you mustn't just replace him with Leo. Be a bit choosy, Anna. And I was going to listen this time.

I walked into the main town and strolled through the market, buying fresh food, wine and kitchen stuff. Both of the bags I'd taken with me were really heavy by the time I'd replaced the wine we'd drunk the night before, and I had to stop twice on the way back for a rest. I wasn't quite sure why I hadn't just got a taxi. Or, actually, why I hadn't yet bought a car.

I scuttled past the taverna door. I hadn't been in since the incident with her and Spiros. I wasn't sure how to approach Maria when she knew that I knew what Spiros had done.

I stopped on the corner leading to my road and wiped my damp face with the back of my hand. A woman in a small red sports car drove slowly past. She turned and stared at me over her shoulder so I looked back. She wasn't smiling, but I gave her a nod anyway. To my surprise, she pulled over and got out. She was slim and slight, unusual in the middle-aged Greek women I had seen so far. Most seemed to succumb to the wonderful food in their forties.

'Kalimera,' she said, hiding behind oversized sunglasses. She had black hair pulled back into a smart ponytail which hung low on the nape of her neck, and was wearing a red cotton sweater and black leather trousers. Très chic.

'Kalimera,' I answered and gave a proper smile as she came up to me with her hand extended.

'I am Delphine Kokorakis,' she said in Greek. 'I live further up the road, past your house. Would you like a lift with your groceries?'

Kokorakis? She must be the wife of Mr K. Mrs K! 'Anna, Anna Georgiou. So pleased to meet you.' I shook her hand, which was cool and dry, unlike mine. 'It's kind of you to offer, the bags are really heavy.'

'No need for you to struggle.' She searched me from top to bottom as I stood there like an idiot, wondering what to say. Then she flipped the boot lid, so I plonked the bags inside and slid into the leather passenger seat.

'So, you have moved to the island from England, I hear?' She slipped seamlessly into English, for which I was grateful.

'Yes, I inherited my grandmother's house.'

'It's many years since I have visited. I like London. I studied there, a long time ago.'

'Me too. Unfortunately, I'm from Manchester where it rains all the time.'

'So you have escaped to the sun?'

'I have.'

'And you are enjoying it here?'

I paused. I wanted to say, I was until I learned a bit about your husband and his activities, but I'm not totally stupid. 'I am. I love my house and the people I have met so far.'

'Do you have a husband, children?'

'No, neither of those. I do seem to have attracted a cat though,' I replied and she laughed gently.

She was a bit direct for me, but exactly like my mother and all the Greek women I'd had to tolerate in the restaurant throughout my whole life – 'Oh, you're so thin, you'll never get a man.' 'No children yet, Anna, you must pray harder.' Bleurrgh. I just learned not to get upset.

'Oh. You are alone. Then what will you do all day?' She drove slowly, far too slowly for the short distance we had to cover.

This was the question I'd been dreading. I wasn't used to being illegal. Ah well, who said I had to tell her the truth? 'My grandmother left me some money to live on while I decide what to do,' I said. 'By training I'm an interior designer. I hope to set up a small business here in the future.'

She finally pulled up in front of the house and I saw Mrs Pantelides' curtain waft.

'I hope I can call you Anna,' she said, 'and you will call me Delphine. It is so nice to have somebody new in the town who has a more professional background, and in an area in which I also have some interest.'

'Thank you,' I spluttered, 'how kind.' I wasn't at all sure I wanted to be friends with her though. I hopped out of the car and stood by the boot.

Delphine, it appeared, was in no hurry. She stood in front of the semi-detached houses and looked at both. 'I can see that you have worked hard. The house had become run-down over the years.' She turned to me and pursed the corners of her mouth, which I think I was supposed to interpret as a smile.

'Could I see what you have done so far? Would you mind? You may be able to help me with a project I am about to start.'

I sent a silent thank you to Mrs Pantelides and her cleaning. Two days before, I would have choked rather than have anybody look round the house, especially this vision of sophistication. 'Of course.' I hefted both bags out of the boot, dropped them on the step and unlocked the door. I'd left the back door open and sunlight flooded through, illuminating the small rooms and framing the view of the White Mountains, glistening in the sun.

Delphine stepped in behind me and I left her to it while I took the bags into the kitchen and stuffed fresh meat and fish into the fridge.

'You have done such a good job, Anna,' said Delphine. 'It's lovely.' She went through both rooms, touching the old dresser, the throws, cushions, and the chunk of black marble acting as a hearth, before finally resting her hand on the wooden kitchen counter.

It made me uneasy, all this touching. What was she after? It could never be as simple as needing a friend, surely? I was aware that my suspicion was entirely about who she was married to, it seemed wrong to think she was the same as him when I had no proof.

'It's very warm and cosy. It has the feel of a real home.'

'Thank you. That's the look I was going for. To keep the spirit of my grandmother, but add in modern pieces where necessary.'

'It's lovely.' She looked out through the back door and smiled at the cat. 'I do like cats. They are so graceful, yet essentially self-centred. They know a good place when they see it. And that is a good thing for survival, I find.'

I was at a loss, so I just smiled. Was she warning me? Threatening me?

'Well, I must be going,' she said. 'Do you have a card?'

I took one from the desk and handed it to her. 'Thanks very much for the lift up the hill. I am planning to get a car soon,' I said, not wanting to look completely hopeless.

She gave me a genuine smile then, displaying perfect, expensive teeth. 'Thank you. I will be in touch regarding the decorative project I have in mind, and perhaps you would like to join my husband and I for dinner one evening? You can bring a friend along, of course.'

She waved as she drove up the street. I was relieved that she'd gone and I was full of mixed feelings toward her. I had no idea what was going on, if anything was, of course, but she made me feel like I was on the menu for dinner, rather than just attending.

I'd barely shut the front door and gone to the kitchen when the back gate creaked and Mrs Pantelides came shuffling up the path.

'Mrs Kokorakis,' she exclaimed. 'Here, in this house!' She clutched both sides of her face, which would have been comical if it hadn't been for the look of shock.

'What is it?' I asked. 'Are you all right? Here, sit down.' I pushed her gently into a kitchen chair and put the kettle on to boil. 'A nice cup of mountain tea will do you good.' I certainly needed one.

I busied myself loading cupboards and filling the fridge until the kettle boiled, then placed the teapot filled with mountain tea, and two mugs onto the table. 'Right, tell me what you mean,' I said.

The old lady didn't look at me. 'There is much to tell, but it is not my place to say. How did you meet her?'

'She gave me a lift from the corner of the road. Just got out of her car and offered. I wasn't going to turn her down. And what do you mean, not your place to say?'

'You have no idea who she is, do you, Anna?' Mrs Pantelides asked.

'Oh, maybe I know a little more than you expect,' I said. 'I know she is the wife of Nikos Kokorakis, a man not to be messed about with.'

'Yes, that is true. But what did she want from you?'

'She wants me to help her with a design project, and she invited me to dinner.'

Mrs Pantelides took a sip of her tea. 'I never thought, after all this time.' She looked down at her cup and swirled the hot liquid. 'Perhaps, this will be for the good. Perhaps it is time.' She stood up carefully and prepared to leave.

'Please don't go yet.'

'I have much to do, I must go,' she said.

'But you haven't told me anything!' Why wouldn't anybody tell me what was going on? 'And I want to know more about Andreas and Nyssa, my other grandparents, and why I never met them.'

She turned at the door. 'I cannot answer these questions for you, Anna. I spoke without thinking. You must ask your parents. Tell them what happened today and ask them to tell you about your other grandparents.' She came back and placed a hand on my cheek. 'It is a story for your father to tell. But, I warn you, Delphine wants something from you, so be careful what you offer.' With that, she walked off back down the path shaking her head.

Whatever was that all about? I sat back down at the table and poured more tea.

What did I actually know about my family history? I knew that Dad moved to England when he was eighteen, to learn the restaurant trade. His father had given him enough money to set up on his own, and that was all I knew. Dad was an only child, and had never mentioned relatives. Now I was here, it seemed most unlikely that there weren't any family members to find. Any normal person would have asked their father, but he was a totally closed book about Crete.

I marvelled now at my own previous lack of interest in his side of the family. Mum had come over from Crete when she was just twenty to join Dad once he had a place to live and a job. They had been together since school. Mum was my contact with the island. I met her parents, a great-aunt or three and my other grandmother, not that I knew it at the time. I didn't remember meeting any men, but that was because they would have been working. I doubted I'd recognise any of them now, if they were still alive. I had obviously met Nyssa and stayed here in her house, but really not known who she was, or that I was in my paternal grandmother's house. Now it made sense. I didn't have strong memories of those holidays in terms of people we met, but I did remember Mum being much closer to one 'great aunt' than she was to Nyssa. I suppose that was her own mother, Cybele, and she was keeping me in the dark so I wouldn't tell Dad about Nyssa. Why couldn't I know? Had Nyssa disowned Dad? It was eating me up, not knowing. I wished I could remember some of the younger people around at the time, but it was a blur. I was too young, I suppose.

I looked around the small house that had become my home. I had shared the second bedroom with my mother, and spent my days with people who were kind, and gave me sweets and cakes, but otherwise ignored me. I was used to this treatment as it was what happened at home. I remembered playing with the china ornaments my grandmother kept on the old dresser, and getting stuck in the tiny cupboard at the top of the stairs. I must have been eight or nine when the visits suddenly stopped. Mum didn't come over for the funeral of Nyssa, and I only knew she had died when the will was read and I was contacted by her solicitor. I'd had my own problems when it had all happened, of course, and didn't think to question the legacy while I was getting divorced. It was a lifeline that had been thrown to me, and I'd grabbed it.

I drank up and rinsed both mugs, then dug in the cupboard for the box into which I'd placed the personal papers that had belonged to my grandmother. I sat at my desk and piled them up, separating out the boring legal stuff and her birth certificate from the photographs. The photos were mostly black and white and many were artificially-posed, stiff family portraits featuring, I assumed, Nyssa's own parents and family. My grandparents and family. Frustratingly, it was impossible to make sense of the people in them without a guide, so I gathered them up and slipped them into a folder ready to take round to Mrs Pantelides so I could ask her about them when she was more receptive.

It was definitely time I went back to Manchester for a visit, although the flights were rubbish at this time of the year and I didn't want to see the parents anyway. I knew it would be difficult dealing with my mother's pleas for me to go back home, and Dad's silence. But if my father had kept his past a secret for forty years, then there was a reason for it, and I had no chance of finding out about it over the phone. I had to be there and force it out of him. Maybe in a couple of weeks.

10

Nikos watched as his wife swung the car into the driveway and parked it roughly in front of the house. She looked almost jaunty, he thought, as she hurried inside. He went through to the kitchen, took the lunch his housekeeper had prepared from the fridge and set two plates, dips and bread onto the edge of the island unit. He hated the formal dining room, even though he knew Delphine loved it. Today they would eat together and he would try to build bridges with her. He rooted through the drawers until he found cutlery and glasses, and poured a delicate white wine from Spina.

'Niko?'

'I am in the kitchen, come in here,' he shouted.

Delphine appeared at the door. She had two spots of pink on her cheeks and looked happier than he had seen her in a long while. 'Is everything okay?' he asked.

'Yes, more than okay. What is this?' She pointed at the food and drink laid out on the island.

'I wanted us to eat lunch together, on our own. Come, sit. Have a small glass of wine and some meats and salad, and you can tell me what happened in Paleochora.'

He could see the usual resistance in her face to any of his ideas, but then, in an instant it had gone and she smiled at him. 'I am very hungry,' she said, sliding onto a high stool. 'This is a nice idea, Niko, thank you.'

He shrugged and took a sip of wine. 'So, how did the Andreanakises take the news?' he asked, spearing a piece of cold chicken and dipping it into the little pot of tzatziki.

'Niko, I will buy them a little house and I have given them money for clothes, but I have had the most marvellous idea. I ran into Anna Georgiou on the way back, and gave her a lift home as she was carrying heavy bags.'

Nikos stopped chewing. 'Did you go into the house?' He could feel tears in the corner of his eyes.

'I did, and it is lovely. So many signs of your mother. Her old china, the big oak dresser, the pine kitchen table, all of these she has kept. But there is a sense of the girl too. I think she may be quite a good designer.'

Nikos wiped his eyes. 'All those years when I was never allowed to visit Mama. I'd drive past and sometimes see her, but that woman next door was always there and I could never get Mother on her own to talk, to explain. Ah, Delphie, I regret so much of that time.'

'I know you do. Drink some wine, I have more news.' Delphine ate a slice of tomato and a piece of Mizithra cheese. Delicious. Why did the food taste better suddenly? 'I realised that she can help me with the Andreanakis project. I will choose a house, and Anna can help me to decorate it for them. It's perfect. That way I get to know her, she sees that we are not horrible rich people who take no care of others, and I have a proper excuse to invite her here to discuss furniture and fabrics. So you can meet her.' She looked at him sideways and sipped her wine. That tasted wonderful, too.

Nikos paused, filled fork dropping its contents back down onto the plate. 'You mean I should tell her, don't you?'

Delphine patted the top of his hand. 'It is time, you know that. Not immediately, of course. She has no idea about all this bad history, but if we handle it well, you may gain a niece and just possibly regain a younger brother. Wouldn't that be worth risking everything?'

'It would, it would.'

Nikos watched his wife eat more than he had seen her eat since he told her about Anna's arrival weeks ago. He hadn't understood how much the story of his past had affected her, and how hard she was trying to sort it out for him. 'You are so good to me, Delphie,' he said. 'Thank you.'

But would it, he wondered, be a warm meeting of long estranged brothers, or the bloodbath that most Cretan feuds ended in? That he didn't know.

11

I had some lunch and worked on the finalising of the altered drawings and plans for the restaurant in Edinburgh. The client had approved the alterations, and I needed to send the actual plans to the architect who would hate the last-minute changes, but that wasn't my problem. It was calming to focus on something I felt I had under control. Once the little clock on the mantel chimed four, I packed it all into a cardboard tube and got ready to go out again. If I got a move on, I could get to town for the afternoon post, and pick up some terracotta paint for the bathroom.

I'd tried to speak to Leo about what had happened in the morning with Delphine, but he must have had his phone switched off, so I left him a text. I wished we had made a firmer arrangement to meet, then I wouldn't be checking the phone quite so much.

~

On the way back from town I called in at the taverna to see Maria. I couldn't get the worry about Spiros' involvement in the burning of the café out of my mind, but I couldn't believe that Maria would have anything to do with it. She was so warm and open. At least I'd thought she was.

Through the window, I could see that Spiros was behind the counter, wiping glasses and looking like thunder, so I didn't go in, but walked around to the back, where I knew I would find Maria sitting on the step, slicing vegetables or doing some other preparation for the evening meals.

She looked up and waved vaguely at me with a small knife. 'Hello, Anna, do you want coffee? Or a glass of wine?' She put the bowl of tomatoes down, threw the knife in and rubbed her hands on her apron.

I'd not seen her looking so careworn. She looked exhausted and like she'd been crying, hard.

'No, Maria, I came to see you,' I said, plonking the tin of paint on the concrete path. 'Are you okay?'

Her eyes flashed with some message that I couldn't decipher. 'Spiro,' she shouted over her shoulder, 'going for a cigarette break.' Then she took my arm and walked me out of the back gate and onto the shingle.

'What is it?' I asked when she stopped marching me along the beach.

Maria sat down onto a flat stone and lit a cigarette. 'I am so angry, Anna. It's him. Despicable,' she spat.

I sat upwind of the cigarette. 'So it's true, he was involved in the fire. I can't believe he would do such a thing.'

Maria gave an ugly laugh. 'Oh, Anna, such an innocent. He was more than "involved".' She did quote marks. 'He is a, how would you say, henchman? But you are right, he would never have done such a thing before he got lost in the drink.'

'So he is the one Mr K uses to do his dirty work?'

She puffed furiously on her cigarette and nodded once.

'Because of him and his stupid, drunken behaviour we will lose everything. I will lose everything. Do you understand?'

'No, I really don't, Maria. I don't think I understand anything.'

'I have paid for the taverna many, many times over in the last twenty years. But he, Kokorakis' – and here she really did spit onto the shingle – 'he holds the deeds. He has given us notice this morning, to get out by the end of the summer season.' She sucked hard on what remained of her cigarette.

I hate smoking, but at that moment I wanted to join her. 'How could he do that? In fact, can he do that?'

'Oh, he can do that because my husband is a drunken fool and he set the fire. It was an accident, he says, a lit cigarette in the bin, but the result is the same, eh?'

I didn't know what to say, so I took her free hand and squeezed it.

'Kokorakis wants to gain some of the money back that he has given Delphine to sort out the mess. It's a lot of money. Spiros has to pay some of it back, so I have to pay also. Kokorakis will sell my home and my business. I'll have nothing left.' Maria broke down and sobbed.

I held her in my arms. How bloody dare they? How dare Kokorakis destroy lives like this? 'He can't treat you like this, Maria. It's inhuman.'

She took a shuddering breath. 'Yes, it is inhuman. It is just business to him. I wish...'

'Go on.'

'I wish he would one day understand what he has done to me.' She used the hem of her apron to dab at her eyes, but she would need much more than that to wipe away the pain.

'Is that all? Personally, I'm wishing him a slow, painful death from cancer and an eternity burning in hell.'

Maria glanced at me and laughed, stubbing out the cigarette

on a rock. 'You are definitely Greek, Anna. But you know there is nothing I can do. It has always been like this.' She moved away from me, got up awkwardly and ran her hands over her face. 'To think he once thought this face was beautiful. Now, he throws me away like dirt.'

I struggled to my feet and linked her arm. Maria and Kokorakis? Never expected that. 'What will you do now?'

We turned and walked slowly back the way we had come.

'Do? We will continue to work in the taverna until the end. What else can I do? I have money saved up, enough to join my daughter in Chania if she will have me. But him?' She cocked her head towards the taverna. 'I don't care what he does, but he is not coming with me.'

'But you're going to have to work together all summer.'

'It will be a first for him. Kokorakis no longer wants him, so I will put him to work full-time. It means one less wage to pay in the summer months. I have lived with him a long time, Anna. He will do as I ask.' She kept her head down as we walked, her shoulders slumped.

I thought she should know about my meeting earlier in the day. 'Maria, I met Delphine Kokorakis today.'

She didn't meet my eye. 'Oh?'

'She wants me to help with a design project. Do you think it's the Andreanakises' house she wants help with?'

'Of course, it makes sense. Spiros told her what you do for a living and she can use you.' She took me by both arms, and shook them. 'Anna, you need to know that they are very interested in you up at the house. Be careful what you say to them.'

'I will. I already feel a little worried to be honest. I'm not in Delphine's league, am I? So why are they interested in me? But, surely if I help to rebuild that old couple's life, then that is a good thing?'

'Yes, probably. Delphine is good underneath and she will not like what has happened, so, a good thing, yes. But him. Watch out for him.' She gave me another intense stare, then ran her hands through her hair, scraping it back from her face. 'I should get back, we will have customers.'

I walked her the rest of the way back, collecting my tin of paint at the back door. I didn't go in. I had a feeling that the taverna would not be a happy place to visit for some time. And I wondered, for the first time, if I might be in some sort of danger here on the island.

Once home, I poured myself a glass of wine and lit the fire in the living room. The air was cold, but the fire soon warmed the space and began to seep upstairs. I flopped onto the sofa and covered myself in a blanket. So much had happened in the last few days, and I still wasn't sure what it all had to do with me. I wanted to talk to someone, and was surprised when that person was Leo, not my mum. It was as if she were too far away now to be of any help, and she was complicit in my father's desire to keep his past a secret. That was an odd feeling to process.

I tried Leo again, but it went to voicemail. His unavailability made me uneasy. I know I wanted to keep it light, blah-blah-blah. I thought we had a good understanding and yet he hadn't even left me a message. What kind of business was he up to? I knew he had to go to the bank to ensure his money had come through from the States, and then he was going to the town hall to discuss permits, but that wouldn't take all day, would it?

I scrolled through my phone for a while and had a look round my pinned boards on Pinterest. The Andreanakises might like a house similar in design to what I had done here, I thought, and began a new pinboard for them.

I took the old photos out of their folder and scrutinised them some more. I thought one might be of a young Nyssa, with several children running around at the beach. It was taken in the fifties, I thought, looking at the clothes. The staring wasn't getting me any closer to learning about my family, though, so I put them away again.

Finally, having put it off all day, I rang and spoke to Mum. She had a few questions to answer. 'Mum, why haven't you told me anything about my other set of grandparents? I'm living in Nyssa's house and I know nothing about her.'

'Darling, it's your father's story to tell, not mine.'

What the hell did that mean? 'Well, Mother, he isn't telling me anything at the moment, is he? And he hasn't for the whole of my life. And, frankly, someone needs to before I really lose my temper.'

'Anna, things are... complicated. Don't be angry.'

'But I am angry, Mum. I feel like an idiot when everyone knows things I need to know and they won't tell me.'

'Your father, he has many regrets. He is...'

'What? What is he? Silent as the grave? Miserable? Just what is he, Mum?'

'He's not very well. Don't worry, the doctor has him on medication for his, you know, waterworks.'

'Is he going to be okay?' My voice trembled over the phone. Oh God. I might be mad at him, but he was my dad.

'Of course, nothing for you to worry about.' She hesitated. 'I will ask him to speak to you when you come home. It's time you knew the truth.'

At last. 'Yes, it is time. I'm sorry I shouted at you. Are you okay?'

'Yes, we're fine. So, tell me about you. Are you ready to come home yet?'

'Yes, I'll come for a visit soon. I want to see Dad. And you, of course.'

'A visit? Tut.'

It continued in that vein: had I changed my mind? Was I ready, having had my little adventure, to go back to that lovely husband of mine and have babies? Ah, the baby question. Babies she so desperately wanted, and I never did. Not with Will, anyway. She went on a bit longer. So long that in order to prevent implosion, I poured another glass of wine, dug out olives and crisps and wondered what to make for supper. I'd bought a large chicken for me and Leo to share. Seemed a bit extravagant for one.

I was relieved when there was a knock on the door. I said a hasty goodbye to my mother and pulled it open, expecting it to be Leo, but it wasn't. Instead, there stood Alex and Cathy from my Greek class. Alex had a bottle of wine in his hand.

'Good evening, Anna,' he said. 'I just met Cathy at the taverna, and we wondered if you could use some company this evening?'

'Please do say if you have plans,' said Cathy. 'We don't want to intrude, but I'd love to see what you have done with the house, and then we could go out to eat, perhaps?'

In truth, I was delighted to see them, even though they were the last people I was expecting. It had been quite a day. Although we had been meeting as a gang for weeks, and had had drinks together, I really hadn't sorted out my social life, and frankly, I needed friends I could talk to, not sleep with. I held the door wide. 'Come in! It's great to see you.'

I gave them the grand tour, and they were appropriately appreciative, and we opened the bottle. 'Stay for dinner,' I said, 'I could do with some company and I'd like to cook for you.'

It was the first time I'd cooked for anybody in Crete, but with these two, I felt no pressure. They sat at the kitchen table and ate nibbles and chatted to me while I cooked. It was as I had imagined life would be with Will, but we had ended up in a cold, marble-and-black kitchen that was rarely used, and certainly not by friends.

I chopped vegetables and added a whole bulb of garlic sliced across the middle into a roasting pan, then oiled, seasoned and herbed the chicken and put lemon inside the carcase. Into the oven it all went, and I sat with them around the kitchen table. Another glass of wine was poured, and I was glad I'd struggled home with the extra bottles. It was the first time I'd felt relaxed all day, and I wondered if they would listen and help me to make sense of what was happening.

'Anna, tell us what happened when you went to Paleochora with Cassia,' said Alex. 'I was quite worried about you, especially Cassia and her brother.'

Cathy's green eyes lit up. 'Yes, do tell. I must say it has been a lot more exciting here in the last couple of weeks than it has been for the last two years!'

While the food cooked, and the aroma of baked chicken, garlic and herbs filled the house, I told them about Constantinos, and about Maria and Spiros, and about Delphine Kokorakis. It honestly didn't make a lot more sense at the end of the tale than it had at the beginning, and they were just as horrified as I was about Spiros and poor Maria.

I sliced green beans and steamed them on the hob, adding them to leftover tomato sauce. It was almost ready.

'Okay,' said Alex, as I took plates from the shelf and warmed them in the oven. I sliced bread and warmed that, too. I was starving. 'So Mrs Kokorakis and you will help the old couple into a new house, Constantinos will go back to Athens, and Maria has lost everything.'

I ran a hand across my forehead, pushing my hair back. 'It's awful, isn't it? It's so difficult being a stranger here. I have no idea if there is any way to actually help Maria, but I'd like to try.'

'No, neither have I, but Spiros deserves all he gets,' added Cathy. 'I know he likes a drink, but to do that and call it an accident? It could have been murder! Beggars belief.' She got up and found the cutlery drawer, placing three settings in between our glasses. 'But I'm sure our collective brains can sort something out. What do you say, Alex?'

Alex turned his almost translucent pale-blue eyes to me. He looked serious, as usual. 'I also would like to help Maria, but I have a feeling Mr K is not a reasonable man. It might be better not to get involved. It could be dangerous.'

That brought the mood down. I didn't reply. How could I abandon Maria now? Instead, I cut up the chicken and loaded up the plates, hoping they were as hungry as I was. Conversation quietened as we tucked in, although there was furious thought happening all around the table. I have to say, it was a pretty decent plate of food.

'Maria needs a job,' said Cathy, pointing her fork at me. 'She knows food. There will be a taverna out there that needs her skills, I'm sure.'

'I can ask around,' said Alex. 'There is no hurry, of course. She will be busy until the autumn.'

'That's true, but at least we can look out for her. And we shouldn't assume she's helpless. Not Maria.' We laughed at that. She was a feisty character, was Maria, and not easy to crush.

'Delicious meal, thank you,' said Cathy around a mouthful of chicken. 'I had no idea you were such a good cook.'

'Truly wonderful,' added Alex and he gave me a dazzling smile. 'I could manage a little more, if there is any,' he said.

'Man after my own heart, Alex,' I said, heaping our plates again. Cathy looked horrified. No wonder she was a tiny thing.

'Learning to cook was an occupational hazard of growing up in a restaurant,' I said. 'I think my mum expected me to take over when they retire, but I wanted to get away. Art and design were my strengths at school. But here I am anyway, in Crete, cooking Greek food.'

'And looking very comfortable while you do it,' said Alex. 'You may be ready to change more than just your home?' His blue eyes twinkled. I hadn't noticed before how gentle he was because he was always so quiet and reserved. 'Change of career, perhaps?'

It hadn't occurred to me until then that I was free to do exactly what I wanted with the rest of my life. It gave me a fluttery feeling in my chest; that the universe might be offering me something entirely new and different from what had gone before. 'You know, you may be right,' I said, grinning at him. 'As I was walking back from the market I saw so many gardens with chickens, sometimes a goat and vegetables already being planted for the summer. I'd love to live a little closer to the land and have some of that for myself.'

'And of course, you can now.' He touched my shoulder. 'We must all be open to change. After all, I never expected to be living on my boat at my age. I thought I would be working in computers until I was in my sixties, but fate took a hand, I made good investments, and here I am, enjoying the good life.'

'Living the dream, eh, Alex?' asked Cathy.

'I have a few investment accounts to keep my brain busy, but yes, you could say I am living the dream.'

I'd never thought about how old Alex was. I'd assumed he was in his late forties, but he could easily have been younger. He had the permanently brown, weather-beaten face of a person who spent many months out at sea, and his hair was so blond it looked silver. 'Will you go off sailing when the weather improves?' I asked him.

'Yes, I go round the islands. People charter the boat and I crew for them.' He tipped his glass at me. 'I could do with a cook in the summer months.'

I laughed. It sounded wonderful, pottering around Greek islands on a boat, cooking lovely food, but the idea was ludicrous. I still had to earn a living for the rest of the year. 'Love the idea, but I don't think it's quite for me, thanks, Alex.'

He looked disappointed. 'Okay, but if you change your mind, you know where to find me.'

I did, he lived on board a beautiful sailing boat in the bay.

'Oh, Alex,' piped up Cathy, and I could detect a definite simpering. 'Anna and I would love to come and see your boat one day. Perhaps you could take us out for a little sail and show us the ropes, as it were?'

Nice work, old gal, I thought. I'd love to have a nosy round and see how it all worked. Just in case I should ever change my mind.

We arranged a possible day out for later in the spring and I refused their offer of help to wash up. While Cathy went to the bathroom I asked Alex to see her safely home; she was definitely the worse for wear.

'You do not need to ask, I will make sure she is safe. And Anna, I will help you if you ever need me, too.' He gave me his telephone number and email address on a card. 'Whenever you need me, I'll be there.'

He gathered me up in a hug and thanked me for dinner. I had a feeling I wasn't the only one feeling a bit lonely out here, despite living the dream. Sometimes it's nicer to share it with someone. Then Cathy came down and she gave me a hug, too, and I felt better than I had in days. Oddly, I hadn't missed Leo at all. This felt like the start of friendship, with people who didn't want anything from me except my company. It felt good.

It was quite late, gone eleven thirty and I was getting ready for bed, when a text came through from Leo. *Sorry not been in touch. Something has come up. Staying over in Chania. Xx.* To the point, I supposed, and it was a message. *Fine,* I sent, *see you soon.* I hoped it felt as dismissive as I intended it to be.

12

A couple of days later, there were two letters lying on the mat behind the door when I came downstairs. One was a formal invitation to dinner with the Kokorakises and a 'few close friends' who would like to meet me, apparently. They had chosen the following Saturday night, over the Easter weekend which was awkward as I still intended to go home for a visit, but I guessed the parents could wait a few more days.

I had mixed feelings about the invitation. On the one hand, entry into the wealthier parts of society could bring me work and recognition for that work. On the other, Kokorakis burnt down people's houses. Well, not him personally, but still. Why would I want to ally myself with such a man? On the other hand, Delphine was trying to help sort out the situation, and I wanted to help her. I took Maria's warning about Kokorakis seriously, but I didn't feel able to refuse.

The other letter was the bill from the builders, which I paid immediately through internet banking. They wouldn't know what to do with themselves, receiving their money so quickly. I then spent a couple of hours completing the restaurant project invoice and sent my bill along to the owner. I'd be lucky if I saw payment for that within three months.

Then I had a much needed proper think about the practicalities of running a business on Crete; paying tax, sorting health insurance, trying for my work visa again, buying a car, all the stuff I'd been avoiding thinking about. I felt better when I stopped for coffee later; I'd made a big decision that needed making. I would call Cassia and ask if she could help me out with the more complex forms, and then I'd complete them, and begin the task of becoming a Greek citizen. Now that the UK was finally out of the EU there was no other option if I wanted to stay permanently, and I liked the idea of dual citizenship – it matched how I felt about myself – a woman balanced between or possibly bestriding two cultures.

I took my coffee out into the garden, and breathed in the cool air, still dusty from the builders' rubble. I had to stop waiting for life to happen, and make my own. First, a car. Next, the garden. There would be room for a vegetable patch in one corner, but probably not enough room for chickens. The sun, which was trying its best to break through cloud, was at the back of the house during the heat of the day, which was the worst direction. It would bake in summer. But if I could plant some trees to make natural screening and provide some shade along the back wall, and incorporate lots of mulch and new soil, I might have a chance. And I needed to get started straight away if I wanted veg this summer. But where on the island would I get soil? Did they have garden centres in Crete? I brought the laptop out and balanced it on my knees. And how did we do anything before Google? After ten minutes browsing, I made another decision. I had to get a car, preferably today, to transport it all. I sipped my drink. Exciting times.

The little grey cat crept through a hole in the wall and rubbed around my legs, looking for food, of course. Mrs P followed the cat, but came via her gate into the little lane, and leant over the back wall to chat.

'Kalimera, Anna,' she said. 'You had a nice time last night, yes? With your friends?'

'I did, thank you. I hope we didn't make too much noise and keep you awake?'

'No, I like to hear you enjoying yourself. It has been a quiet house for so long.' She straightened her headscarf, tying it more tightly behind her head. 'I must shop for food today,' she said, 'but perhaps we can share tea later when I come home? You have not yet been to my house since you arrived.'

'I would love to! Thank you so much. But, are you fasting for Lent? Will it be okay for you to give me tea?'

'We do not eat animal products, oil or fish leading up to Easter, but everything else is fine. I can still bake. Shall we say four o'clock? That is the time for you English to have tea, is it not?' She waved at me and chuckled her way round to the road.

Excellent, a chance to get to know her a little better at last.

I rang Cassia and she agreed to meet me in town, next to the car sales dealership. I was happy about managing the Greek for a transaction, but I'd only ever had a car on a three-year renewing lease, and had little idea of what to look out for.

'Cassia, thank you so much for coming,' I said, and kissed her on both cheeks. Something had changed in our relationship since we had shared the horror of what had happened to her brother. It felt warm, more like friends than teacher and pupil. I wasn't expecting to see Tinos standing there as well though.

'Hello, Anna,' he said. 'I thought I would be more help in choosing a car than she would.' He laughed, and received a punch to his good arm from his twin.

'That may be true,' I said, 'but you'll both be better than me. It's good to see you looking better, Tino.'

He smiled at me, wistfully. 'I feel that I have lost part of me, but I can, and will start again elsewhere. I am young after all,' he said, and winked. I hadn't been winked at so much in years.

An overweight, balding man in a suit too tight for him stood just inside the sales room door, eyeing us up.

'Okay,' I said, 'we should see what Mr Charisma has to say. I can always go to Chania if the deal isn't good enough.' We strolled around the dozen or so cars on the lot, and I took a fancy to a smallish white one. Tinos gave his approval when he had checked the mileage and looked under the bonnet. Why do they do that? Men? What can you see under a bonnet that tells you anything useful? I just liked the simplicity of the controls, and that it had working air conditioning and wasn't yellow. Or orange.

After a half hour of bargaining conducted by Tinos, and the scrutiny of my passport, international driving licence, English driving licence and proof of address, I was able to purchase a four-year old Fiat Punto in white. I passed over my credit card, then we waited and drank his awful coffee while he did the paperwork and gave me the papers that proved it was a road-worthy vehicle. Hurray! The easiest first step of my plan was complete. The fact that I had never driven abroad didn't dawn on me until I put the key in the ignition and had to remember to drive on the wrong side of the road, and not to keep trying to change gear with my right hand which would only result in me pulling on the handbrake. Yes, Will had always driven when we went to Italy or France. The litany of shame continued.

'Don't worry,' said Tinos, 'you'll soon learn, and now you will be free!'

I drove them, as slowly as an arthritic grandma, to a fish restaurant on the promenade. I wanted to treat them both for helping me, and we all wanted to avoid Maria's. Especially Tinos.

Over fresh bouillabaisse we talked over the taking out of dual citizenship. Cassia agreed that it was a good idea. She had spent years trying to find ways for refugees to be accepted into Greece, and understood the system. My Greek parentage meant that it would be a formality, but I still wanted her help as my Greek wasn't good enough for the more formal stuff. I'd have to settle for three-month residency passes for the moment though. I hadn't realised it would be years before I could apply for permanency.

'What are you going to do now, Tino?' I asked, as he finished his glass of white wine and folded his napkin.

Tinos ran his finger around the rim of the glass. 'I am a chef by training,' he said. 'I know Cassia and our parents would like me to go home to Athens for safety, but I have made my home here. There are still many young people who need my help. And' – he drew himself up in his chair – 'I am not of a mind to allow *him*' – he gestured over his shoulder and up the road with his thumb – 'to bully me off the island. No, I shall look for a job, save money, and then try again.'

'Meanwhile, I have lost my home office,' said Cassia, 'but I am sort of enjoying the company of my annoying little brother.'

'Five minutes younger,' he said, 'and she never lets me forget it.'

They were such nice people, I couldn't help but feel a little jealous. How I used to long for a brother or sister to share what had been a lonely childhood. I'd had pretty much anything I wanted as a child, except my parents' time. The restaurant always came first. And there were no more children after me. For long, countless evenings alone in the flat upstairs, all I had was the TV and my books, drawing and painting and the fantasy worlds into which I escaped.

I hadn't had any wine with lunch, I was way too scared to drink and drive. I paid the bill and then drove the twins up the street and along the main road to Cassia's apartment. Having dropped them off, I negotiated the petrol station, filling the car up to the top and buying a bunch of flowers for Mrs P, and then found the smaller road that led to my house. There were cars parked and even double-parked at odd angles all the way up the road. Nothing stood in the way of a Cretan ready for his lunch, especially not road markings. I was dreading having to reverse at any point, but luckily, the fact that it was still siesta time meant that the roads were quiet, and I was able to draw up outside my house without mishap. Well, possibly I could have got a bit closer to the kerb, but who was checking?

Once inside, and having checked at least three times that the car lock worked, I let out a little whoop and danced around the living room. I was mobile. I could get soil and plants for my garden, carry groceries, go for drives across the mountains, visit historical sites. The island was mine to explore. I was a resourceful, independent woman, on the verge of my new life.

I drank down a pint of water, standing at the sink. I think I may have sweated it out trying not to run anybody down.

I can honestly say that at that moment I was happier than I had been for a very long time. I was home.

Four o'clock came quickly. The flowers looked better when I rewrapped them in plain paper and hand-tied the bunch with raffia, so I held them in front of me as I tapped on the door. Mrs Pantelides appeared and gave me a warm smile, taking the flowers from me and kissing me on the cheek. She looked completely different. It was the first time I had ever seen her without a headscarf. It revealed hair dyed an interesting shade of brown and carefully curled. Gone was the permanent apron over the long black skirt, and in their place was a flowery dress and silver earrings. 'Wow, Mrs Pantelides,' I said, 'you look wonderful!'

She blushed and ushered me inside. The living room took my breath away. Every single shelf, corner, tabletop and cupboard was covered in Cretan pottery. It looked like the inside of an artisan shop. 'This is amazing. Have you collected all of this?' I couldn't help picking some pieces up and looking at them. 'So delicate and so beautifully painted.'

There were ranks of photographs on the shelves of the old oak dresser that backed against the adjoining wall. It felt rude to do more than glance at them, but I could see proud young men dressed all in black carrying rifles, and young children sitting on the knees of old ladies. Priests and a younger Mrs Pantelides dressed in traditional costume celebrating Easter, perhaps. What a wonderful family history in this small room. How I would love to have had something like this. I patted the folder of photos that was tucked under my arm. Surely I could get some answers here?

I was so engrossed I didn't notice that someone else was there, sitting in the kitchen. He was a priest, a large, portly man with a huge beard and a kindly face, dressed entirely in black, of course. He pulled himself to his feet but remained where he was behind the table. I walked through and shook his hand, feeling a bit embarrassed that I hadn't noticed him. 'How nice to meet you, Father,' I said in Greek.

He, of course, replied in English. 'Father Georgiou, but Stav will do fine here with family. It is good to meet you too,' he said. 'My mother has told me much about you.'

'Sit down, Anna, sit down,' said Mrs Pantelides, before I could ask what she'd been saying about me, and settled me at the table. The table was also covered in Cretan pottery, but each bowl and plate was full of pastries, fruit, and cake. It was a feast, and not what I had been expecting. Clearly Easter fasting in Crete was a bit different from how people did it in England. Not that I took part anyway. I'd walked away from religion as quickly as I had walked away from home. Ran, truthfully. Even now, meeting a nun unexpectedly kicks my 'fight or flight' response into action. A childhood spent in a catholic school with a sarcastic nun had firstly frightened me to death with the fear of damnation, and then made me angry that they got away with such behaviour towards children.

'Help yourself,' she said, handing me a small plate. 'Would you like tea?' She poured it from a huge black metal teapot, and returned it to her range, from which heat warmed the room.

Father Georgiou, how could I call him Stav? Father Georgiou said, 'My mother didn't collect the pottery, Anna, she decorated it. She is a well-known pottery painter in Crete. Very famous, eh, Mama?'

Mrs Pantelides blushed and shushed him.

'You decorated it all? It's beautiful work.'

Mrs P wafted her face with her hand, but she was pleased, I could see. 'It was my job, Anna. I don't do it anymore, I am too old, but I keep my favourite designs and pieces. They comfort me.' She bit at the corner of a sweet cake dripping in honey and I observed her new look while we ate.

Older Greek women still go into mourning and wear black when their husbands die before them. I thought the tradition was only meant to last a couple of years, but I had seen many old ladies wearing black for the rest of their lives. Probably because there's always someone popping their clogs that you know, I supposed. I wondered what had caused the change. 'You look very nice in your dress, Mrs Pantelides. I've only seen you in black until now.'

She shook her head sadly. 'It is twenty-three years since my beloved first husband died, five years since the second, but only two years since your grandmother passed over,' she replied. 'My son tells me I should come out of mourning, at least on some days of the week, even though I feel it is too soon. But he is the priest, so how could I disobey? This seemed like a good day to start.' She patted her hair. 'You don't think it looks too young for me?'

Father Georgiou kicked my foot under the table and I got the message. 'No, I really do think you look lovely, and you have a beautiful home.'

We ate and drank some more. The honey cakes were delicious even if they did spray crumbs all over the tablecloth. 'How long have you lived here?'

'Oh, many years,' she said. 'I remember you as a tiny child coming to stay with your mother. You won't remember, but Stavros took you to the beach when he was back from the seminary for holidays.'

I looked hard at the priest, who was jaw-deep into pastry. If he'd shaved the beard off, and lost thirty years, and at least thirty pounds, I might have been able to place him. 'No, I must have been very young. I don't remember you, Father.' Then I looked properly at Mrs P. 'It's strange, I think I do remember you, though, Mrs Pantelides, now that I see you dressed so differently. You used to come to see my grandmother, with my great aunt. Is that right?'

The priest swigged down tea, cleared both his throat and the front of his cassock and gave his mother a look and a nod.

It was happening again. People knowing things without telling me. I felt like Alice in bloody Wonderland sometimes.

'Anna, you should know that Pantelides is my married name from my second husband.' She crossed herself and gave a deep sigh. 'To lose two husbands, eh? No, I was once a Georgiou, like you and like Stavros, who is my child from my first husband.'

'Oh! Are we related? Are you my cousin, Stav?' I felt quite excited, even if an Orthodox priest wasn't top of my list of lost relatives.

Mrs Pantelides reached over and took my hand. 'My first husband was your mother's uncle. I am not sure what that makes us, so call me Irini, please.' She smiled. 'I'm very pleased to meet you!'

'So you're my what? I mean what relative are you to me? Great aunt?' I was beginning to sound like someone off an episode of *Long Lost Family*, but I was completely taken by surprise. 'No, that's not right.'

I tried again. 'Okay, so you are my great aunt by marriage? Possibly?' I would have to get to grips with the family tree later. Were they all called Georgiou? The same surname on both sides of the family, or were we all related? Yipes, that could be interesting. 'So I can call you Aunt Irini, perhaps? But why didn't you tell me? Why have I lived next to you for six weeks and you haven't said a word? I feel like an idiot.'

Father Georgiou intervened. 'It seemed like a good idea to wait, as we know your mother has told you little of your family on the island. Since your father left, things have changed here in Kissamos. It seemed better to say nothing.'

I thought about Kokorakis, and wondered if he had something to do with my father leaving the island all those years ago. 'Do you know why my father left? And why he won't talk to me about Crete?'

'I have already told you, Anna,' said Mrs P, or Irini as I should now call her, 'the story is your father's to tell. But Stavros and I, we feel there are things you should know.' She got stiffly to her feet and went into the front room, returning with a gilt-framed photograph. She put the picture on the table and stood between me and Stavros, leaning heavily with one hand on the back of my chair. 'So, this was taken when you were a very little girl,' she said. 'Who do you see?'

A younger Irini holding an enormous teapot, and Stavros who was a plump youth lurking in the background, and there was my mother, only in her early twenties, with me, no more than three or four years old sitting on her lap. 'It's me and Mum,' I said, tracing Mum's face with my finger.

'And this lady.' Irini pointed to the chair next to Mum's, where a vigorous-looking woman with black hair and large eyes sat with a plate in her lap. 'This is Nyssa, your paternal grandmother.'

The breath caught in my throat. What? 'So who's this?' I asked, pointing to the other woman sitting next to Mum.

'That is your maternal grandmother, Cybele.'

I was struggling a little. I'd never seen pictures of my father's parents, of course, but this was the grandmother I had stayed with as a child. Nyssa. The other woman was an aunt, I thought, who we visited. 'So, Mum and I stayed with Nyssa, whilst my dad thought we were staying with Cybele?'

'Yes. That way Nyssa could get to know you. And, until today, we have never told anybody about what your mother did. It was a great secret.'

'And risky. If Dad had found out, he'd have been furious. It was a betrayal of him.'

Stavros chuckled. 'That is a harsh interpretation. Your grandmother had done nothing wrong, except to be married to your grandfather, so why shouldn't she see her only grandchild?'

I sat back in my chair. This was a lot to take in. So my mother had lied to Dad for years, thirty-five years to be exact. 'Nyssa's wearing black, did my grandfather die young?'

Stavros sent a warning glance to his mother. 'He died some time after this picture was taken. Nyssa lived alone in your house.'

'So they didn't live together.' I searched the photo, trying to bring it back. 'There was no man in the house that I remember.' I thought about my dad again, and wondered for the hundredth time if this was all about an actual family feud, and now I wanted to know if Nyssa had been a victim as well as her son. 'Is this all to do with the reason my father left and moved to the UK? To do with his father?'

'Yes, this we can tell you,' he said, topping up his tea.

Maybe, finally I was going to get some answers. I leaned forward and placed the folder of photographs on the table, taking each photo and placing it between the plates. 'What else can you tell me? Who are these people?'

They looked at each picture, Irini sighing at some of them. 'They are your family, Anna, but I cannot say more.' She pointed at the one of the young woman with children on the beach. 'That is your grandmother and some of the local children.'

'Is one of them my father?'

Reluctantly, she pointed out a small boy with his back turned to the camera, playing with the sand.

I picked it up and looked more closely. 'And the other children?'

Irini didn't answer, but got up and poured yet more tea.

Father Georgiou wriggled on his hard chair. 'It is difficult to break a promise,' he said, 'but, I believe you have met the Kokorakis family?'

'Yes, I met Delphine Kokorakis a few days ago. She has invited me for dinner.' Why was he changing the subject?

Aunt Irini covered her mouth with her hand. 'I wonder what she really wants from you,' she murmured.

'She wants me to help put right a wrong that her husband committed,' I said. 'You know about the fire in Paleochora?'

Father Georgiou crossed himself and held onto the crucifix that sat on his ample stomach amongst the cake crumbs. 'A terrible deed that I fear cannot be put right with money. What does she want with you, Anna?'

'She wants me to help her decorate the interior of the new house she is going to buy for the Andreanakis family. That's all.'

The priest caught his mother's eye. 'Then maybe that is all, God willing. Delphine might have a good heart under her hard face.'

Aunt Irini clutched at my hand, however. 'Be careful with that family.'

'I will,' I said, squeezing her hand, 'I've been to Paleochora. I've seen what Kokorakis can do. The young man whose business was burned down is the brother of my Greek teacher. I want to help, but I will take care, I promise.' I took my hand back and drank the tea, stewed though it had become.

'Well, that is what we wanted to tell you,' said Aunt Irini. 'To be careful. Perhaps that is enough for now.' She picked up her teacup, but her eyes were fixed on those of her son.

'I know there's more,' I said quietly. 'I'm not a child. You can tell me what you are hiding.' I gathered up the photos and stuffed them back in the folder.

Irini took a deep breath. 'No, I cannot. But, yesterday I talked to your mother on the telephone, and she agreed that despite what your father says, it is time that you met some of your Greek family as you have come home to live, and here we are, meeting you.'

'You talked to my mother?' I couldn't quite get my head around the fact that Irini had hidden her identity from me, and that she and my mother were obviously talking about me behind my back.

'I talk to her every so often, she is like a daughter to me, and I like to know how the restaurant is going, and how you are.' She dropped her eyes to the tabletop. 'I have to tell you that I have been reporting back on how you are doing. But I have said only good things, please believe me. You are fitting in so well here, making friends, even a boyfriend.'

Her unstinting help with the builders suddenly became clear. My mother would have asked her to step in and make sure it all went well, because I was clearly unable to manage it on my own. Obviously. Do mothers ever stop interfering? Do they ever allow their children to grow up?

Suddenly it was all too much. Too much information and too much lack of information. I wiped my fingers on the paper napkin and stood up. 'Thank you so much for a delicious afternoon tea, Aunt Irini. It was lovely to meet you, too, Stav. I hope we'll see more of each other soon. I have to go now,' I said and tucked the folder back under my arm.

Irini's old face was a map of worry as I slipped out the door and went home.

I slammed my door tight behind me, flopped down onto the sofa by the window and sulked. After several minutes of fuming I had a self-pitying weep and found myself using the bottom of my T-shirt as a handkerchief. So I got up, found a tissue, blew my nose and went upstairs to wash my face. It was not a pretty sight. I couldn't have explained to anyone exactly why I was feeling sorry for myself, except that I felt I could never get away from the prying eyes. From all the people who knew best how I should live my life. Even when I was gifted the house, and thought I was finally free to make my own way in life, my mother was still there, interfering, spying on me. And I'd bet a million pounds she was feeding it all back to Will, who had already told her he was waiting for me to 'get over my midlife crisis' and go back to him. As if. I glared at the phone. I should ring Mum and question her about her secret double life, but I couldn't, I'd get angry, or upset, and that wouldn't get me anywhere. Cool and calm I needed to be when I had that particular conversation.

Darkness had fallen while I'd been feeling sorry for myself, so I pulled down the blinds, cleared the grate from the day before and set a fire. As it got going, I ran a bath and found bubbles and bath oil and put them both in.

It was odd that, apart from one text, Leo had not been back in touch. For the first time I felt a niggle of worry. It was gone six o'clock, which meant he had been out of touch for almost two days. I texted him again, and took the phone into the bathroom with me. I hoped he wasn't in any sort of trouble. Especially with Kokorakis. He wouldn't be so stupid, would he?

The warmth of the water calmed me down, and enabled me to think. I did understand that Irini felt unable to tell me my father's story if he had expressly forbidden her from doing so, but it was getting ridiculous. There was obviously a secret that I didn't understand, and it was about my father leaving the island. Why did his mother live alone in this little house? How could something from forty years ago, before I was even born, be of such importance now?

Dry and wrapped in my fleecy dressing gown, I made scrambled eggs on toast and a huge mug of camomile tea, and took them through into the living room, which was warm and cosy. I didn't want to think about family for the rest of the night. I was tempted to watch a film on Netflix, but didn't trust myself not to end up in tears again, so I played some music, dug out the laptop, and lost myself in designing another little house just like mine for an elderly couple who had lost everything.

13

I lay snuggled under my duvet, with only the slowly lightening stripe down the side of the blind indicating that dawn was on its way. Going to bed early had been an excellent idea, but I was now wide awake. I was contemplating moving into the smaller bedroom during the winter for the morning light, and then into the front room in the summer when the light at the back would be too strong, when there was a quiet, tentative knock on the front door.

I leapt out of bed, worried that it might be Aunt Irini in trouble. She was an old lady after all. I struggled into my dressing gown and trotted downstairs on cold feet. I opened the door to find not her, but Leo on the doorstep. He was wearing a heavy coat against the cold wind coming down from the mountains and looked awful; tired, baggy-eyed and with several days' beard growth.

'Hi,' he said, 'sorry to wake you. Can I come in?'

I let him in, of course, and he enveloped me in a hug that didn't smell too good. 'What on earth have you been up to?' I asked, locking the door behind him and pushing him into the living room. The remnants of the fire were still putting out a little heat so I added a log and stirred the embers a bit. It might catch. 'Do you need a drink, some food?'

'I'm just tired, Anna,' he said. 'Would it be all right if I took a bath and then crashed here for a few hours? It gets so noisy at the hotel during the day and I need to sleep.'

'What's going on? Why haven't you been to bed?' I was at a loss.

He took my hand. 'Oh, you know, got drinking and talking with some boys on the Athens boat and one thing led to another.' He sighed. 'I may be several hundred euros worse off than I was some hours ago.'

I'm not sure quite what I'd been imagining he'd been up to, but none of it was drunken gambling on the night boat from Athens. 'Athens? I thought you'd been in Chania? And I thought you'd been in trouble, you look so awful. I can't believe you've just been playing cards,' I said. 'Leo, why won't you tell me what you're up to?'

There was no reply, of course. He stood silent, and almost sullen at the foot of the stairs. So I gave in. 'Of course you can have a bath and get into bed. I'm awake now anyway, so sort yourself out. I'll just collect some clothes and then I won't need to disturb you.' We headed upstairs and I ran the bath for him.

'Thank you.' He cupped my chin and breathed beer and cigarettes over me. 'You're wonderful, in case I haven't told you that already.' He sat on the edge of the bed, looking ready to drop, until the bath was deemed deep enough. Then he stripped off his clothes and dumped them in a pile on the bedroom floor, and got into the bath with a splash and a sigh.

I let the door close and looked back into my pretty bedroom, now decidedly untidy. For a giddy moment, I was tempted to do that thing you always see on the TV, where the woman checks the wallet of the man and finds something that reveals he is the serial killer or already married or whatever. I didn't do it. She always gets caught on the TV too, and I didn't want him to catch me out. How embarrassing would that be? However, he told me he was going to Chania, not Athens. I couldn't work out why he was lying. It wasn't a nice feeling. Everybody had their secrets. Except me, it appeared.

I shook out the duvet, put a towel on the end of the bed for him and took my clothes downstairs to get dressed. It was still cold, colder still than it had been in March, and here we were at the end of April and the winds were getting colder. Snow was quite possible in spring, my mother had warned me. Crete has an almost alpine climate because of the huge mountains, she said, and Cassia had said it too. Great. I added logs to the fire and wondered about getting central heating, but as the sun rose over the mountains, the heat came with it and I realised it would be one of those glorious clear days, just right for starting a garden.

Above my head, the floor creaked as Leo got into bed, and I heard nothing more from him all morning.

So, with tea, yogurt and honey and toast, and seated at the kitchen table, I planned my trip back to my parents. I'd need to fly to Athens and then catch a plane to Manchester, and I wouldn't get in until the middle of the night. Great. At least the flights back were closer together. I regarded the wall connecting me to Irini next door. It would be a hell of a lot cheaper, and much easier to force the old lady to tell me the truth. I really did not want to go back home. It was duty that called. Dad was always so gregarious in the restaurant, the life and soul, but in the house he said little. He was too tired to play when I was young, and too busy to talk to me when I was older. I guess we grew apart. I didn't have the open, argumentative relationship I have with my mother, and I didn't know how to get him to open up and tell me what I wanted to know either.

Maybe it was too soon to go back. I felt sure there was more I could learn about my family here, on the island. And it would be typical of my mother to read all sorts of messages into my return and invite bloody Will over. I saved the information and closed the laptop. There was plenty of time to book it later.

More interestingly, I thought, pouring more tea, was what Leo had been up to. How had a stopover in Chania turned into a trip to Athens? I had no idea of the permissions he would need to convert the old ruin of a house into a restaurant and casino, but it wouldn't be cheap, or easy. He obviously came from money over in the States. His clothes said it all. He lived in New York but didn't have that broad accent that you heard in films. Leo sounded privately educated, and his father owned a string of restaurants, not a humble single one, like my parents. So he had the money and the desire to set up his business here in Crete, even if the country was still suffering a horrible depression and nobody would make it easy for him.

I wondered what it was that had driven so many young men away from Crete after the war. Poverty? Loss of the freedom they had grown used to? Being wanted for arson, or murder? I didn't know. The Cretans had fought so hard against the Germans to save their island, but many of the young men left and started again all over the world. I'd always understood that my parents went to England for the same reason, in the eighties. To start a new life. Ironic then, that I should retrace their journey back here but for a similar reason.

Cheered, I made a list of what I needed to start my gardening project and headed over to the nearest garden centre, which was in Plaka on the other side of the bay. It was quiet on a Sunday morning, so the drive was less stressful than it could have been and I arrived at the garden centre in better condition than I'd expected. Piece of cake, this driving abroad stuff.

Firstly, I bought a car boot liner in the shape of a large tarpaulin and spread it over the boot and up the sides of the car. No way was I messing up my nice, clean vehicle.

I was the only customer that early on a Sunday, and the owner helped me load compost, trowels, spade and fork, buckets and lots of tiny seedlings into the car boot. I had kept the old fig tree that had become lodged into the garden wall, and bought a peach to go next to it. And, as a late brainwave, four plastic cloches to protect the little plants if the weather changed for the worse. That would get me started, at least. The drive back passed quickly; I was full of plans.

I was on my knees and up to my elbows in soil when Leo finally appeared at the back door, looking rather sexy in just his jeans.

'Good morning, Earth Mother,' he said. 'Do you have coffee?'

'It's in the cupboard, make a pot. I'll stop and get cleaned up.' I stood and stretched my poor back. It was hard work, digging up old soil and mixing it with the new stuff, but it was going to be a good garden, I knew it. I poured water from my new watering can over the short lines of seedlings and kept fingers crossed that I could at least have a coffee before things crawled out from under stones and ate them. Lettuce, cucumber, tomatoes and green beans looked fragile in the soil, but I had to try.

Leo was hungry, as was I after all the exercise, so I scrambled eggs and spinach and we had lunch together.

'This is great,' he said, shovelling the food in. I made more toast and poured more coffee. The guy could eat.

'So, things didn't go according to plan in Chania then,' I tried, more to see what he might say than in expectation of a straight answer. I was learning that Leo liked to keep his life in compartments.

'Oh, I hadn't got all the paperwork that I needed, so I had to go across the water and see a few people, put a few things in place, you know.' He waved his hand about, then put his head back down and forked up more food.

Like a locked safe. 'So have you got a lawyer for the purchase? I can give you the name of mine? She was fantastic, did all the paperwork for me on this place, managed all the legal Greek.' I sipped coffee and nibbled on a last piece of toast, watching him eating. I have a thing about men's forearms, which I justify as being completely legal and above board. I couldn't take my gaze away from his right arm, as he flexed the muscle and all the little curly hairs around his wrist caught the light. I'd already noticed that they were strong hands with flat, wide palms and long fingers. I thought of Michelangelo's sketches for his statue of Adam in the Sistine Chapel, all languid pointing and charged with the painter's obsession for his model.

'Hey, dreamer,' Leo interrupted. 'I lost you there for a minute. I said, going to Athens was part of getting a lawyer. I wanted my own guy from back home to help me sort this out. He's Greek-American like me. Okay?' He pushed a lock of hair out of my eyes with his equally strong left hand. 'But we don't have to talk about all that, do we?' he murmured, and dragged my chair across to his. 'How about we catch up for lost time? I've missed you.' He kissed the nape of my neck and a shiver ran through me. All thoughts of my seedlings quite disappeared as we wasted the rest of Sunday afternoon in the most delicious way.

∼

I mentioned the invitation to the Kokorakises' dinner party as he was preparing to leave, much later in the day. Leo stood near the door, holding me tightly and I caught a glimpse of the envelope lying on my desk. 'Oh, I forgot to mention, I've met Delphine Kokorakis and she wants me to help her make a new home for the Andreanakises.'

His face was blank.

'You know, the old couple we saw in Paleochora with Tino.'

'Of course, sorry. But why you? Why did she speak to you?' He dropped his coat on the floor and flopped onto the sofa, patting the space next to him.

'Well, I am an interior designer, Leo. But actually, I think Spiros was spying for them, and perhaps Maria was, too. I think they have known everything about me since I came. Maria was my only friend when I arrived. I suppose I told her lots about myself. More fool me. I bet they know about you as well.'

I realised at that point that I had told Leo nothing of the past few days. Of Maria and Mr Kokorakis, of Aunt Irini, of Delphine. I felt oddly reluctant to discuss my family revelations; instead I told him about meeting Delphine and the dinner invitation, and the terrible revenge exacted on Maria for Spiros' stupidity. 'Anyway, there is little we can do to stop that man evicting Maria and Spiros, but I don't want to miss the chance to help the Andreanakises. They did nothing wrong, and I can help Delphine. At least she is trying to put things right. Perhaps I can ask her to intervene about Maria too.'

Leo had watched my face so closely as I'd told him my news I thought he might take a bite off the end of my nose. 'So,' I continued, 'I will have to respond soon to the dinner invitation as it's happening next Saturday. Would you like to come with me, Leo?' As soon as it was out of my mouth I regretted it. Did I really want him with me? Didn't that tie us together as a couple?

A tie I didn't want? What was the matter with me? Afraid to go to a party alone, or ashamed to be alone?

Leo's eyes had veered off toward the low burn of the fire. I could almost feel him evaluating the information.

He turned back to me and grinned his huge toothy grin. 'Will I? Will I come and meet Mr K in his mansion at the top of the hill, and be wined and dined by the guy who is selling me my restaurant? Or, rather, failing to sell me my restaurant?' He leapt up and pulled me to my feet. 'Too right I will. What an introduction! You know, I could have waited months for a chance like this, but you just waltz straight in there. Amazing. You are my lucky charm, Anna.' He kissed me, hard, and danced me round the small space.

'So that's a yes, then?'

'That's a definite yes. Hooeee!' He put me down. 'Okay, honey, I have to go and get my paperwork up to date, then I'm off again for a couple of days on business to meet my lawyer and do some more legal stuff. But I promise I will be here, in time to pick you up for dinner, in my good suit, on Saturday evening. You've done so well!' He kissed me again then left, racing off towards his hotel and smoking like a man possessed.

I stood at the door and watched him disappear. What the hell was all that about? I had the worst feeling that I had manipulated myself into doing what Leo wanted without even knowing I was doing it. And he'd been so bloody patronising too. *You've done so well.* I'm not twelve.

I felt a bit sick. And, if Kokorakis was the higher society Leo wanted to be in with, then I wasn't at all sure he was a person I wanted in my new life. Never mind how beautiful his arms were. And I hated the cigarettes. I actually can't stand smoking. I'd tried to ignore it, but it wouldn't go away. He smelled.

I put the overhead light on in the kitchen to illuminate the darkening garden, and attempted to cover the seedlings in the cloches to save them from the birds. My earlier good mood had vanished. I wasn't at all sure I liked Leo Arakis, even if my body betrayed me every time he looked at me. I reminded myself that right at the start of this affair, only a week or so ago, I knew that Leo was not a keeper, and that I should play, enjoy, then move on. So that's what I would do, I'd take my own advice for once. I wished I hadn't invited him to the party, but it was too late now, he was coming.

14

On Monday morning, response to Delphine written, I added my phone number and sealed it in an envelope. Then, on impulse, I pulled on a jacket and set out into the chill morning sunshine to walk up the road and see what her house looked like. I knew there was a large wall surrounding the property, and I'd had a look on Google Maps to get a feel for the size, but nothing beats seeing it yourself. It was a pleasant walk. When I complain about the hill, it isn't actually a hill, it's more of a slope, but I'm so unfit it feels like a mountain track. The road only starts getting steeper as it heads up into the White Mountains which stand over us all in Kissamos. They took my eye every time I looked up, like a full moon does on a clear night. Tops sparkling with snow, sunlight creating dark shadows, the mountains were the permanent face of the island.

I stopped outside the wrought-iron gate and peered in through the bars. The house had been built in the nineties, I guessed. It was all huge windows, concrete and glass. The original house stood off to the left, a more typical Greek villa with verandahs and smaller windows to keep out the heat. The main house was definitely more the status symbol of a successful man, but I thought it was interesting that Kokorakis had kept his old home. A tie to a simpler past, perhaps.

I pushed the envelope into the mailbox and wandered back down the hill towards Maria's. I wanted to support her but not get involved with Spiros. I was worried that I might say something I shouldn't. I walked a bit further and thought a bit harder. Spiros was being punished enough, wasn't he? I couldn't see anybody else wanting to employ him now that Kokorakis had let him go. And I should support my friend. I doubted she had wanted to spy for Kokorakis, and deep down, I didn't believe Spiros had intended to set the fire.

The taverna was quiet except for the regulars, who now nodded and said 'Kalimera' as I entered, which was an improvement. Maria looked up from a newspaper she had spread out across the countertop.

'Anna, how lovely. We haven't seen you for days. Coffee?'

'Are you okay, Maria?'

She shook her head briefly, then gave me a look that said: not here, not now and pointed a finger at the stairway. So I hopped up onto a stool in front of her. 'That would be great, and I'll have a bougatsa, too,' I said. I needed a cream pie to balance the effort I'd made in walking two whole miles. 'I'm going to have to get fit, Maria,' I said. 'Gardening yesterday nearly killed me, and I've just walked...' I stopped mid-sentence. Maria didn't need to know what I was doing with Delphine, '... at least two miles, and I'm exhausted.'

A hint of a smile lit her face. 'And if I don't make a mistake, I think I saw Mr Handsome running back to the hotel early this morning. That also makes you tired, eh?'

I laughed. 'You see far too much, Maria! But yes, there may be a little romance. But, you know, I don't think it's going to last.'

Maria poured the coffee and placed a pie on a small plate

and lowered her voice. 'You think he isn't all that you expect?' Her eyes followed mine.

'Yes, that's exactly it. He disappeared off for a few days last week and arrived at my place on Sunday morning filthy and shattered, having been to Athens and back on the boat, or so he said.'

Her expression was hard to read. 'What do you think he is up to?'

'I don't know. It doesn't seem like normal behaviour when you're buying a property, does it?'

'It may be time to find out a little more about Mr Handsome,' Maria said.

'Ooh, do you have a plan?'

'No. I'm just interested. A bit of excitement to take my mind off this mess.' She picked up my coffee spoon and polished it vigorously.

'Really? You always seem a little... guarded around Leo. Don't you like him?'

'No, it is nothing. He is your friend,' she muttered, and went off to clear tables and stayed chatting to an elderly man about the latest political scandal.

Frustrated, I ate my pie and drank my sweet coffee and wondered what she wasn't telling me about Leo Arakis. I should have waited and questioned her further.

I turned her newspaper around, and, as I had suspected saw that it was open on the job vacancies page. She'd been circling jobs for Spiros. The taverna could not make enough money to feed them during the winter, and they had relied on Spiros' building job with Kokorakis. It was sad, but at least summer was coming and I hoped it was going to be a busy one for her.

Quietly, I shrugged on my coat, slid a five euro note under the saucer and slipped out before she finished her animated conversation with the elderly customer about the state of the current government. Our topic for the next Greek conversation class was 'How to talk politics with a Cretan'. I thought it might involve shouting and waving one's arms about in a similar fashion. I'd not met a Greek yet who didn't hold strong opinions about everything from the horrors of the EU to the Italians 'stealing' their best olive oil after a poor trade deal in about 1983. It would be good fun to have a chance to join in without needing a translation app. I was probably in a better position than the rest of the class, though, as I'd listened to my dad rattling on for years. He might not have wanted to ever return to Crete, but he still behaved as if he was living here and should have a say in the government.

I strolled along the beach for a while, enjoying the growing warmth and the soft sound of waves breaking on the shingle, wondering just what Leo was up to, and why he was so secretive about it. I was having a battle between my desire for him and my instinct which was telling me to run.

Yet again, there was not another soul on the beach for as far as I could see. It would be easy to be lonely here. I could see why people would come out here to live the dream and find it too hard to stay. You needed to be able to adjust to this very different way of life, and to know that Cretans aren't like Brits, or Americans. The culture is so different from back home. The heart of a Cretan is low down, it's fire in his belly, not a philosophical debate in his head like an Athenian would have. He would shoot you rather than surrender to you, and that was the essential difference. With Will, I'd been escaping from my roots into a highbrow world I found fascinating, but alien. I was never comfortable there, despite how he tried to mould me. It was the difference between the hardness of life in the mountains which bred people who were resilient and tough, and the softness of the tourists, who lay on the beach, wallowed in the warm water and toasted themselves brown. Their worlds could not meet.

This island was home for me, though, I could feel it. I needed friends, of course, and I needed a purpose, both of which were coming together. I'd already made friends in Alex and Cathy, Cassia and Tinos, and I think I could still count Maria as a friend. As for Leo, who knew? He was hiding something, and perhaps I wasn't included in his plans.

I'd reached the hotel where Leo was staying. There was no sign of his car, so I assumed he would be out on business somewhere. Then I did something way out of character. I gave in to my nosiness. I wondered if he might have left paperwork or something in his room that might tell me more about what he was up to. I wanted to take a peek. How to gain access to his room was the problem. After a moment's thought, I removed one earring and slipped it into my jacket pocket, and, heart pounding, entered the hotel and approached the reception area.

'Kalimera,' I said to the young man behind the desk. 'Err... would you check and see if my friend, Leo Arakis, is in his room, please?'

The boy phoned the room. I could hear it ringing and there was no answer. So far so good. 'Oh, what a shame.' I pointed at my ear. 'It's just that I seem to have left my earring in his room, and I wondered if I could go up and look for it? It wouldn't take more than a minute.' I gave him my best smile.

'I can't leave the desk, madam,' he said, and smiled back at me.

'I understand. Do you remember me from the other night? We had dinner here in the restaurant?' I didn't add, and we were practically eating each other, never mind the food.

The young man flushed. Yes, he'd remembered.

I went pink as well. 'I'm sure he wouldn't mind me having a quick search, I'll be very careful not to disturb anything, I promise.'

He was wavering.

'These earrings were a present from my mother, and I would hate to lose one. Please?'

He passed the key over and hissed, 'Be quick, please.'

I didn't need telling twice. I shot up the stairs and was inside the room within twenty seconds. It was a mess. I stood for a moment to adjust to the gloom as the blinds were still down, then scanned the room. On the table under the window was the bag he had had with him when he came into the taverna and showed me the plans. I stepped over dropped towels and discarded underwear. Inside was the folder containing all the plans and paperwork for the purchase of the land and house. I opened it and discovered that the 'paperwork' was in fact, just paper, there was nothing on the pages except for the top page which held the estate agents' details and the folded map. I was stumped. If Leo was off sorting out official business to do with the purchase, why hadn't he taken this stuff with him? *Was* that what he was doing? Of course, he could have had all that he needed with him, I supposed.

I had a quick scan of the rest of the room, but there wasn't much to see. Quickly, I retrieved the 'lost' earring and tripped down the stairs, thanked the boy behind the desk, and wandered down onto the beach where I sat on a rock and pondered. Was I being ridiculous to suspect that Leo was up to something? Possibly. Yet... there was something about him I didn't trust.

15

As I had anticipated, as soon as Aunt Irini heard me digging another bed out in the garden, and cursing at the number of rocks buried in the flinty soil, she was leaning over the wall to see what I was up to. I got off my knees and stretched my poor back. It wasn't getting any easier. 'Hello,' I said, going over to stand closer to her. 'I'm sorry I was rude the other day. I should not have run off like I did.'

Irini gave me a sad smile. 'I understand. It was a shock to you. Yes, your grandmother and I lived next door to each other for many years.' She reached across the wall and placed her hand on my arm. 'I know it is hard for you to understand why we are keeping information from you, but there are reasons for it.' She shrugged. 'I have a feeling that soon you will know everything, and then, who knows what might happen?'

'What does that mean? Please, Aunt Irini, please tell me what this is all about.'

'No, you must talk to your parents for the full story. This is up to your father, and he must tell you.' She gave me a sly look. 'He does know that you will be asking him, you know.'

'Does he? You and Mum been talking again, have you?'

Aunt Irini lowered her gaze. 'We all want the best for you, Anna. I can say that I'm hoping that you being here will bring an old and bitter feud to an end.'

Aha! A feud *was* at the heart of this. As I suspected. I was in Crete, home of the feud, after all. And my father, with all his moods and coldness, had the ideal personality to hold a very long grudge. 'So, that is why Dad left the island? Because of a feud?'

Irini inclined her head. 'It was many years ago, but it didn't end in bloodshed as so many have done before.'

'Did it end in exile?'

'Yes,' she said. 'So now you know more than you did before, yes?' Irini turned away from the adjoining wall and went back towards her house.

'Yes, thank you. Thank you for telling me that much,' I shouted to her retreating figure. I slumped onto my little wooden bench and drank some water. At last, answers were coming. A feud between families would explain why Dad never wanted to come back. Possibly he never could come back. That, of course, set me to wondering who exactly had been involved in the feud. And what my father had done to warrant exile from his homeland. Could he be wanted by the police? Unlikely. He'd stayed in exactly the same place for years. Easy to find. The sweat on my brow dripped into my eyes as I stretched out my legs. Whatever my father had done, it was going to have to be serious to have had such a long-standing consequence.

Above me, the sky was darkening by the minute, and the tops of the mountains had disappeared behind low cloud, so I stopped worrying about Dad, and Leo and everything else and tried to finish the beds before I got soaked.

I used the bigger rocks I'd dug out of the soil to make a border for the second bed, and added compost. The tiny salad seedlings didn't look like they could survive, but the man at the garden centre said it was time to plant, so in they went. Finally, I dug a huge hole for the tiny peach tree, filled it with a good soil mix and watered it in. It was placed against the side wall, and would get afternoon sun. I was already salivating at the thought of fresh peaches, although I'd need a regular supply of water to make them juicy.

As if awaiting their cue, the roiling black clouds that had been growing up and over the mountains began to unleash their power. Time for a long bath and some supper, I thought.

Delphine, however, rang as soon as I got inside the house, and asked if I would like to look at two possible houses with her and the Andreanakises the following day. So the job was on! I was quite excited and said yes immediately.

A quick dip substituted for the long soak, and I was down at my laptop within half an hour, putting together colour schemes and ideas for furniture. I had a feeling that Mrs Andreanakis would want traditional Greek furnishings, but I was starting from scratch in Crete and didn't have my enormous stash of materials and textiles that I would normally offer on a mood board to help people make up their minds. Instead, I raided my house for Grandmother's tablecloths, shawls, bowls, cushion covers. I took photos of the old dresser, kitchen stool and the wooden panel which decorated the wall of the spare bedroom. I opened the box I had brought with me from home and dug out paint colour panels and coloured swatches of materials. After an hour or so, I had a collection of images and objects which might help Mrs A start again. Judging by the walls of Aunt Irini's home, the hardest things to replace would be the photographs of her family. But perhaps her children could help with that.

And, to add to my good mood, Mr Andreiou rang and said he could do the tiling and electrics the following day if it suited me and the walls were dry. It did. Especially as I would be out all day. I had a feeling Irini would keep an eye on him for me.

As I prepared for bed that night, I realised that I'd had another day without communication from Leo. Whatever he was doing, I didn't think I figured much in his plans except as a way in to the Kokorakises. Happily, I realised I didn't care.

Next morning, I let the builders in and made them promise not to wreck the place. Then I shut the door on them and alerted Irini, my spy and slave driver.

Delphine picked me up in a big silver Lexus and drove me over the mountains once again to Paleochora. Even just a week later the hillsides were covered in flowering purple and pink and white plants. It was beautiful. I needed to get out here and explore, walk the Agia Irini Gorge, stretch my legs on the mountainside. Actually, find my legs. There were muscles in there somewhere.

It was different this time with Delphine. I was more relaxed with her, and that helped the conversation. I told her a little of my training and background, but was relieved when we stopped at Topolia Gorge and picked up Mrs Andreanakis from her sister's. Now I'd have my Greek tested.

She was apologetic before she even got in the car, until Delphine told her she had to stop. 'This is my husband's money we are spending, so let's enjoy it! We are going to look at two houses, and you must say if you like either of them. If not, there is no problem and I will look again. Understood?'

'Understood,' said Mrs Andreanakis, smiling shyly.

'You haven't brought your husband,' I said.

She smiled, fastening her seat belt. 'He will only argue with me, and I decide what we will have. The house is my domain.'

We laughed. 'Good for you,' I said. I'd put her in her late sixties, I thought, but it was hard to tell as all Greek women tend to look old once they adopt the black uniform. Aunt Irini, back in black since our tea party, had been transformed in a flowery frock.

The first house we saw was modern, not more than two or three years old. Apart from moving furniture in, there was nothing to be done. Centrally-heated, solar panels on the roof, all done in white throughout. It had no soul whatsoever. We looked around its two downstairs rooms, two bedrooms and a bathroom. 'It's clean and easy to look after,' I ventured.

'And there is a little area to sit outside in the sun,' added Delphine.

But I watched Mrs Andreanakis's shoulders slump, and knew it wasn't for her.

'Come,' said Delphine, 'let us see the other one.'

We walked slowly past the wreckage of Mrs Andreanakis's former home, and it was all I could do not to cry. Mrs A did, caring little about what anybody thought. The scene was devastating for her.

Delphine set her jaw. 'Come on,' she said. 'There is nothing for you here now,' and she took Mrs A by the elbow and led her gently away.

The second house was better. The estate agent, who was hovering in her heels on the doorstep as we arrived, told us a little about the house. Built before the Second World War, it was on a side street a short walk up the hill leading out of the town. It had views over the sea and a proper garden in which people could grow vegetables and sit out. The house needed redecorating, but had a working range in the kitchen and an open fireplace which had seen many winters. The owner had died recently, and much of the furniture would be sold with the house.

I stood in the doorway with Delphine and smiled as Mrs

Andreanakis nodded vigorously as the woman talked, saying, 'I like this, it's very good. Very good.'

'I think she likes it,' said Delphine, grinning at me.

Mrs A wandered from room to room, touching tables and sofas, deciding what she wanted where. Her eyes were shining when she returned. 'I'd like this house very much, please,' she said. 'If it is all right for me to say?'

'Of course it is, that's why we're here. Now, let's have a think about what you want to keep and get rid of.'

Delphine beckoned the estate agent over and said, 'We'll take this.' She wrote a figure on a slip of paper and handed it to the wide-eyed woman. 'Offer this amount. If there is any difficulty' – she passed over her card – 'ring me straight away. There will be no difficulty.' Then she told the estate agent we wouldn't need her for the rest of the day. 'We need time to decide on things. Make the offer, then ring me. I will return the key later,' she said, and the woman did.

Doesn't matter where you live, money talks.

'Anna is here to help you, Mrs Andreanakis,' Delphine said, turning back to us as if she hadn't just bought a house in fifteen minutes. 'She has lots of things with her to help you decide what to have in your new home. Shall we make a list?'

I got my suitcase out of the car, and took out the contents to spread around the living room. 'See any colours or fabrics you like?' I asked, and Mrs A's eyes gleamed. 'Pick them up, touch them. You could put one or two things in each room, so I can get an idea of what colours and materials you might like.'

Delphine took me on one side and passed me an envelope stuffed with euros. 'That should cover furniture and other things for the house. I expect you to spend it all,' she said, with a twinkle in her eye.

'Your husband is certainly paying for his mistake,' I said, and zipped the money into my bag.

'He is. He's a businessman, Anna, not a monster. He never intended to hurt these people, He has to make hard decisions sometimes, but he will always make amends to the local people.'

I smiled at her. 'I think you might be his conscience though.'

'That may well be so.'

Mrs A skipped around like a child, placing cloths and objects and colour swatches in each room, then changing her mind and moving them all again. I pottered to the café opposite and brought back coffees and pastries for us. This was going to be a long morning.

I opened my notebook once the initial flurry had subsided. 'Shall we start in the kitchen?' I asked, and off we went.

The rest of the morning passed in the most enjoyable way. I love my work, Delphine had a good eye and Mrs A was delighted to finally get to choose what she really wanted, which was much more modern than I had expected.

'I inherited so much from my parents, and from his,' she said. 'The house was like a museum, stuffed with things. It's why it burned so well.' She shrugged. 'Yes, I have lost many things, but' – she tapped her head – 'the memories are in here with me. At least we got out with our lives, and now I will have a beautiful new home.' She patted Delphine on the hand. 'My angel,' she said.

Delphine was embarrassed. I gathered this wasn't how she was usually referred to. I could see she was moved though. Hard only on the outside, as Father Georgiou had said.

Things are never as black and white as we would like them to be, are they? I knew who Delphine was, of course, and so did Mrs Andreanakis, but we were both warming to her, even though her husband had no doubt broken many laws. Should I have refused to help her because she stayed with Kokorakis? Perhaps, but I had stayed with Will for ten unhappy years, and had only got away because it became possible to move to Crete. I would like to hear her story one day, and find out why she had stayed. I started to gather up my things. Perhaps she loved him. Simple as that.

16

I was exhausted by the time Delphine dropped me at home. I had a huge list of things to organise and buy, but not as much as Mrs Andreanakis, who had been charged with equipping her kitchen and dining room. I assumed that the house conveyancing would go through quickly and without difficulty, as Delphine had said, so I gave myself two weeks to put together the designs and plans.

Mr Andreiou had already gone by the time I got home. All was quiet. I raced upstairs into the bathroom, and there was the shower corner, tiled and neat, and a cubicle waiting to be fitted. There was hot water on, too. I rang him immediately and thanked him. What a great day.

I couldn't face cooking because I was so tired, so I rang Alex and Cathy. I fancied some easy company where I could speak English and celebrate a very good day. Cathy was busy with the production of the local English language newspaper that seemed to take up a lot of her time, but Alex sounded delighted, and we agreed to meet at the fish restaurant on the promenade where I'd had lunch with Cassia the week before.

I felt much more relaxed about going out for dinner with

Alex than I ever did with Leo. I chose my rose-pink cashmere jumper, black jeans and flat boots, shrugged on my old thick poncho to keep out the keen wind, and strolled down to the quayside feeling hungry and ready to relax.

Alex was waiting outside. He kissed me on the cheek and held the door open for me, which was nice. Inside, the restaurant was quiet as it was only just eight o'clock, but the lighting was subtle and we could watch the sea rolling gently onto the beach. It felt intimate and warm.

'What would you like to drink?' the waiter asked in Greek.

I was amazed. He was the first person to assume I was Greek and not some other nationality. He suggested a local red, which was strong and rough, but would taste wonderful with moussaka, so that's what we ordered.

'How is the house purchase proceeding?' asked Alex, pouring the first glass of wine.

'Brilliantly! Mrs Andreanakis is so excited, and likes my ideas, and I think we have found her the right house in Paleochora. Between us, I reckon we can make a cosy home for the two of them.'

'And Mrs Kokorakis, how is she?' He lifted an eyebrow at me over the rim of his glass.

I took a moment. How was she indeed? 'You know, she isn't like some sort of gangster's wife. I mean, she's got all the status symbols and the bling, but she's sweet under all that. I quite warmed to her, and enjoyed her company. She has a very good eye for interiors.'

He looked at me thoughtfully. 'That's interesting to know. I wonder why she has stayed with that man? She must know what he's like.'

'That's easy. Security, wealth, privilege, fear of being alone. Maybe she loves him. Why does any woman stay with a man who is bad for her?' I blushed. Hadn't I done exactly the same thing? Perhaps that's why I liked Delphine; I recognised her.

'And once you're settled into the world your husband creates for you, it is hard to escape, yes?'

'Too right it is. I think I lost the ability to take a decision on my own. Mine even chose my clothes, for goodness' sake.' I took a swig of wine. 'Sorry, this is not what I want to talk about. Tell me about boat renovations.'

Alex laughed and showed me his hands, which were paint-spattered and roughened from barnacle-scraping. 'This is me in the winter. I clean, mend and replace worn-out parts ready for the summer.' He drank a little wine. 'And then I sail the Med with small groups of people who want to see the less well-known islands.'

'It does sound wonderful,' I said, thinking of his offer.

'Do you get lonely here in winter when it's so quiet?'

'Sometimes, but I joined the language class and met you, and Cathy takes me under her "making new people welcome" wing. You should come along to some of the expat events she organises, they can be fun. We're joining in the Easter hat parade on Saturday and having a huge feast in the square. Come.'

'I will at some point, but not on Saturday, sorry. At the moment I'm trying not to be so obviously a foreigner. At least my Greek is coming along.'

'And mine, at last.

'Tell me a bit about you, Alex,' I said. 'Have you ever been married?'

He poured us more wine. 'I have been married, twice.' He looked up at me under his eyebrows. 'That must make me seem like a gigolo?'

I giggled. I couldn't imagine anyone less like a gigolo. 'Are you?'

'I might be...' Then he chuckled. 'Sadly, I'm not. Wife one was my childhood sweetheart who left me as soon as she grew up and realised she wanted a very different lifestyle.'

'She didn't want to be married to a computer geek?'

'No, she wanted to be married to a woman.' He laughed at the look on my face. 'It takes time to know these things. I'm happy for them both. They are good friends of mine now. You can meet them sometime if you like?'

'Okay. It's good that you could stay friends.'

'Yes, with her, but not with my second wife. She and I parted badly, and I don't get to see my children as often as I should.'

'You have kids?' I was stumped. Why hadn't I known this? What had we been talking about for weeks after class? Me, I supposed. Or listening to Leo was more likely.

'I have two boys, aged fourteen and seventeen. You'll meet them in the summer when they come for a holiday.'

The waiter appeared with two steaming dishes of moussaka and a bowl of local greens. I was glad of a moment to process all this information. Alex was a dad. I bet he was a good one. 'Are they still in Sweden?'

'Yes, at school there. I miss them. They love to sail, and fish, and swim. They are good boys.' He dug the spoon into the greens and added them to his plate. 'Shall we talk about something else?'

'Of course, sorry for being nosy.' I poked at the moussaka to let out some steam. 'Something odd has happened actually,' I said, helping myself to greens, 'that I would like your advice on.'

'Odd good, or odd bad?'

'Good. I knew I must have relatives on the island, and it turns out I'm living next door to my mother's second cousin, or great something or other, Irini. She didn't tell me until the other day.'

'Extraordinary coincidence?' asked Alex. 'Or was she shy?'

I chewed down a forkful of moussaka and followed it with a sip of wine. The waiter was right, it tasted great. A more expensive bottle would have been lost in the rich lamb mince of the dish.

'I think she was waiting to see what I was like. Then she invited me to afternoon tea with her son, who is the local priest. I like both of them.' I chewed for a few more moments, unsure of whether to tell Alex about the strange history of my parents and their relatives. In the end I thought it might help me sort out what I should do. 'The thing is, the house I inherited is my paternal grandmother's house, even though I think Irini's family may once have owned it. So, the mystery is, why won't my father tell me anything about his parents? I obviously must have met my grandmother, she was called Nyssa, when I holidayed here as a child. And why did she live on her own?'

Oh, of course, what an idiot I was. 'And I never understood why Mum and I stopped coming here, but we must have been coming to see my maternal grandmother, too, and when she died, Mum had no more strong ties to the island.'

Alex put down his fork. 'This is indeed a mystery. Do you know why your father left the island?'

'I can only think that he fell out really badly with his own father. It must have been something terrible. Irini referred to it as exile. He has never returned, not even for his own father's or mother's funeral. He doesn't talk about Crete, or answer any of my questions, and neither will my mother. Irini said I would have to ask my father to get to the truth. That it is not her story to tell.'

'That is probably true. To keep back information in families is common, I find. Getting to the truth is not an easy path.'

'I know, but it's quite important. Irini specifically warned me away from Kokorakis, and I have a sick feeling in my stomach that he might be at the back of all this. It's all a bit complicated, isn't it?'

Alex took my hand and squeezed it. 'Some things are safer left buried, you know.'

'I know, but I can't leave it. I'm like a dog with a bone, I keep worrying away at it.' I laughed and squeezed his hand back. 'Thanks for listening to all this.'

'It's intriguing. I can see why you cannot let it go.'

'I'm invited to a dinner party at the Kokorakis' house on Saturday night. Perhaps that will reveal a little more.' I took my hand back and drank more wine. 'It's eating away at me. No, the only thing I can do is to go home and ask my father directly what happened all those years ago.' I looked into his blue, blue eyes. 'I have to know.'

He grinned. 'And so, our heroine throws herself into the path of danger, and takes on the local bigwig in order to clear the name of her dishonoured father... It would make a good movie.'

'Heroic Swede comes to her rescue when she falls on her backside at the first obstacle, more like. I'm sure it's nothing so exciting, but I'll book a flight home next week and go ask.' I had a sudden mad moment of wanting to cancel Leo and take Alex to the party instead, but Leo had been so excited I felt I couldn't let him down. Alex read my mind.

'Will you be taking Leo with you on Saturday night?' he asked, his eyes drifting sideways to the slow rolling sea.

'Yes, I've already arranged it with him. He was as excited as a child at Christmas,' I said, and for the second time, wondered why.

'He has not been around much these last couple of weeks,' said Alex. 'Are there difficulties in purchasing the property?'

'Not so far as I know. I think the difficulties are in persuading the authorities to allow him to build a casino here. Kokorakis holds the lease to the building, I know that. That's why Leo's so keen to meet him on Saturday night. I know very little about what he's up to and I'm fast losing interest.'

Alex merely shrugged. 'I suppose he must do whatever it takes, but it worries me that he is trying to move so quickly. Here, tradition is as important as the law. He should take time to learn the customs, and not upset the system.' Alex shrugged again. 'Americans, always in a hurry.'

I felt a bit deflated at the mention of Leo. I was so confused about him. We had little in common except sex and his need for a designer. Nothing wrong with a fling based on sex, of course. It was certainly a novelty being with someone so passionate and urgent. But he kept disappearing and I'd still like to know what he was actually up to, my mystery man.

'Hello, earth calling Anna.' Alex topped up my glass with the last of the wine.

We'd eaten the food and I was feeling warm and sleepy. I hadn't even noticed that several other tables had filled up during the course of the evening. 'Sorry, I was thinking,' I said.

'Are you okay, Anna?' he asked. 'Is all the family intrigue worrying you?'

'No, it's not that. I'm a bit confused about Leo, that's all. Like you, I'm worried that he'll get into serious trouble and end up angering Kokorakis, or the authorities in Chania.' I took a deep breath. 'Still, it's not my problem, is it?'

'No, it's not,' said Alex with a grin that may have been relief. 'I'm glad you are not thinking that. Cheers,' he said.

I yawned, one of those where you try not to yawn and stretch your lips into a ridiculous rictus grin. 'Sorry, I guess I'm tired. It's months since I did an honest day's work.'

He laughed. 'Come on then, as I'm boring you, I'll get the bill and walk you home. A walk will help to digest the food.'

'Oh no, I'm getting the bill. I invited you, remember?'

He struggled a bit, but then he gave in. 'Next time, it is my turn to pay. Okay, independent woman?'

'Very okay, kind sir. It's been lovely, Alex. Thanks for being such good company and listening to my story.'

'It's my pleasure. I haven't had such good company for a long time, either. We should definitely do this again.'

I smiled up at him. So it had been a date then. Get me, newly divorced and seeing two blokes at the same time. Racy.

Alex took my arm as we left the restaurant and we strolled back in silence, enjoying the sound of waves against the shore and the occasional sleepless seagull calling for a mate.

At my door he kissed me on the cheek and left, striding out with his long legs and whistling under his breath.

Inside, making mint tea, I felt quite odd. I'd wanted Alex to come in, to stay longer, but I knew where that would lead, and he probably did too. It was all so complicated with Leo still in the picture.

17

Delphine sat up in bed, supported by pillows and cosy under the duvet. No matter how hard she tried, she couldn't get the staff to keep the house warm enough for her. She clattered her nails on the laptop, cutting quickly through emails and rubbish so she could go back to snooping online. The previous day, delighted by Anna's involvement and expertise in the world of interior design, she had done a thorough search on the internet and found Anna named as one-time partner in Hunter Design, a well-established design house in Alderley Edge, Cheshire, England. The gallery photos were almost all in tasteful shades of taupe, grey and black, with an occasional flash of beige or cream to lighten the palette. Even Anna, who looked thin and sad, was wearing the corporate colours, which washed out her sallow skin. Only the ex-husband, Will, looked at home. He was looking off into the distance, as if focused on things far more important than a website. She snorted. Pompous fool. Still, she bet he wasn't so pleased with himself now.

Nikos came into the bedroom with coffee and little buns on a tray. He placed them carefully on the bed and peered over her shoulder at the screen. 'You've found her. What do you think? Is my brother's daughter a threat to me?'

Delphine tutted. 'Niko, leave it. She's lovely, and wants only to live here and enjoy her work. Stop being so melodramatic. What harm could she bring to you? No, I like her very much, and I want to tell her that I am her aunt on Saturday night after the dinner.' Her eyes drifted away from him. 'For me, it is like having a daughter after all these years.'

Nikos withdrew his arm from her shoulder and slumped into a nearby chair. 'It is, I suppose, time. Time I faced up to what I did all those years ago. But what will she think? Her father has clearly told her nothing about me. She may hate us both, for what we are.'

'That's not the way to look at this. In the same way that your mother told you nothing about Anna's birth, so Anna's father followed your instructions to stay away and keep silent. So many stupid secrets are still carried in this family. What a waste of years when we could have shared so much.' She stopped then; she could see how much he hated it when she told him the truth. He was a child in so many ways. 'Well, you can work on your confession and be ready to talk to her on Saturday.'

He turned to go, already dressed and ready for the day's meetings.

'Wait, I haven't finished.' She cleared her throat and thought about what she wanted to say. 'I truly believe Anna will be pleased to know who we are, but that so-called boyfriend of hers, Leonidas Arakis, he is an oddity.'

'Why? Have you found something out about him? He seems to be hopping about between here and the mainland, but he hasn't been talking to my land agent about the land he suppos-edly wishes to buy. I've been waiting to see what he will do.'

'No, I haven't found out anything about him. That's my point. There is nothing on social media or any of the business sites about him at all.'

'He is a ghost?'

'Exactly. And why would that be the case, do you think?'

Nikos scratched his ear. 'Hiding his identity? Why would he do that? Did you find my younger brother, Stephanos, on the computer?'

She pressed another few keys. 'Yes, he has a successful chain of restaurants in America, and three sons, but he kept the family name, unlike Theo, and there is no son called Leonidas.'

He thrust his hands into his trouser pockets and grunted. 'That means nothing. It has begun, hasn't it? Do I look weak, Delphie? Are the vultures circling?'

'No, don't be so gloomy. You have loyalty and status here amongst the other businessmen. Why assume he has bad intentions?'

'Because he's not doing what he said he would. That makes me suspicious. Still, I will make sure he and I have a chat on Saturday night, over brandy at the end of the meal. That may loosen his tongue and I can get the measure of him. I will find out who he is, and he won't find me an easy target if that is what he's thinking.' Nikos gave her a wave and walked from the room with his head down, lost in thought.

He's not getting paranoid, thought Delphine, even though he sounded it. She glanced through the window at the rows of vines climbing away up the field, and watched their workers weeding early spring growth. He's getting old and there is no heir to all this. The vultures will indeed be circling, and we must be careful who we trust.

Her phone pinged. A message from the solicitor. The paperwork for the house in Paleochora was awaiting her signature. If she could bring the Andreanakises across to his office, they could have the keys by the following weekend. Delphine smiled. There were advantages to being Nikos' wife that she very much enjoyed.

18

Delphine rang me early in the morning and gave me the good news about the house, so I collected Mrs Andreanakis to take her shopping in Chania. Driving over the mountain, picking her up and driving back across the mountain to the city was the furthest I'd driven so far. Apart from a hairy moment with a goat who wanted to take her kids across the road in front of the car, we arrived in one piece.

The sensation of accompanying a senior Greek woman on her home territory was liberating. Nobody spoke to me in English, and my accent and understanding was improving all the time. Mrs A also knew all the haberdashers, material shops, furniture warehouses, and most importantly (after three hours of relentless shopping), the best restaurants.

'Please can we stop for a break? My feet are killing me,' I finally asked in desperation. The woman was a machine.

Over lunch of stifado and a glass of wine for her, water for me, we discussed our purchases. I'd tried to persuade her that we only had two hands each, and couldn't get everything in one day, but we loaded up the car twice and had still more bags with us. The furniture would arrive at the house in parts, but the warehouse was sending someone to assemble it for her. I had one pang of guilt about how much we were spending, but it was Kokorakis' money, so I was otherwise enjoying it.

Mrs Andreanakis' eyes shone as she chattered about her new start, new home and new life to the waitress. I relaxed, slipped my feet out of my shoes and looked out onto the street. It was deserted as most people had gone for lunch and there were few tourists about.

There was some noise coming from the bar across the street, however. It was filled with a bunch of men, uniformly dark and swarthy, locals no doubt. They were standing at the bar, eating cheese pies and swilling them down with tiny cups of coffee and gulps of raki. Then I had that peculiar experience you get when you see yourself in a mirror unexpectedly, only this time it was Leo I saw, right in the middle of the gang. He had several days' growth of beard and looked dishevelled, just as he had the previous week when he'd turned up at my door. There was no way he was doing business with land officials and solicitors. Liar. What the hell was he up to? I watched for a few minutes as he slapped a man on the back and shared a joke, and I became even more determined to snoop.

I knew he wasn't what he said he was, or probably even who he said he was. He was up to something shady and I didn't know what to do about it. There was no actual evidence apart from him clamping down on my questions, and obviously not being in the kind of talks that would require a suit, or even a bath, but I wasn't going to let that minor problem stop me from speculating. Maybe he was a spy? Maybe he was spying on Kokorakis, which would explain his excitement at being invited to the party. But why? I was desperate to talk to Maria about it. She'd understand and enjoy helping me, especially as she was no longer spying on me for Kokorakis. I hoped. And there must be a reason why she didn't like Leo, mustn't there? I'd trust her intuition. I could tell Alex, of course. And Cathy. Cathy would bring her science teacher skills to analyse the problem, I'd bet. I could see another rather drunken evening looming enjoyably ahead.

'More coffee?' asked the waitress.

'No, thanks. The meal was delicious.' I paid the bill using yet more of the wad of cash, which was somewhat depleted now. Good job I'd already ordered paint.

Mrs Andreanakis looked on anxiously as I counted out the cash. 'Have we spent it all?' she asked.

'No, there's enough to get anything else you might need. Don't worry. But if you're ready, we should make a move.' I wanted to get out of there before Leo noticed me spying on him.

I kept my head down as we struggled back to the car, unnoticed, I hoped, and took the mountain road to her sister's house, where I unloaded her, three bags of linen, cutlery and crockery, and a pile of material. Mrs A was in charge of making the curtains and cushion covers.

Mrs A's sister lived in a tiny village at the top end of Topolia Gorge so I drove a short way and stopped at a parking area at the side of the road just before the road tunnel. I needed a little time to myself, and a walk along the top of the gorge looked possible without proper footwear. I strolled down a dirt path, the steep sides of the gorge soon drowning out traffic noise from the road. It was warm, and I could hear so many birds it could not have been described as quiet. In gullies fed by rainwater grew wild thyme, oregano and new season Malotira that would be harvested for mountain tea later in the summer. It smelt wonderful already. I headed down a little further towards a farm, where the farmhouse nestled against the gorge wall, and the flat land in front of it was cultivated with ranks of olive trees. It wasn't the trees that made me gasp, however, it was that the whole area was a mass of scarlet poppies and yellow camomile. It was breathtaking. I walked into the field and knelt down. The heady scent of the camomile was almost overpowering, but to kneel and brush my hands across the heads of the flowers, and to spot early orchids and rosemary poking up amongst it all was wonderful. I took out my phone and did my best to capture some of the views. I'd certainly be back later in the summer for some wild herbs. The first day of May, coming up soon, was when families came up onto the mountain and collected flowers for wreaths that they use to decorate their doors. I'd come with them this year, if I could.

I got to my feet reluctantly and spotted the farmer's wife standing in her doorway, laughing at me. 'Take the flowers,' she yelled, 'my husband will cut them all down soon.'

I supposed they might count as weeds in a farmer's eyes. Philistine. So I got to work and collected a huge bunch, glad that I had her approval, and had gathered them before they became just mulch.

Approaching home, I could see that the bathroom window was open wide, and I could hear tinny music coming from Mr Andreiou's old radio. Both he and Vasilis were singing along at the tops of their voices, which I took to be a good sign.

'Hello?' I shouted up the stairs, and all went quiet.

Vasilis' head appeared around the top of the banister. 'Hello, Miss. Come up, please.'

I was amazed, I didn't know he could speak. I took the stairs two at a time and squashed into the bathroom, where both men were also packed in. The shower was in. 'Fantastic!' I said, then remembered to speak in Greek and to thank them.

'Not long now, almost finished,' said Mr Andreiou, wiping his brow.

'Thank you so much, it's wonderful.'

His face crinkled into well-worn laughter lines and he went back to work.

I brought my things in from the car to the sound of the pair of them singing their hearts out to Ed Sheeran, and wondered at the conflict between the medieval attitudes towards business and the clash of the modern on this island.

Later, once they had gone, and I had inspected my beautiful new shower again, I sat outside as the sun went down and drank mountain tea with the little grey cat on my lap. We both stared at the mountain and I was grateful to have its solidity at my back. The cat was starting to fatten up, but I knew she would be pregnant soon, and never have enough to feed her family. I could do something about that.

Mainly, though, I was consumed with the need to know what Leo was up to, and frustrated because I couldn't see how I could find out if he wouldn't tell me. It's hard for those of us with a nosy disposition to let things go, or 'see how things turn out'. A nosy disposition and lack of trust in the object of my suspicions made it even more infuriating for me.

I picked the cat up and carried her round to Irini's house. She came to the back door immediately; she had been cooking her evening meal. 'I'm sorry, didn't mean to interrupt you,' I said. The cat jumped down and went to her bowl. Irini ushered me into the kitchen, where the range was hot and a wonderful aroma came bubbling out of the pot on the top.

'It's lovely to see you, Anna. Come in and sit. Have you had a nice day? I could see that your car was gone all day, and the builders have been back to finish your shower.' She poured tea into her best china cups and sat heavily opposite me.

'Thank you, I've had a lovely, but tiring day.' I told her about Mrs Andreanakis and what Delphine was doing for her. 'I don't know if she has changed, or what, but being kind suits her.'

'I hope she is learning to be kind. It would be good for all of us.' She gave me the sideways glance I was coming to expect. 'Nikos is getting older now, he must be in his sixties.'

'Much older than Delphine, then?'

'They married late. Nikos liked the ladies, but finally realised that he must marry and produce an heir when he was already in his forties. But, of course, that never happened.'

'Right, I thought Delphine mustn't have children as she never mentions them. So who will inherit his businesses?'

'Ah, you have grasped the problem. Who indeed? All I know is there will be war amongst the wealthy families if he dies without naming a worthy successor.'

'War, over a vineyard and some olive trees?' I laughed. 'Cretan men!'

Irini drank her tea, measuring me like she had the last time I had sat at this table. And like last time, I had to say, 'You can tell me. What else does he own that could cause a war?'

'Kokorakis is a businessman. He has olives, fruit and wine, some of the best land in the area, but he makes most of his money from building new houses for tourists, hotels, and factories. As you see, though, his methods if you fall behind on your rent are crude.'

I struggled a bit. 'So what you're saying is that he is an important businessman in the area?'

'He is the most powerful man in the area. One day you should drive out to his country estate. Stavros will show you where it is. The house you will see on Saturday, that is for show. Nikos likes to stay in the middle of the island, where he has a... a fortress, you may say. His business base. It is full of the building materials he requires, his farms are based up there, and it is where his teams work from.'

I was agog. 'Why a fortress?'

She twisted the side of her mouth. 'You will see if you go. He has a lot to protect up there. But now, at least you know why I asked you to be careful. He is not just an oil and wine business-man, he is the biggest builder on this side of the island. He oper-ates only just inside the law, and well out of it if you talk to his tenants. He expects a level of loyalty that is very difficult to live up to. So do not get involved, Anna, it could be dangerous for you.'

I thought of Spiros and Maria, and how much power he had over them, and felt a little of my anger towards Spiros soften. I finished my tea. 'I hear you. I'm going to carry on working with Delphine while the work on the house goes ahead. After that I don't think our paths will cross. I'm at the poorer end of society, not someone they would cultivate as a friend, I'm sure.'

The strangest expression crossed her face.

'What is it?'

'You have not yet talked to your father.'

'No. I'm intending to go home to see him face to face. Mum says he's ill.'

She gave a sad smile. 'That would be a good thing to do. Go soon, then it will all be out in the open.'

The cat jumped back into my lap and I stroked her silky back. 'Oh, I came to ask if you would mind me taking her to the vet and getting her spayed? I don't know the Greek word for it,' I said to her blank face. 'An operation so that she won't have kittens, and can live here with you safely.'

'Oh, of course. I didn't think about it. Yes, that would be fine. She is a friend for me, and kittens are a nuisance. Do you mind?'

'Not at all, I'll take her as soon as I can.'

Her eyes lost focus for a moment.

'Are you okay, Aunt Irini?' I looked around her neat kitchen. 'Do you need help with cleaning or cooking or anything? I can help. I'd like to.'

She placed her old hand on top of mine. 'You are kind but I'm fine. We are strong, us Cretan women!'

I laughed. 'I know you are, my mother's a tough one too. But, you know, if you need help in the night, or at any time, bang on the wall with your broom handle and I'll come.'

'Thank you, Anna, it is good of you. I can always phone my daughter, but it is good to have you close by.'

I gave her a kiss on my way out. I had to stop being such a selfish ratbag. Irini was family after all, and I could help to look after her, couldn't I?

That night was a largely sleepless one. I couldn't relax, despite a hot shower and herbal tea. I was concerned about my dad, even though Mum said he would be okay. And then I had the issue of Mr K turning out to be a rather unpleasant landlord to work through. I didn't like any of it, couldn't solve any of it, but I couldn't get it out of my head. It went round and round, and then, of course, because that kind of thinking always does, it turned into me dissecting my failed marriage, lack of kids (why hadn't we had any?) and then it became a beating-myself-up fest that I hadn't indulged in for weeks.

19

Thursday morning was language class again, talking about politics. It was great to catch up with Cassia especially as she had Tinos in tow for the class. He had not gone back to Athens then, and his arm was out of plaster but in a sling. There was no sign of Leo, but Alex and Cathy soon arrived and we began. Cassia gave us some phrases and got us started on the EU, guaranteed to spark strong opinions, especially from those of us whose countries were out whether they liked it or not.

It was fun, and I picked up some useful phrases, and learnt some new vocabulary, especially from Tinos, who was hotheaded compared to his sister, and easy for Cathy to provoke with her carefully rehearsed questions. As a Scot, she was still furious about the Westminster decision to leave the EU. Tinos didn't understand when she was winding him up, which made it funnier.

Alex was his usual calm, collected self, enjoying the banter, but keeping himself apart. I found myself looking to him for support when I was struggling with expressing my ideas.

We went, as usual, to the taverna for coffee after class. I hadn't seen Maria for several days and was glad that she was on duty and not Spiros. We ordered drinks and cakes, and Maria looked almost back to her old self, although I knew that couldn't be the case.

'Right, everybody listen up,' I said. 'It is time I had a supper party, and I'd like to invite you all to eat with me tonight. What do you think?' I caught Maria's eye. 'You too, Maria, if Spiros will cover for you.'

Cathy laughed. 'Well, I can't fault your ambition but can you fit six around that table of yours?'

'Hmm. I may need to move the table, but I think we can squash in. Well?'

Alex said, 'I can say that she is a very good cook. Isn't she, Cathy?'

'To die for. Really.'

I went a bit pink. I didn't want accolades, I just wanted to talk through everything that had happened with friends. Still, it was nice to hear. 'Okay, if you can all come, shall we say eight o'clock, to give me time to cook something?'

Maria, having recovered from her surprise said, 'That would be lovely. I can't remember the last time I ate at someone's home. I would like to bring something, please.'

Cassia also tried to offer, but I hate that, I like to do it all myself. Ungracious, *moi*? 'I can't have you all bringing food, it's enough that you want to come and bring yourselves. Wine or beer would be welcome though.'

Cathy interrupted: 'Please could Maria bring some of her chocolate baklava for dessert? It's so delicious.'

I had to agree. 'Right, that would be great, thank you. I'm deserting you now, though, I have shopping to do.' I passed over some euros for my coffee and stood up. 'See you later.' I left feeling great. I had friends, and I could cook for them.

I had a couple of hours before the market shut for lunch, and spent them happily buying food. Going to the market was one of the highlights of my week. Even early in the year, tomatoes were ripening, and spring vegetables burst out of their baskets. I got a bit lost in the cheese counter and also bought thyme-infused olive oil, just because it was there. Finally, I bought lamb from the butcher and struggled back home with yet more heavy bags. There was a learning point somewhere there. What could have been better than a spot of cooking for helping me forget about all the other stuff that had been crowding my head?

The afternoon passed in a flurry of roasting a leg of lamb, meze-making and table-setting. Irini allowed me to steal fresh rosemary from her garden. I took one extra cutting and planted it in my fledgling garden. You never knew. It might take.

When my guests arrived, I'd had a few minutes to get changed, but was hardly the vision of cool loveliness I'd been intending. Roasting a leg of lamb in a small kitchen made it hot, but I'd lit the fire in the living room anyway, just for the atmosphere.

Alex arrived first and gave me a kiss that felt so nice. He smelled good, and looked great in a blue linen shirt that emphasised his eyes. I had no idea how Leo had bowled me over so quickly. Why hadn't I been looking in the right direction?

He handed me a bottle of the same brand of wine we had drunk in the fish restaurant a couple of days before. 'I thought as we had enjoyed it...'

'It's perfect, thank you,' I said, and gave him another kiss. Just because.

He took the chair by the fire and wafted his face with his hand. 'You like to keep the house warm,' he said. 'I like your top, good colour on you.' He tipped his head to one side. 'You look lovely.'

I was quite relieved when the doorbell rang; it wasn't just the fire making me warm. Cassia and Tinos had collected Cathy and given her a lift, and Maria arrived just as I got them settled with a drink.

One of the things I love most about Cretan cooking is the meze first course. Everybody dives in and takes a little from all the plates in the middle of the table. It's relaxed and casual, and the cook doesn't have to get up and do things all the time. I surveyed the vast quantities laid out, and hoped they were all hungry. 'Let's eat,' I said, and we scrambled round the table until we were all in. I hadn't ever thought I would have enough friends to invite five of them to dinner all at once.

We chatted in a mishmash of Greek and English, and drank wine and laughed at each other's linguistic mistakes. It was like an extension of the language class. I enjoyed seeing Maria out of context, too. She was good company at the table. Sad that Spiros had fallen so far.

Once we had finished eating the meze, I sat back in my chair, sipped my wine and watched them. Tinos and Cathy were still in heated debate mode about the EU, Cassia and Maria were chatting about the unemployment problem, and Alex? Well, as far as I could tell, Alex was watching me. So I got him to help pile the empty dishes into the sink, and to carve the lamb, which we had with roasted potatoes and onions, green beans in tomato sauce and onion gravy. Scrumptious, if I say so myself.

Over Maria's delectable baklava and coffee, I finally got around to the purpose of the evening. 'So, now I have you all relaxed and receptive, I have a mystery I want you to help solve.'

Cathy rubbed her hands together. 'Do tell,' she said, 'I love a mystery.'

'Who is Leo Arakis?' I asked them. 'He may have been on the island longer than me, and he may not be who we think he is. So who exactly is he?' Having set the scene I told them about his disappearances, and the state in which he returned, and my visit to his room where he appeared to have left all his paperwork behind.

'You really got into his room?' asked Tinos, laughing.

'I don't know what came over me,' I said. 'Not that I found much.'

'Sounds as if you may make a good spy,' he replied, and toasted me with his beer bottle.

'But what do you think it means?' asked Cassia, topping up her and Cathy's glasses.

'Do you think he isn't intending to buy the land, and that the paperwork and maps are a cover-up?' ventured Alex.

Cassia objected. 'But what else could he want? Kokorakis owns nearly all the land around here. Nothing happens to do with land without him knowing.'

That brought me up short. 'Really?'

'Could Leo be a taxation officer working undercover?' asked Cathy.

That took a bit of translation, but they got there eventually. 'I don't know, but I was thinking he might be a spy of some sort. I saw him in Chania yesterday, and he was all scruffy again and in a bar chatting with local men. There is no way he is in business meetings this week, not looking like that.'

'I'd be surprised if Kokorakis is paying his taxes as he should,' offered Alex, 'so he could be under investigation, but not by an American with rusty Greek, surely?'

'Now you have us all interested, Anna,' said Cathy. 'What can Leo be up to?'

'Well, I have more news that might help. I'm going to the Kokorakises for dinner on Saturday and I invited Leo and he was very excited. Far more excited than he should be, I thought.'

Maria let out a long sigh. 'This is hard for me, Anna. You know, I think you all know now, that Kokorakis holds the deeds to my taverna, and you all know why he has sacked Spiros.'

'He has also told you to be out by the end of the summer, hasn't he?' I said.

She shrugged, her mouth turned down. 'It has always been like this on the island. They could not have been local men with Leo in the bar. Not if they were plotting against Kokorakis in his own town. He has bought loyalty here. So they were either foreigners, or you are wrong about Leo. Maybe he was just having a drink.'

'But money talks,' said Alex, 'and it may be talking louder than their fear of Mr K.'

We were all quiet for a moment. That was true, and there were enough unemployed men on the island to be bought. 'But what does it mean? What could they be doing?'

Maria snorted. 'Wouldn't it be wonderful if someone could bring Kokorakis down, after all that he has done to me?'

'I can't believe you are paying the price for your husband's appalling behaviour, Maria,' said Cathy, drawing herself up to her full height. 'It's barbaric.' She held up her hand to prevent interruption. 'And don't anyone say, "it has always been like this on the island" or I'll slap them. It's wrong, and should not happen. There are laws.'

I poured more coffee, time to change the subject back again. 'Leo's American, but Cretan-American. He has ties to the island, just as I do, which may mean that he's finding his place here, same as me. I suppose he might not be a master criminal' – I arched an eyebrow – 'but what if he is?'

Maria cleared her throat. 'I have seen him leaving the hotel late at night, heading up towards the mountain road.'

'Is that what you were hinting at the other day?'

'It did not seem right to arouse your suspicions if it was nothing, but as you have doubts already, I cannot see that it would matter.'

'It all adds to the mystery, doesn't it?'

'Look, shall we let it lie?' asked Tinos. 'Leo was kind to me when...' He hesitated and glanced at Maria.

'It's okay, Tino, say it,' said Maria.

He smiled at her. 'Thank you. When Spiros set fire to my café. Maybe Leo is not a bad person, but a person who wants to find out all he can about Kokorakis before he commits to buying land from him. And that is all.' He gave me an apologetic look. 'Sorry, Anna, to ruin your good story.'

I sighed. Maybe the whole Leo Arakis thing was entirely in my head because I was so fed up at his unavailability. 'You're probably right,' I said. 'Leo did tell me he was bringing an American lawyer over to sort out the paperwork. I suppose that would fit if he doesn't trust Kokorakis to give him a fair deal.'

'But we can keep our eyes open, can't we?' asked Cathy. 'Maria can see him going past, and we can watch who he meets?'

'But what if he is just an ordinary businessman?' said Cassia. 'He does have rights to privacy, even on Crete.'

In the end, we'd had enough of Leo, and I told them about Irini, my second great cousin, or whatever she was, living next door. 'I have to call her Aunt Irini, though, otherwise it's very confusing.'

'I am so glad you have met your relatives, Anna. It will help you to settle on the island.' Maria beamed at me.

'Me too. I have a Greek orthodox priest as a cousin, too. Not everyone can say that.'

Cassia laughed. 'They can in Crete!'

I then told them about my parents leaving Crete in the late seventies and the feud that apparently existed between my father and possibly Kokorakis or even his own father. 'I don't know any more as no one will talk to me until I have asked my father what happened all those years ago.'

'But,' spluttered Cathy, 'they would have been boys forty years ago. Perhaps it was the fathers who began it all?'

'Of course, you're right. Unless it was a fight over a girl or something?'

'Do you think your father will tell you the truth now, after all those years of silence?' asked Alex.

'Not willingly. I think Dad must have upset Mr K, or Mr K senior just like Spiros did, and has paid the price. But I guess we'll find out once I've been home and asked him.'

The evening broke up then as it was late and Maria had to work the next day. Alex offered to wash the dishes, but I wanted a bit of time on my own to think through what I'd learnt. And I knew that if he stayed over, then my little complication, that I didn't like or trust the man I was actually sleeping with, would spill over into a big one. Life certainly was no longer boring. But as for letting it all go, as Tinos had suggested. No way. Leo was up to something, and I would find out what it was, one way or another. And as it turned out, sooner than I expected.

20

I hate being late. It had become a problem over the years. Will cultivated lateness because above all, he liked to make an entrance, but that only made me worse. I hate being thought rude. I'd loved living a life for the past few weeks where time was more fluid and flexible and I wasn't so driven, but the anxiety was still lurking.

However, I could remember those relaxed feelings when I was in a better mood, and not about to be late for a dinner party. I pulled the curtains aside and looked once again down the dark street. There were lots of people about as it was Easter Saturday, but all were headed down into the harbour for a huge midnight feast and fireworks after the usual church service. Only the honoured few would be going up the hill to Kokorakis mansion. Seven thirty and still no sign of him. Where was he?

I'd dressed in my favourite crimson silk shift dress, which was a bit tighter than I remembered around the hips, but still looked fine. With carefully applied makeup and a serious conditioning of the wild mop that passed for my hair, I'd been feeling pretty good by the time I'd finished dressing.

I checked again. Still no sign of him. Still no text since early in the week.

I poured a cold glass of deliciously scented white wine and sipped it as I perched on the very edge of the chair. No point creasing the dress before I got there. I was apprehensive, but also excited. I checked my watch. It was an old one my father had given me on my twenty-first birthday. Silver-and-gold bracelet with a tiny face and ornate numbers. He said it had been his grandmother's. It was the only time I remember him ever mentioning her. I added silver earrings and my chunky ring, and checked my hair once again.

Ten minutes to walk up the hill, so I should leave at seven forty-five. Or maybe leave at eight, if I was going to have to go on my own. There was no way I was getting there first. I put lipstick, my newly-printed business cards and tissues into my beaded shoulder bag, and added my phone, which had remained silent since a quick call from my mother earlier in the day. Then I stared moodily at the cold fireplace.

Finally, there was a rap on the door, and Leo was there, looking very cool in a black dinner jacket and a bow tie.

'Well, you look a bit better than last time I saw you,' I said, and let him in.

Leo scooped me into a close hug and aimed for my freshly-painted mouth. I struggled back a little. 'Watch it,' I spluttered, 'don't wreck all my hard work!'

He settled for a kiss on the cheek. I wondered if he sensed that I wasn't as bowled over by him as I had been.

'Said I'd be here, clean and sober, ma'am,' he said and saluted me. He offered his arm. 'Shall we walk?'

'Perfect timing. Let's mingle with the rich and famous of Crete.' I was excited now that the plan had come together.

I'd forgotten how to walk in strappy sandals after months in boots and trainers, so it was a slower walk up the hill than planned, and we were overtaken by two large, expensive-looking cars that Leo insisted on naming as we walked.

'So, how did your meetings in Athens go?' I asked.

'Fine, I think everything is in place. At least I hope it is.'

'So no drama then? No problems with leases or our host for the evening muscling in?'

'I doubt Kokorakis even knows who I am,' said Leo. 'In fact, I'm looking forward to meeting him tonight. I've been dealing with his land agent, not the man himself, of course.'

And that was the end of the conversation. Still lying, I reckoned.

Leo was jumpy on the walk, laughing quickly and commenting on everything from slinky cats crossing our path to quirkily-painted front doors. I half-listened to his inane nervous chatter and thought about Alex's blue eyes and calm smile.

The first thing I saw when we reached the house were the lights. A whole spectrum of colours washed slowly over the front facade and up into the night sky. It was breathtaking. Delphine had decorated her plain, modern house with light, and it was wonderful.

We walked up the path and were greeted by the housekeeper who took us into the sitting room. It was a large room with a vaulted ceiling, the plainness of the walls disappeared under lighting which glowed in soft tones of peach and apricot. 'Oh my God, Leo, it's beautiful.'

'Classy,' he said, 'she must be a classy lady.'

There were uplit pieces of glass and sculptures on plinths, long, low leather sofas and coffee tables. On the walls were huge abstract prints which would have dwarfed a room with normal proportions. In the corner, a baby grand piano stood with the lid open, ready to be played. It was all gorgeous, and the real log fire in the granite-and-slate fireplace gave the room a warmth it would lack in daylight. I realised I had little to teach Delphine about interior design. 'It's just a party room, isn't it though? You couldn't actually live in it, could you? Too vast and empty.' I thought about what Maria had said the other night, about the farmhouse in the mountains being Kokorakis' preferred home.

'I could get used to it,' said Leo, scanning every corner. 'He takes his security seriously,' he murmured, smile gone from his face. 'Alarms all over the place, and I doubt that guy over there is a waiter.'

I hadn't noticed the man standing alone by the door in a dinner suit. I'd assumed he was a guest until I realised he wasn't talking to anybody, or drinking anything. It brought it home to me that I was about to move in very different circles from those I was used to.

A short man in his sixties came towards us. His eyes were hooded but almost black in a long face. A good suit hid his paunch, and there was a sense of strength, of ownership about him.

'You must be Anna Georgiou,' he said, taking my hand. 'Nikos Kokorakis. It is very good to meet you. My wife has been telling me about the wonderful work you are doing with her. Thank you, and if you need anything else, you must ask. It was a terrible mistake, what happened, and I want to put it right.' He squeezed my hand and stared into my eyes.

I was surprised. He genuinely sounded like he cared. The trouble with listening to rumours is you only get half the picture, I thought. And then I remembered what he had done to Maria.

Kokorakis turned to Leo. 'And who have we here?'

'This is my friend, Leo Arakis,' I said, and released Leo's right hand. I hadn't realised I'd been holding it.

'It is very good to meet you, sir,' said Leo, falling into that faux respectful tone that a certain class of American seems to find natural. I could see that Kokorakis liked it. Or was used to it. 'You have a beautiful house,' he added.

'My wife's work. I think, in another life she would have liked to be a designer, like you, Miss Georgiou. Perhaps you could teach her?'

I glanced around the room. 'There is little I could teach her, Mr Kokorakis. She has a strong style already. Unique. This is fabulous.'

On cue, Delphine left the couple she had been talking to and came across. She kissed me on the cheek, which was unexpected, murmured that I looked beautiful, also unexpected, and shook Leo's hand. Both of them were examining Leo like he was a specimen in a jar.

'I hear that you are planning on buying land here in Kissamos,' said Kokorakis, his English slightly stumbling and not often used, I suspected. 'Come and talk to me later, after dinner, about your plans.'

'I will. Thank you, sir,' said Leo to Kokorakis' back as he went off to circulate.

Delphine waved a waiter over and we took glasses of champagne. 'To new beginnings.' We clinked glasses. 'I'll catch up with you later,' she said, 'I have a couple more people to greet,' and headed for the front door once more.

I walked Leo across to a set of double doors and we looked into the dining room, set with ten places. It was a room that would have stunning views over the town and out to sea in the summer. Now, in the darkness, the windows were covered in gauzy curtains, and the table glowed silver. 'It really is something,' I whispered.

'It's just showing off, Anna,' said Leo, a little sharply. 'They want to impress their wealthy friends.'

I took a look at his eyes which were darting around, avoiding my gaze. 'Well, you're doing all right if Mr K wants to see you later,' I said, giggling a bit as champagne bubbles went up my nose. 'You might be one of the wealthy friends soon.'

'I sure am, and it's thanks to you. I wonder how I could repay the favour?' he said, and kissed me just under the ear, which sent a small explosion of pleasure down my spine. See? Complicated. My head said avoid this man, he bad; the rest of me said, go for it, girl, he's hot.

Another glass of bubbly settled my nerves and I was able to study the other guests. There were three other couples, most of whom seemed to know each other, so naturally they headed straight over to us, the newcomers. 'Fresh bait,' I muttered to Leo as one woman took my arm and led me towards a gaggle of them standing by the log fire, leaving Leo to fend for himself with the men.

Some of the women spoke excellent English, but we settled in the end to Greek with English translations when I got stuck. It was incredibly useful to be dropped into ordinary-speed conversations, if a little terrifying. One of the women was a dress designer, another an architect. I gave my card to several of them, and realised that Delphine had invited people she thought might be able to help me.

She grinned at me from across the room at one point, and I felt suddenly grateful that I had met this talented woman and that she might want to be my friend.

I took tiny canapés from a waitress, and relaxed into the atmosphere. I was admiring my surroundings and watching Nikos chatting as Delphine flitted between her guests, charming them. Every time I met Delphine I had to reassess how I felt about her and her husband. It was obvious that he had aimed high to capture Delphine. She was a natural at all this stuff, and fitted far better into his lifestyle than Maria ever would have done.

A quiet gong sounded to call us in for dinner. I was really looking forward to the meal. My expectation was that the food would be of the highest standard, and I was hoping not to be disappointed. Kokorakis seated me on his left and the dress designer on his right. Leo was down the table near Delphine which suited me. I felt uncomfortable in his presence now. It was hard to pretend that I was enjoying his company, when I'd been accusing him of being a spy, or worse, only a few days ago.

Over tiny individual dishes of tempura calamari, squid stuffed with prawns and plates of salmon and caviar, I got to know my host a little better.

Kokorakis poured me a dry and delicate white wine. 'I am so glad to meet you, Anna,' he said. 'So you have come to the island from England to live?'

I answered him in Greek. It seemed wrong to let him struggle, and I needed the practice. 'Yes, I have inherited my grandmother's house in the town, and it was time for me to move on and find a new life. It came at the right time, I suppose.'

'Welcome, welcome. Tell me a little about yourself. I know you are a designer, but what about your family? Were they happy for you to go away?' He speared a piece of caviar-topped salmon and chewed on it.

'I'm an only child, so they were quite unhappy to see me go, but I feel like I'm coming home, Mr Kokorakis.' I drank more wine. Oh God, what if he asked me more about my parents, and what if the feud Irini mentioned is real? I felt a bit panicky. What could I say?

His hooded black eyes widened. 'Are your family local? There are some Georgious in the area.'

Well, I couldn't refuse to answer. 'I think so. Dad's mother lived here, of course. To be honest, Mum and Dad worked hard to buy our restaurant in Manchester and we never talked about Dad's background at all. He has made his home and life in Manchester.' I concentrated on my food, and breathed in relief when the woman on Kokorakis' other side asked him a question. For some reason, I never expected to have to talk to him about my family, and I didn't want to lie, so I turned to the man on my other side, the husband of the architect, and talked to him about interior design, and his love of fast cars. Riveting it was not, but it saved me from further embarrassment with my host.

The main course was actually two courses, a fish stew in little bowls followed by lamb, traditional at Easter, roasted and served with vegetables. Although dessert was served, I hadn't even a squeak of room left. Expectations had been more than satisfied.

I'd relaxed a bit, and was more able to chat to Kokorakis, who said, 'Please call me Niko,' after an hour or so. He wanted to know about my work with Delphine and about what I had done to my own house. He seemed genuinely interested in me and my work, and it felt fine, not intrusive or seedy.

Kokorakis would have been one amongst many self-made businessmen in the city where I used to live. They, or rather their wives, made up the biggest proportion of my client base. If I wanted to pursue a friendship with Delphine, I'd need to be friendly with her husband, and he was making it easy. He poured the wine generously, and because I was eating at the same time, I matched him glass for glass.

'Anna, that is a very old watch you are wearing, I think?' he asked, and took my wrist to have a closer look. He looked for a long time, tracing the gold filigree design on the silver. 'Is it a family heirloom?'

'Yes, it was my great-grandmother's. Dad gave it to me when I was twenty-one. I love it very much.'

He looked misty-eyed for a moment. 'Take good care of it. I

am sure your great-grandmother would be proud to know that you are looking after it,' he said.

'I will. I never knew her, and this is a connection to her, in a way.'

At the other end of the table, Leo had been working his way steadily through the wine, too, and his loud stories and laughter were interrupting other conversations. He was boorish as soon as alcohol loosened his private school training. He and I were going to have a serious conversation at the end of the evening. Then I asked myself why I was wasting my time wondering about him, when really I just needed to dump him.

After dinner, those of us who had actually been eating, i.e., not Delphine, staggered into the sitting room and fell onto the sofas, groaning quietly. Coffee appeared as if by magic. I was quite drunk, and drank two cups down quickly. I needed at least two pints of water as well.

As soon as we were all settled, Delphine delighted me by sitting at the piano and playing some gentle jazz. She was good. It washed over me, and I suddenly felt sleepy. Time had gone by quickly and my watch said almost twelve. Smokers wandered off to stand outside on the patio, and I saw Kokorakis grip Leo firmly by the elbow and take him out of the room for a chat, as promised.

I lay back against the soft leather for several minutes, enjoying the music. I didn't feel the need to talk to anyone, I was simply enjoying the mood. After she had finished playing, Delphine sat next to me. I gave her a round of applause.

'So have you had a good time, Anna? My husband wasn't too nosy, I hope?'

'Not at all. I've had a lovely time, and the food was exquisite, even if I did eat too much of it.'

She smiled in appreciation. 'Eleni and her husband, Panos' – she indicated the man we had seen earlier at the door – 'look after us. We have extra staff for dinner parties, and managing the garden, but otherwise we keep a small staff here. Eleni was trained in Paris and Athens.'

'Ah! That explains everything. She's a gifted cook. Please thank her for me.' And ask her if she'll give me lessons, I didn't add. 'I'd love to be able to cook like her.'

We chatted about the next steps for the Andreanakis house for a few more minutes, until I became aware of raised voices coming from outside the room. Delphine excused herself and slipped away through the door, patting the air with her hands to assure us everything was fine.

Fine? I wished for the ground to swallow me up, because the only two people out there were Leo and Kokorakis, and everyone in the room had stopped talking so they could listen to the American, shouting.

There was an abrupt stop, the sudden crash of the front door slamming, and then nothing. I caught Ekaterina, the architect, raising her eyebrows at me, and managed a mortified shrug. Well, I didn't know what had happened, did I? But it didn't mean I couldn't find out. I followed Delphine out the door, along the corridor and stood in the entrance to what looked like a study. Delphine stood with her hands on her husband's chest. His face was a dark, blotchy red, anger leaking from every pore. He turned to glare at me.

'I'm sorry,' I said, 'I wondered what happened. Is everything all right?' Clearly something awful had happened. 'What did he say?'

Delphine turned from her husband and came toward me, head on one side. 'A disagreement, that is all. But I think your companion has left without you. Stay here, and I will collect your things, then you don't have to go back into the sitting room.'

I nodded, dumbly. She wanted me out, that was clear.

Kokorakis moved and stood behind his desk. 'Is that man a good friend of yours, Anna?'

I flushed. 'No. No, he's not. I didn't feel able to tell him not to come tonight after I had invited him, but he is no longer a friend of mine. I'm so sorry to bring trouble to your house, Niko. I would never have brought him here had I known...'

'Known? Do you know who he is? Who he really is?'

He gave me such a hard look my legs wobbled and I had to lean against the door jamb. I struggled to clear my head. 'No, I don't, honestly. I know he *isn't* who he says he is. I know he's been lying about what he's doing on the island, but I don't know who he is. Unless you can tell me?'

Kokorakis poured himself a drink from a decanter on the table while I tried to get my drunken thoughts into some sort of order. So, was Leo a spy? Had he threatened Kokorakis in some way?

Behind me, Delphine arrived with my shawl and bag, wrapped the shawl around my shoulders and stuffed the bag into my hand. 'Are you throwing me out?' I asked.

Delphine shook her head, and held me in a brief hug. 'Of course not. All the guests will be leaving soon. But I need to talk to Nikos now. I will call you in a day or two and explain what has happened. In the meantime, and you must promise me this, Anna, you must have nothing to do with Leo Arakis. He is a dangerous man. Do you promise?' She held onto my free hand and squeezed it, hard.

'I promise. I don't want to see him anyway, but please, can't you tell me anything about what he said?'

She cast a glance at her husband, who was still a terrible colour. 'As you can see, this has been hard for Nikos. Trust me, Anna, soon you will know everything.'

With that, she bundled me out through the door and into

the night. More secrets, more lies. More not telling Anna anything. It was becoming the story of my life.

I stumbled down the road, feeling and looking like an abandoned drunk. Around me exploded the fireworks of the Easter celebrations, voices and music came from doors and open windows, and ahead of me, in the town's tavernas, people were having a wonderful time. I thought of Alex, out with the expats on what would be a raucous night, and felt small, and lonely, and like I had made a terrible mistake when I had smiled back at Leo Arakis that very first time.

As soon as Delphine had sent her guests away, citing a sudden headache on Nikos' behalf, she went back into the study and closed the door. 'What happened?'

'He wants in on my business. Listed the areas of weakness that he has studied, told me I should say yes and avoid any unpleasantness.'

'But who the hell is he? How dare he come up here demanding anything from you at all? Does he have any idea who you are?'

Nikos' face turned puce once more. 'Everything, not anything; the wine and oil and the building business. He said I owed it to him after what I did to his father; that he should be my heir; that he had been studying the business carefully over the past few months, and knew all its weak points. And wouldn't the tax office like to know exactly how many people I employed, and how much business I was actually doing? He has been spying on me.'

'His father?'

'He is apparently Leontes Kokorakis, Stephanos' son.'

Delphine sat heavily on a chair. 'So he changed his name to fool us.'

'And fool us he did.'

'Oh God, Niko, what did you say to him?'

'I refused to believe him at first and attempted to throw him out.' He held up a bruised wrist, finger marks turning blue where the blood had risen to the surface. 'But he was too strong for me.' He took a long swallow of his brandy, and breathed out a sigh. 'So then he tried to bargain with me, and get me to give him a chance, working alongside me. As if I would give in to his puny threats. I asked him why he hadn't come to me openly as my nephew first, and asked to learn the business in the normal way, and said then it might have been an option.'

'What did he say? The feud?'

'Exactly. He will inherit nothing from his own father, who appears to have taken the same stance with his children as mine did with us. And he believes that he can only get something from me through threats and bribery, because of the feud. And possibly because of the way he has been raised.' He wiped a shaking hand across his brow. 'All those years ago, and the actions of my father are still visited on his sons and their sons. Will it ever stop?'

'What then? How did you get him to go?'

'I could see he was getting very angry, so I told him to get out, and that he would get nothing from me. I called Panos, who got him out after a little struggle. He left, but said this was not over, and he would be back.'

'Was it wise to throw him out? Who knows what he may do now, Niko? We may be in danger.'

'How could I negotiate with him when he came into my house and threatened me? How could I give my business to him? I'd rather lose it all. No, he does not have the qualities I am looking for in an heir.'

He pushed himself to his feet, walked around the desk and drew Delphine up so he could hold her tightly. 'No,' he said into her hair, 'Anna will inherit. She can have it all.'

She pulled back. 'Anna knows nothing about this business.'

'But she can learn, Delphie, and we like her. I think she has a good heart and a strong mind.'

He took her by the hand. 'Let's go up to bed, I have had enough of today. A few weeks ago I did not think I had any relatives. Now I have many, and I don't want all of them. I'm very tired, let's talk in the morning. I must plan carefully if we are to survive this attack.'

21

The sunlight streamed in through the sides of the window blind as usual and beat on my face. I woke to find myself caught up in a hot tangle of duvet.

It was after nine on a beautiful Easter Sunday and somehow I had slept through bells, fireworks and drunken people staggering home. Which was a blessing.

What I needed was an easy day where I could process Leo the Liar out of my brain and focus on a future made much simpler without him in it.

I took a couple of headache pills and made tea and ate toast. I was starving, as usual, despite all the food the night before. Food always makes me feel better, and I was at least calmer by the time I settled with my phone and composed a short text to Leo. *Thanks for last night. Embarrassing me in front of people is not my idea of having a good time. I'm deleting your number. Do not try to contact me again.* I removed the first sentence, not at all sure he would understand sarcasm, and sent the text.

Mum called. Dad was not very well at all, could I come home soon? I had a panic, what if he was really ill and they, naturally, hadn't told me? 'Mum, tell me what exactly is wrong with him. When you said his waterworks, did you mean his prostate?'

'Yes, but it's okay, darling, he is having the treatment. It's quite common for men of his age, I believe. He would just love to see you, he is very low in spirit.'

'Right, then I'll come as soon as I can. I'll book the flights and let you know. I can be there by the end of the week.'

'Good, that will be perfect. We'll see you soon. Love you.' And she ended the call. Home it was then. I'd be happier off the island for now, with an angry Leo marauding about.

I checked local news and read some reports of the night's festivities. A ridiculous Easter bonnet parade run by expats which featured Cathy prominently marching at the front sporting a bird's nest on her head was the most interesting article. Nothing else came up of interest.

Tentatively, I texted Delphine to thank her for the evening and to ask if they were okay. Nothing came back from her.

A tap on the door brought Irini into the kitchen. She had returned from church, dressed once again in black with her head covered. 'Did you have a good evening? I noticed that you came home alone.'

'You don't miss much, Aunt Irini.'

She shrugged. 'I'm an old lady, I don't sleep much. Was it a nice party?'

'Take a seat, I'll make tea. It's a long story. It started well, Nikos and Delphine were very good hosts, and I had a lovely time. Their house is beautiful, and the food was fabulous.' I added water to the kettle, tea to the pot and found two pottery mugs in the cupboard.

'Yet you came home alone.'

I watched the kettle come to a boil and poured water onto the leaves. 'Leo behaved badly. We were all drinking but he got loud and difficult. Then Nikos took him into the study and there were raised voices and Leo left, slamming the door like a child. I was really embarrassed.'

'Hmm. I wonder what they were talking about?'

'I thought Nikos was going to talk to Leo about the house and land he wants to buy. Perhaps there is some problem with it.' I poured us tea and sat next to her. 'Anyway, Aunt Irini, I will not be seeing Leo Arakis again. I have finished with him for good, and I'm glad.'

She touched her mug against mine. 'In that case, let's drink to independent women.'

'I'm going to book a flight home for later in the week, to see my parents. It is about time I sorted out all this mystery,' I said, pouring more tea and breathing in the fragrance.

'Yes, do go home. I think also it is time for it all to come out, especially now that you are living in the town.'

We drank our tea and she told me more about Stavros, and her daughter and grandchildren, all of whom I was to meet now that the Lent fast was over. 'There will be feasting, Anna, I must warn you!'

Finally, she pulled herself up from the chair. 'It's a beautiful day for a walk. The spring flowers are all out. You will feel better if you do something nice. It is a tradition to walk today, after all. Forget about all this nonsense with the young man.'

I opened the back door and saw her through it. 'You look after yourself,' I called after her, and closed the door and locked it. Just in case a certain someone was around.

It was indeed a nice day for a walk, perhaps in the mountains, near the fortress. Well, I couldn't hang about all day waiting to see if Delphine told me anything about Leo, and I'd quite like to have a look myself at the Kokorakis base of operations to see if it was as extensive as Irini said.

I rang Maria and asked if she knew exactly where the fortress was located. Or rather if Spiros did. She sent me a grid reference within minutes, and a warning to take care as it was guarded.

I then rang Alex. 'Hi, did you have a good time at the celebrations?'

'I did have a little too much raki,' he said, 'I have a thick head.'

'Well, I have the perfect antidote for that. How about a drive up into the mountains and a nice walk to clear your head?'

'Sounds perfect.'

I filled him in on the problem with Leo and how angry and hopeless it had made me feel, and came clean on wanting to see Kokorakis' business base for myself. Just to get an idea of the size of the operation.

'You can't go up and just ask to be let in, Anna. They might have men with guns guarding the place.'

'Guns? He's a builder, Alex, not a gangster. We don't have to go in, I just want to see the place.'

'Maybe not, but this is not such a good idea. Why do you want to see the place anyway? Let's go for a beach walk instead.'

I don't think I could honestly say why I wanted to go. I was still trying to square the warnings from Maria and Irini with the charming couple I had begun to know. I guess I needed to see for myself.

It took a good ten minutes to talk him round. My last argument, that it was Easter Sunday and there would be families all over the mountains walking and picking flowers, seemed to win him over. 'So, I'll make a picnic. Do you have binoculars?' He had. 'And we'll be looking from far away.'

I packed lunch and wore my walking boots and jeans. It would be cooler in the mountains, so I packed a light waterproof jacket and a fleece into my backpack and was ready when Alex knocked on the door.

He kissed me lightly on the cheek, then gave me a tight hug

that almost winded me. 'I'm glad you are okay,' he muttered into my hair. 'You worried me with that phone call this morning. I'm glad you have finished it with Leo. He isn't a good man, I know that now.'

He let me go and loaded his backpack into my car. I stood for a moment, having a little bask. Alex cared about me. He would come with me even though he didn't want to. Sneaking up as close as we could get, and having a look at the set-up were my only aims for the afternoon, and then dinner when we got back. It was a good, if basic plan, I thought.

Once I'd loaded the directions into his phone we set off, following the Falasarna road up into the mountains. The sun was strong on the windscreen and it felt good to roll the windows down and feel the air on our faces. It would help to clear our heads after our overindulgences the night before.

Alex brought up Maps on his phone. 'It is a region full of olive trees and grapevines, as one would expect. But here' – he pointed to a spot on the map that I couldn't see because I was concentrating so hard on the road – 'is an isolated farm with many barns and outbuildings. It's a big place. The property business must bring in more than the farming altogether,' he said.

'Yes, I suppose it must.' We drove in silence for a few kilometres as I negotiated switchback bends and dizzying drops to the plains below. I was feeling a bit sick from the bends and wondering if driving had been such a good idea when Alex spoke up.

'I will show you where to park,' he said as we neared the grid reference. 'We should walk from there. There is a little chapel on a hill that will give us a good view down onto the fortress, as it is called.'

The phone announced that we should take the right fork off the main road which meant we were getting close to where we would need to get out and walk. The chapel was about two kilometres from where we could park, and the fortress was downhill from there, another kilometre or so. It felt like a long way away, but it would have to do.

I parked as far under a large cypress tree as I could get, aiming to disguise our presence somewhat, in case we were trespassing. We ate lunch before we set off, sitting under a stand of Holm oak trees bearing luminous new green leaves and marvelling at a clump of pink orchids growing nearby. I took a photo, having no idea what kind of orchid they were.

I slathered bread in hummus, cheese and wedges of tomato and passed one to Alex, who devoured it even faster than I did. There is something about being outside in the crisp air that stimulates the appetite, although from the looks Alex was sending my way, it wasn't just his stomach he was interested in. At least the 'complication' of Leo was well out of the way. I grinned at him. 'Not such a bad way to spend a Sunday?'

'Not so bad at all,' he said, and took a drink from his water bottle.

The walk was uphill, through wild, forested areas along a trail that had been used in the past. And still would be used now, I realised, by whoever it was who tended to the little chapel and the goats which could be spotted roaming all over the hills. When we reached it there were wild flowers in a small vase at the door, and inside, a gold-painted icon of Mary and a lacy cloth covered the altar. It was tiny, and much loved by somebody.

In the open space around the chapel, beehives buzzed in the afternoon warmth and poppies poked up from the earth. There were goats clanging the bells around their necks as they leapt from rock to rock and clambered into gnarled trees in search of the best new leaves. It was idyllic. I let out a breath and gave a silent thanks to the mountains for what they gave us, especially in spring. We were among them now, their limestone crags glittering in the sharp sun and snow caps slowly melting into rivers that would be bone dry in a month or so.

Alex called me over to a large, flat rock on which he had perched. He was scanning the area with his binoculars. The views were huge from up there; olive groves and orange groves and forests crowded the nearby slopes. Rows of vines, cut and already sprouting in new growth, marched away over the hill-sides and the whole valley meandered down towards the sea at Falasarna. 'Look,' Alex said, 'there is the place.'

I followed the line of his arm down the valley to a spread of buildings. There was one enormous central building that looked like it had been extended many times from the original farm-house, and as Alex had noticed on the map, six outbuildings, a wine-production facility and huge amounts of machinery and materials for building houses. There were lorries and white vans parked all over the place, probably because it was a holiday.

I scrambled up next to him, took the binoculars and refocused them for my long sight. At first I could see little, but then my eyes focused and I could see quite well. 'Wow, do you think they make the bricks as well as put the buildings together?' I asked, pointing him towards an enormous cement mixer.

'It's possible. He can massively cut costs by keeping it in-house. It is a big operation for one man to control.'

'And that can go wrong, can't it? Especially if you send someone like Spiros to do your dirty work. Why on earth didn't he get a solicitor to send a letter, like normal people do when someone defaults on the rent?'

He laughed at me. 'That is not the Cretan way, Anna, you know that.'

I laughed too. 'Good point. Still, it went horribly wrong, didn't it?'

I moved the binoculars down into the yard between the farm and the outbuildings and spotted a man standing in the middle of the yard, hands on hips. I ducked down automatically. He had been looking straight at me.

'There's someone looking up at us,' I murmured, 'and he must have good eyesight. As long as he's not overprotective we should be okay. Surely the path to the chapel is a public right of way?'

Alex turned over and lay on his stomach, shading his eyes to see better. 'It's a big business,' he said, 'security will be tight.'

I kept looking. 'The farmhouse has been extended. Many Cretans built big family houses with multiple doors and links to each other in case of invasion. Mum said they would head for these houses in the hills at the first sign of invaders. That's why they were such trouble for the Nazis in the war, it was almost impossible to track them down and they were always ready to go.'

'And it would be fertile up here during the summer, so they could survive well.'

'They're a tough lot,' I said, and took a closer look at the layout of the farmhouse. There was a front door set into what looked like one large room, then a series of rooms ran off in either direction. 'I'd guess there are at least four doors leading out, one from each of those sections. It's interesting.'

'No secret tunnel?' asked Alex, lying back on his elbows and smiling lazily at me.

'I wouldn't be at all surprised if there was.'

We basked on the warm rock for an hour or so, chatting, sunbathing, and finding out a little about each other. Our second date. 'See, it's fine,' I said. 'We're not trespassing, and now I understand a bit more about the size of his business.' I spread my arms as wide as they would go. 'Huge.'

'Enormous,' Alex said.

'Gigantic.'

'Massive.'

'Extensive.'

'I can't think of any more adjectives in English,' he said. 'Quit, you have an unfair advantage.'

I laughed and he leaned over and kissed me, quite gently, on the lips. Before I could go back for more, there was a cough from behind us.

I'd heard nothing, but then we had been a little distracted. I swung round and found two rough-looking men standing at the foot of the rock. One of them had a hunting rifle over his shoulder. I squeaked, 'Alex!' but that's as far as I got.

'You come down, now,' the bigger of the two men growled. He was young, but built like a rugby player, with meaty arms and leg muscles bulging through his jeans. The other one moved away, signalling us down with his rifle.

Alex saw the panic in my eyes and pulled me to my feet, holding me steady. He gestured at the man. 'We will. No need for weapons,' he said. 'We're just enjoying a walk and looking at the view. If we have trespassed, then I am sorry, and we will go.'

He jumped from the rock and helped me to the ground, where I collapsed into a heap against him. I was so scared, and so angry with myself. I'd put me, and worse, someone I cared about in danger. Why did I have to find out about everything? What was the matter with me? Why couldn't I let things be? I got up shakily and held onto Alex's hand, and put on my best wavery English lady voice. 'Please, we are just tourists.' I couldn't take my eyes off the weapon that hung so casually over the guy's shoulder.

The older man looked us over. 'Then why,' he asked in broken English, 'you look at farmhouse with those?' He indicated the binoculars.

'No,' said Alex, 'we have no interest in houses. We are bird-watching. Vultures.'

'Vultures? I see the sun on the glass. Looking at the house.'

Alex grasped my hand tighter as the men spoke rapidly in Greek, deciding whether or not to believe us, or whether they should call the police or the boss after what had happened last night. Did they mean Leo? Was he spying after all? I could feel the thump of my heart in my head. I'd be mortified if they told Nikos I'd been up here spying on him, too. I had to think of something.

So I did what women have had to do for eternity when confronted with superior male strength: I started to cry, loudly. It wasn't a dramatic stretch to be honest, I was scared. 'What have we done wrong? Oh, please let us go. We're on holiday, please!' I sobbed. 'We're looking at the birds, not your house. I'm so sorry.' I sobbed more.

Alex played along, shushing me and patting me on the back. 'My wife,' he said, 'she is pregnant, and this has been a terrible shock. I must get her to a doctor to make sure the baby is safe. Please may we go? We will go straight back to the hotel.'

I gave them my best, rather snotty, pleading look.

More debate followed, about the pros and cons of having to alert the boss, who was in a foul mood. And what if we really were tourists? Then they would be in trouble. Apparently I didn't look like a spy. No names that I recognised were mentioned, which was frustrating although I was sure I knew who they were looking out for.

Finally, our acting must have been good enough; they sent us on our way, but followed us until we reached my car and I drove off down the hill, shaking so much I could hardly change gear. They had parked their large SUV right up behind my little Fiat. Even the car looked intimidated.

Once onto the main road to Falasarna, the men turned back to head up towards the farmhouse and when I figured we were far enough away, I pulled over into the nearest lay-by, where I stopped the car and had to prise my hands off the steering wheel. I couldn't look at Alex. 'I'm so, so sorry, Alex, getting you involved in this. I was just being nosy, but it's all gone wrong. I feel awful.' I couldn't stop the tears that followed, they just fell out of my eyes and onto my shirt. Real tears, not ones just for effect.

There was a snort from next to me, then Alex said in a high-pitched squeal, 'We are looking at the vultures!' and he began to laugh and pound the dashboard. Big belly laughs that left me astonished. It was infectious. Once I started I couldn't stop laughing until the tears were running freely down my face and we had exhausted all the tissues in the pack.

'My wife is pregnant!' Alex snorted, and started us off all over again.

'Please let us go, we are tourists,' I added through my hysteria.

I finally sobered, and found that I felt better, and calmer. 'Thank you for that,' I said, sniffling, 'it really helped.' I knew I looked an absolute mess, but it didn't seem to matter. He'd sorted me out. After a final shuddering breath, I was okay. I pulled down the little mirror on the sun visor and observed the blotched skin and swollen lips and pink nose. Nice.

Alex took my hand. 'When something happens that is a shock, the only thing to do is laugh, I find. Laughing takes away its power, don't you think?'

'Yes, but I might have put you in danger because of my nosiness.'

He shrugged. 'Nobody has been killed, Anna. They are just guards for the business. The rifle was broken across his shoulder. He had no intention of firing on us. It is all fine, isn't it?'

I squeezed his hand. 'I guess I was more upset by Leo's behaviour last night than I thought. Did you catch the comment about the boss being in a foul mood? I really need to know what Leo said to upset him so much.' I caught myself out. 'I'm being nosy again, aren't I? You know, all I really want is to live quietly, to work, to get to know my family and to enjoy life. And my friends,' I added, squeezing his hand again.

Alex passed me the bottle of water from my backpack. 'Now that is the most sensible thing you have said today, Miss Marple. Drink this and we'll go back to your place. You promised me dinner.'

The afternoon sun warmed us as we made our way down to the coast and through the town to my little house. The atmosphere between us had changed since that interrupted kiss, and I was both excited and nervous about what the night might bring. Alex kept sneaking little glances at me, as if he too had seen something different. We were treading lightly, chatting about growing plants and getting the boat ready to go back in the water. All inconsequential things, like the ads before the film, when they make you sit through them before you get to the good stuff. At the risk of sounding trite, I'd never felt like this before. As if the next few hours would seal my future, and I had to get it right.

I need not have worried. We had barely closed the door when Alex took me in his arms, kissed my eyes, the tip of my nose and then found my mouth, and I knew it would be all right, now. I was home.

22

Alex curled up beside me in my bed for the first time that night. We had eaten lightly, and given the alcohol a break after our respective heavy nights, and we slept well. I was comforted by his presence. I still didn't feel safe with Leo prowling around being angry.

In the morning, while he lay quietly asleep, I took his callused hand and traced the marks made by ropes; the small scars and cuts and grazes. A man who could be serious, but also silly. A man who liked me and didn't want to mould me into somebody else. A father to two sons. I felt a huge tug around my heart and pressed a hand against my belly. Maybe, one day.

My phone, charging on the bedside table, buzzed. It was Delphine, could I come up to the house after breakfast as she and Nikos had something to discuss with me? I replied asking if it was okay to bring Alex, and she said she would prefer it if I didn't, as they didn't know him. I understood. How could they know what he had become to me?

When I'd finished the text, I noticed that his blue, blue eyes were open and looking my way.

'That is an extremely attractive shoulder that you are brandishing at me in a very provocative manner, Miss Georgiou. Please bring it closer so I may inspect it for freckles.'

I lent him the shoulder, but after a few minutes, I had to call a halt before he wanted more than the shoulder. 'We have to get up. I must go to Delphine's, she has something to discuss with me. They promised to explain what has been going on with Leo. Can I see you later?'

He sighed. 'I only just got you, and now I have to share you?'

'Only temporarily. This is really important to me, Alex. I'm finally going to find out what's been going on, and, if I'm feeling really brave, I may ask Nikos if he did know my father all those years ago. I can't see why Irini would have made a mistake.'

'I understand. I have work to do as well. I plan to get my boat back into the water this week, and I have a lot of work to do on it. Although I would prefer to stay here with you.' He gave me one last kiss, rolled out of bed and stretched his long body so that his hands touched the ceiling. 'Don't worry about breakfast. I'll have a quick shower and go.'

'Will you come back tonight?'

'Every night, if you'll have me.'

The large house looked less imposing in the white morning light. I couldn't decide, on the short walk, whether I was excited, or worried to find out about Leo. Or indeed, whether there would be anything to find out. I knocked on the door and it was opened by Panos, who nodded at me and took me straight into the study, where Delphine and Nikos were seated across from each other on small sofas.

Delphine got up, kissed me on the cheek and seated me next to her. 'I am glad you could come, Anna. We have a lot to talk about.'

Nikos rose and stood in front of an empty fireplace. He spoke formally. 'Anna, I understand that you would like to know about what Leo said, but there are more important things that you need to know first.'

He stuffed his hands deep into his trouser pockets, which made him at once less imposing, and a little vulnerable.

'Forty years ago, before you were even born, my father made a decision which has caused more pain than you know. He had three sons, and I am the eldest. When I was twenty-one he said I was to inherit all of the business he had built up, and that the others, just boys really, were to leave and not return on pain of death.'

I threw my hands up to cover my mouth before I blurted anything out. Be quiet, Anna. Listen.

Nikos understood. 'Yes, your father, Theo, is my middle brother. He went to live in England with Galena, and I have not heard from him since, as our father demanded. The youngest and best of us, Stephanos, went to America and I had not heard from him either. Until now, when his son confronted me on Saturday night.'

'His son?' My heart thudded slowly in my head. His son? The blood rushed down to my feet and the room went dark red and then black.

Delphine caught me as I fell forward, and pulled me back up to lie on the sofa. 'Oh, Anna, breathe deeply,' she said, and held me round the shoulders until the nausea passed. 'I didn't realise you would be so upset.' She dashed off to the kitchen and brought me water.

Of course, it wasn't the separation of the brothers that upset me the most, I'd figured out a lot of that on my own, even if I hadn't known that Dad had brothers, or been sure that his own father had sent him away.

'Leo is my cousin?' I stammered, taking a long drink of water to clean the bile from my mouth. I'd slept with my own cousin?

Delphine caught on. 'Oh my goodness. Yes, I am so sorry. You didn't know, but neither did he.' She glanced up at her husband. 'At least, I don't think he knew?'

That didn't help. I felt... dirty. Used. 'I feel awful,' I murmured, 'like I've done something really bad.' A Catholic childhood means the guilt runs deep and long.

Nikos shrugged. 'That cannot be helped, you were ignorant.'

That was marginally better. Marginally. Then I got a grip and actually listened. 'I'm your niece,' I said and shook my head. "Curiouser and curiouser", thought Alice, and Anna. There didn't seem to be much left for Dad to hide from me now.

Nikos sighed. 'At last, you understand.'

Delphine took my hand again. 'We wanted to tell you after the party, but of course it all went badly wrong. Welcome now,' she said, 'welcome to our family.' And she gave me a squeeze round the shoulders.

Dully, I finished the water, put the glass down carefully on the side table and settled back onto the sofa. I couldn't think of a single thing to say.

Delphine looked at me anxiously, then at her husband. 'Niko, perhaps we should have coffee?'

He went to the door and shouted for Eleni to bring coffee, then returned and sat opposite me. 'I am not proud of what I did all those years ago. I should have stood up to my father. I should have refused to accept his decision and then my brothers would have been able to stand up to him too. But the truth is we were all terrified of him. Only my mother stood firm when he sent my brothers away.'

'She moved into my little house.'

'And never set foot in the villa again. She never forgave my father, or me.' He wiped away a tear. 'I should not feel sorry for myself, but because of my weakness, I have lost all those years with my family, and now I am getting old and we have no children of our own.'

Delphine interrupted: 'It was a miracle when you moved into Nyssa's house. We realised that your mother must have kept in touch with Nyssa when you were a child. And when you arrived, it was as if we were being given a second chance...'

'A chance to put things right, Anna. To make it right with Theo and Galena.' Nikos stared at me with such intensity I knew he meant what he said. My dad, exiled all those years over a cruel and hasty decision made by a bully. Perhaps it was time for a reunion after all. I wanted some good to come from this. 'What do you want with me?'

Nikos cleared his throat. 'Anna, I want you to be my heir. To inherit my businesses when I retire.'

No, no, no, no. That could not possibly be right. 'Heir? But you hardly know me.'

'I don't need to know you, you are my blood.'

The odd thudding began in my head again. I took a couple of deep breaths and ignored their worried faces. 'Leo is also your blood. He's your nephew. What did he want on Saturday night?'

They exchanged a glance. 'He wants the business,' said Delphine, 'but he wants it now. He threatened Nikos with the tax investigators if he doesn't sign it over and allow Leo to come in and run it all.'

'I will not do that, Anna,' Nikos said, thumping a fist into his other hand. 'I will not give in to this blackmail. I will not give *him* my life's work. Why couldn't he come openly and ask to speak to me? Then, perhaps we could have talked. Now, I will not let him have a penny. I want you to have it all. Will you say yes?' He took my hands in his. 'There will be nothing for you to do for many years, God willing, while I am healthy and well. It would mean so much to me to know that all I have worked for has not been a waste.'

I pulled away, stood up, and had to clutch at the arm of the sofa for support. 'Can I go into the garden for a moment?' I asked, and headed out through the patio doors behind his desk. It was still morning, although it felt to me as if a month had passed. The whole world had turned the wrong way, and I was struggling to catch up. I could process the Leo thing as an accident, even though it made me squirm. But the rest?

I walked onto the grass of a huge lawn, idly wondered if it was watered from underneath in the summer, and took in the view of the mountains, cool and purple, with snowy caps and deep, shadowy ravines. They had stood, endured, for so many thousands of years, and witnessed so much death, and love and change. All that could happen in our petty little lives made so little difference to them. And here was a little more for them to observe. I'd been itching to know what was going on, and now I had my answer, didn't I? I would be rich one day. But is that what I wanted? To own that huge business? Never.

Yet again other people were manipulating my life, of course. But surely I could stand up to this? I didn't want the inheritance, true, but I also didn't want Leo to have it. At least it was clear now what he'd been up to on his jaunts away, he'd been staking out the fortress and learning what he could about it, ready to go on the attack. I was just an unfortunate coincidence.

My dream, of a simple life with family around me might still come true, however, and that was something to hold onto. The end of the stupid feud could happen; I was sure of that at least. I walked a bit further and stood under a pergola, heavy with bougainvillea, ready to burst.

Finally, I was in a position to change things for myself, and for those I had come to care about. I'd seen how money talked. I made my mind up. I would only agree to inherit if Nikos would do a few things for me before he retired. There were wrongs to be righted.

But that negotiation could come later. For now, I needed to let them know what I had decided. I turned back and saw them standing, hand in hand, side by side on the patio and recognised the same vulnerability that I had seen in my parents' eyes as they said goodbye to me a few short months ago. Bereft, they were. So I would do it for them, for my new family and for Mum and Dad, who deserved an end to the feud.

I walked back, and summoned up a smile. 'Okay, I'll do it. I would be honoured to be your heir, Niko,' I said, laughing a little. 'This is not how I thought my life would turn out, to be honest, but it's wonderful that I have found my family out here, and I want to share this with my parents, too. I'll try not to let you down.'

For the first time since I had met him, Nikos enveloped me in a hug. He smelt so much like my father I felt weepy, and clung onto him. It had been a week of shocks, and a body can only take so much. How did I not notice the resemblance between him and Dad the other night at the dinner? And how did I not realise that when Maria questioned Leo about relatives on the island, it was his resemblance to Nikos that had troubled her?

Back inside, calmer than I had been all morning, I saw that coffee and little almond biscuits had been laid out on the side table. Delphine poured while Nikos sat at the desk and completed some paperwork. He called me over and I sat and read every single line, asking for translations where necessary, and getting to grips with exactly what was being offered. It was an enormous fortune, and an enormous responsibility. I drank coffee and ate a biscuit, buying thinking time, while Delphine fussed around me and Nikos rang someone, most likely his lawyer. Finally, I could see no reason to delay further and signed on the dotted line. I felt as if I had lost control of my life yet again. This inheritance would give me power I had never wanted to wield. I just hoped it wouldn't be for a very long time.

Nikos spoke in Greek too rapid for me to follow properly, but it appeared he was changing his will in my favour. I still felt stunned. How did I get here from where I was two months ago?

'So,' I said, still a little shakily, when he came back and sat down opposite me, 'what did you actually say to Leo at the party?'

'I told him that I had already chosen an heir, that he would get nothing after coming into my home and threatening me, and that if I saw him again I would set the police on him.' Nikos pulled back the sleeve of his shirt and showed dark bruises around his wrist. 'He did not want to take no for an answer. Luckily, I had Panos to help me.'

'He hurt you?' I was horrified. How could he?

'It was nothing.'

Didn't look like nothing. I had a wobble. 'Did you mention my name?'

He had the grace to look ashamed. 'It came out. We were arguing. He called me a liar, saying that I had no other heirs except him and his two brothers. So I told him who you are. I'm so sorry, Anna.'

Delphine saw the shock on my face. She grabbed my hand again. 'He won't come back, Anna. He said he was going to do something about it with his big-shot lawyers.'

I felt a little better. 'Right, he'll have gone to see his American lawyer in Athens, no doubt. How can you be sure he won't come harassing me?'

Nikos looked at his feet. 'I am still alive, so it will be me he wants to damage, or persuade, not you. Thank you, Anna. Thank you for doing this.' He smiled for the first time that morning, and I saw that there was the possibility for change in his eyes. Perhaps this would work out after all. Or perhaps I was heading straight into danger.

The rest of the day was bizarre. Nikos took me up to the fortress for a grand tour of the business I would one day inherit. I kept wanting to laugh as we passed the two guards who had stopped Alex and me the day before. They were scanning the roads and hillsides, looking for Leo, I guessed. I was hoping they couldn't see into the black windows of the Lexus.

Nikos led me around the site. He proudly showed me all that he had achieved; the mechanisation of the oil and wine production, the bottling machines and presses, and he told me that he acted as the centre for the co-op of local producers, and that they had pushed up standards across the region.

Delphine went off to organise lunch in the farmhouse and left Nikos to continue the tour. We walked downhill to the fenced-in building business part. It took up a huge section of the land and, as I'd noticed before, was surrounded by barbed wire. 'Do you have everything here to make a house from beginning to end?' I asked, impressed.

Nikos' chest puffed up a little. 'It is how I like to work. I owe nobody anything. We make as much as we can in-house, and employ local people to do the work.' He gave a smile at the look of surprise on my face. 'You have been talking to Maria. She is bitter, and Spiros was out of control. I should never have sent him to speak to the Papadikis boy, but Spiros has a drink problem, and I could not trust him on the machinery anymore.' He shrugged. 'I am used to being painted as an evil man, but in truth, many people here are in my employment, and I look after them.'

I couldn't quite marry up this apparently saintly person with the successful business owner and the 'monster' Maria had talked about, but it gave me a way in to ask a difficult question. Walking and talking has always been the best way to do that, I find. 'I know that you want to punish Spiros for what he did, but what you have really done is destroy Maria, and she had nothing to do with what happened. She has nothing left without the taverna. She will be out on the street, without a job or a home.' I stopped walking and looked at him. 'Uncle Niko, change your mind. Better still, give Maria the deeds to the taverna. Give her some reward for all the years she has served you well. Please.'

His mouth dropped open. 'Give the taverna away? But it brings me income! I'm not a charity, Anna. Be reasonable.'

Reasonable was not in my vocabulary that day. I'd done something huge to help him out, now it was my turn. I waved a hand to encompass all that he owned. 'You have all this, how can the few thousand that you get from Maria make a difference to you?'

I hadn't noticed Delphine arriving until she stood by my side. 'What have I missed?' she asked.

Nikos gave a rueful laugh. 'One hour she has been my heir and already she is ruining my profits. She wants me to give Maria the deeds to the taverna.'

Delphine's eyes sparkled at me. She raised her delicately-arched eyebrows. 'So, you want Niko to show kindness, and that he can forgive?'

I chose to ignore the sarcastic smile playing on her lips. 'I do. Exactly. Thank you for understanding. Look, I don't know how a business like this runs, but I do know about doing what is right, and taking away Maria's self-respect isn't right.'

Delphine took my hand so that we stood together against Nikos. 'So what do you say, husband of mine? Do I dig out the deeds? Will you grant your niece this one wish?'

I watched his face and decided this definitely wasn't the time to ask for the other wish yet. All in good time.

Nikos rubbed a hand across his eyes and began to lead us back towards the farmhouse.

I held my breath. So did Delphine, who kept squeezing my hand.

'Okay,' he said, after sixty-two paces. I counted. 'I will do this. But I do not want to look weak. What if other tenants refuse to pay their rent, am I expected to just let it go? To be kind? Kind and poor, eh? Is that how you want me?'

'Oh, thank you. Thank you, Uncle Niko. Yes, be kind this time because when you're fair, then people see it as a kindness, not a weakness and they won't take advantage. It's similar to what Delphine and I are doing for the Andreanakises. Restitution is a strong thing to do, not a sign of weakness.' I hoped.

Delphine laughed her tinkling laugh. 'She has you there, Niko. Let's eat, and we can talk about Maria and the taverna for a little while, and I'll tell you all about the new Andreanakis house and what has been done so far.'

So we did. And I felt better than I had in several stressful days. He wasn't a monster at all, my uncle. He just needed reminding about how to be a human being as well as a businessman. And I was beginning to enjoy my role as Kissamos' own Mother Teresa, too, even though I had no idea how far I could push Nikos before he said no.

After a late lunch, which had been simple salads, cold meats, cheeses and bread, Nikos phoned his lawyer again, and arranged to have the deeds transferred over to Maria, but not to Spiros. I wanted her to have something of her own. Something that he couldn't drink away.

Later, when I took a moment to myself, I rang Alex and told him about my day, and he was just as excited as me about the taverna and Maria. 'But don't say anything, Alex, I want to talk to her after she has received the paperwork, and knows that it's true.'

He laughed. 'Are you feeling good about this? I can hear the excitement in your voice. It seems you have tamed the dragon in his den!'

'Hmm, we shall see. I have another request for him, and he may not feel so good about that. Anyway, will I see you later? We had a late lunch, but I could do us a supper if you came over around eight?'

'Lunch? Is it past lunchtime? Oh, I have missed it again. Yes, I'll get a sandwich now, and see you then. I love you, Anna.'

He said it. He said it. I whispered, 'Love you too,' back at him and ended the call, heart pounding. I hadn't said those words in almost ten years. 'Please don't let me mess this up,' I muttered and made my way back into Nikos' office, ready to be driven home.

'I want to stop at my very special vineyard on the way home, if that is okay?' asked my uncle.

Who was I to disagree? I hoped the visit would result in us having a glass of wine or two. I felt like celebrating. The shock of the first part of the day had faded enough for me to understand that not much in my life would change for the time being, and I had plenty of time to formulate the nebulous idea I had floating about in my head. An idea that might just help Tinos. Which was the other thing that Nikos had to put right.

23

It was after seven when Nikos dropped me and two boxes of wine from his vineyard outside the house. He helped me unload but I refused his offer to take it into the kitchen. I said goodbye to them both on the doorstep, and all the awkwardness of earlier in the day was gone. I was simply saying goodbye to my aunt and uncle.

As soon as I lugged the boxes into the living room and plonked them on the floor, something felt wrong. I had left the kitchen door open when I left that morning. I was sure I had. Then I smelt smoke. Cigarette smoke. Oh God, had Leo been in my house? I froze and listened hard. Nothing, but the smoke smell was strong. Perhaps he'd gone when he realised I wasn't there. But what if he was on the other side of the door? Instead of listening to my gut, which was telling me to run and call the police, something else took hold. How bloody dare he? I slammed open the kitchen door and there he was, calmly sitting at the table, blowing smoke straight at me.

I could only focus on the broken lock on my back door. 'You broke into my house! What the hell do you think you're doing?' I pulled the door back and examined the lock. The wood was ruined. I swung back to face him, absolutely boiling. 'How dare you break into my house? I thought I'd made my feelings perfectly clear on the phone.' I held the door open wider. 'Get out. Go back the way you came, sneaking in through the back door. You lied to me and hurt Nikos.' He didn't move. 'Go on, go.' When he still didn't move I looked down at the floor. I shouldn't have said what I said next, but I did, it was like bile that had to be spat out. 'You're disgusting. I don't want to see you anymore.'

Leo leaned forward on the kitchen chair, hands on his knees. I wished I'd been looking more closely at his face. I had no idea how angry he was. He leapt up and grabbed me round my throat, squeezing my neck until I couldn't breathe. I felt my body go slack as lack of oxygen hit my brain. I'd die if he didn't stop. I kicked back against his shin as hard as I could.

Something must have got through his rage, because he loosened his grip until I was panting to get my breath. He shoved me back against the cupboard and was so close in my face I could smell his foul breath.

'You don't get to speak to me like that,' he hissed. 'Who are you anyway?'

He squeezed my neck again and I felt the panic rise.

'A nobody kid of a nobody father. You're nothing.'

I tried to speak but he wouldn't release the hand under my chin even a millimetre. I held onto his arm with both hands and tried to drag it off but I couldn't shift his grip. I tried desperately not to cry but the tears slid out towards the edges of my eyes anyway. I had to think, not collapse.

'No, sweet cousin. You and I are going to have a nice sit down at the table and talk about our uncle and what we do next.'

Abruptly, he pulled away and shoved me toward the table. I sank down onto a chair, trying to think a bit more clearly now that I could breathe again. I put my head onto my folded arms and breathed deeply. It would be a while until Alex came, so there was no point expecting rescue. My phone was in my bag in the living room. I couldn't fight Leo, he was strong and there was a cruelty to him I had never suspected. He slid in opposite me, hands on the table, loose and ready to react if I tried to run. My options were few.

I raised my head and indicated the tap and he let me get up and pour a glass of water which I drank standing up. I took in some more deep breaths and steadied my racing heart. I leaned back against the sink, it gave me the tiny advantage that I was standing and he was sitting. 'Leo, can we just talk?' I said. Croaked really. 'You've hurt me, and you didn't have to do that. I thought you were going to see your top lawyer to take your claim through the courts?' I coughed and drank more water. My voice was an octave deeper. I hoped it wasn't permanent.

'I didn't mean to hurt you,' he said, hands working on each other. 'You just don't get to talk to me like... like I'm some sort of idiot.'

'I'm sorry, I was angry because you broke my door down.' I was trying to be calm, but I was so annoyed I blurted out, 'Why didn't you wait on the bench until I came home? Then we could have talked over a glass of wine, rather than this mess. You almost killed me.'

Leo banged both fists hard on the table, signalling frustration like a child would. 'Stop talking. Sign the business over to me, Anna. Just do it and all this will go away and you can go back to your small, pathetic life. You couldn't run that business anyway, could you? Admit it. It's mine, my father promised me.'

I was scared again, but I daren't agree with him, even to get him out of my house. If I gave him any sign that I might give the business to him, he'd never leave me alone. 'It's all new to me,' I said slowly, 'but I'm going to learn about it, and in a few years, maybe I will be able to...' Wrong thing to say. His face turned purple. I had to get out. He really would kill me.

He was up on his feet and blocking me before I could move. 'No, that's not good enough. Say I can have it now and this will go away. If not...' He shook me hard, rattling my teeth against each other. 'Don't you get it? You can't say no.'

He made a grab for my throat again but I ducked down and he caught my hair in both hands. I screamed and pulled away, feeling chunks of hair coming away in his fists. I screamed again, beating him off with my hands.

'No, no!' I yelled, squirming in his grasp.

There was a sudden banging at the front door, and Alex's voice shouting, 'Anna? Are you okay?'

I screamed louder and twisted in Leo's grip so I faced the back door. If only I could...

Leo let go of my hair and grabbed me round the waist as I made a dash for the back door. I wriggled and fought and scratched at his hands but he held on, snarling.

I'd managed to drag us both outside when he tripped my back foot and sent me sprawling onto the path. The last thing I remember was him delivering a kick to the back of my head and another kick to my side.

I must have blacked out for a few minutes, because when I opened my eyes, Alex was holding me. I was still on the path, lying on my side.

Alex rolled me over gently. 'Anna? Please open your eyes. Please.'

I managed to get one eye open, although all I needed was to go to sleep, and smiled at him. 'Hello,' I said, usefully.

'Thank God you're conscious. Can you move?'

Good question. Could I? I turned slowly, very slowly onto my front, then got onto all fours. I had the most appalling pain in the back of my head, and my ribs hurt. 'I think so,' I whispered and let him help me up and half carry me back into the house.

He settled me onto a chair in the kitchen, and closed the

back door, wedging it shut with another chair. I was dreading him turning the lights on, because if I looked the way I felt, he was in for a shock. 'Has he gone?' I muttered.

'Leo? I saw him running down the street as I came round to the back of the house. Yes, he has gone. Oh God, Anna, look at you.' Carefully, he examined the back of my head, on which a lump was growing.

'I hope he broke his foot,' I croaked.

He came back to the front and tilted my head to each side. 'And your neck will be bruised, too. The bastard, how dare he do this to you? He could have killed you, Anna.'

I rolled up my T-shirt and looked at my left ribs. 'Yes, I know. This was his parting shot.' It was turning blue already.

Alex knelt on the floor in front of me and held my hands. 'Why did he do this?'

I asked myself the question. 'Frustration? Nikos made me his heir, Leo wants me to sign over the business to him. At any cost. Especially to me, apparently. I'm an easier target than Nikos. Simple as that, I think. He thought he could bully me into signing it over. I don't think he was actually trying to kill me.' I touched my neck carefully. The bruises told a different story.

'That wasn't bullying. It was attempted murder. Right, I'm calling the police. There is no way he can get away with this. I'll get a doctor, too. You may have concussion,' he said.

'No, I think I'll be...' I dropped my head on my arms on the table and was asleep in seconds, only for Alex to wake me up. Swine.

'No, you must stay awake until the doctor gets here.'

Alex busied himself making a pot of mountain tea while we waited, but I could tell, because he kept waking me up with such concern in his eyes, that he was angry. And that was fair enough, because I was angry too. Or I would be once I'd had a good sleep.

The local police officer ambled in and took a statement a short while later. He must have been expecting a burglary or something minor. As soon as I mentioned the Kokorakis link, he smartened up, and was much more alert when I told him what had happened. He took pictures of my injuries, and put a message out on his radio for Leo to be arrested on sight. I knew Leo's car make, but not the registration number, and gave the officer Leo's hotel address. I hoped they would find him quickly. I didn't feel safe with him out and about. What if he came back?

The doctor arrived a few minutes later. She agreed that I had mild concussion, bruised but not broken ribs, and a bruised larynx, all of which should heal with time. She gave me painkillers, and nodded with approval at the mug of mountain tea. 'She can stay at home, but you will be with her?' she asked Alex, who nodded, thank goodness.

Alex came back into the kitchen after filling the police officer in on the rest of the story while I was being treated by the doctor. Alex told the officer to contact Nikos, because he too might be in danger, although he could have saved his breath; that was the first thing the officer would do, I expected. Once he had assured the doctor and the police officer that I would be well looked after, we were left alone.

'Bath and bed for you, my darling,' he said, and walked me through to the bottom of the stairs, and, hands on my butt, guided me gently up the stairs so I didn't fall backwards. I would have laughed if I'd had the energy.

I perched on the edge of the bed while Alex ran a shallow bath, and he stayed with me so I didn't fall asleep while I was in it. He couldn't hide the distress on his face when he saw the extent of the bruising. 'Don't worry,' I said, 'it will heal. I'm just relieved that you came when you did. I'm okay.' I hoped.

I remembered little else of that night.

24

The sunlight warmed my face and played across my eyes. I had been dreaming, something about a doll I'd had when I was a child, when I heard soft chat and realised I wasn't alone. It was a struggle to open my eyes. First there was pain, and fear, and then the whole horrible night flooded back in and I woke up properly.

On one side of the bed sat Delphine, and on the other was Alex. I hadn't realised my breathing had become ragged until I took in a proper breath and let it out again. I was safe.

'How are you, you poor girl?' asked Delphine, eyes full of concern.

I dragged myself up onto the pillow and let Alex prop me up. I did an inventory. 'I'm not too bad,' I said, 'the head is pounding but I can talk. Even if I do have a sexy croak.' Alex passed me water and I drank. 'That's better. I must have slept really late. Is it afternoon already?'

He laughed. 'It is, late afternoon. Welcome back.'

'I did need to sleep, once you let me do so.' Then all conversation was halted by my need to empty a very full bladder. I insisted on getting out of bed on my own and going to the bathroom, and then wished for soundproofing, as the human bladder is a very stretchy thing. I'd slept for over sixteen hours.

Shakily, I stood and faced myself in the mirror. The bump on my head was showing through my hair at the back and pulsing quietly, and I had two very interesting bald patches at the temples. Both sides of my neck were bruised, with a clear thumb mark on one side and finger marks on the other. How on earth could I disguise that mess? Carefully, I lifted up my nightdress and looked at the bruising on my left side, which was coming up beautifully into a rainbow of pain. It was sore to the touch, but low on the ribs and my breathing felt fine. So that was that. Inventory done. I started a bath running and wobbled back into the bedroom.

'Have the police caught him?' I asked, falling back onto the bed. I felt weak, and not completely in the room. Part of me wanted to go back to the dream I'd been having, where I was a child and didn't need to know about men beating women up to get what they wanted.

'No,' said Alex, 'but they are convinced he isn't on the island anymore. They found the car, and he had already checked out of the hotel. They are looking at airports and ferries. They're doing a good job.'

'I'll bet they're not. Not for a foreigner. I'm last on their list.'

He pulled a cover over me, but I was hot and threw it back. 'No, don't,' I said, tetchily.

Delphine, who had observed my mood, asked Alex to fix me the soup she had brought. 'One of Eleni's best,' she said, and Alex went downstairs to do that. I realised I was starving.

'Right,' she said. 'I know you must be feeling strange and confused, but you are not to take it out on Alex, who has looked after you since this happened. Your anger should be directed at Leo, who has behaved abominably, and not at the people who love you.'

Tears came quickly. 'I'm sorry,' I mumbled. 'I'm not angry with Alex, or you.'

'I know.' She took my hand. 'Have soup, have a bath, and get up. You need to be on your feet to get better. Go and sit in your garden, get the sun on your face. Tomorrow I will get my hairdresser to come and sort out your hair and bring makeup for your poor neck. After all, you have to go home and see your parents, and I hope, bring them back with you. Don't you?'

I pushed myself up. 'Yes, of course. I should already have gone home. Dad's ill and I'm still here.' I was tearful again. 'Why did he have to hurt me, Delphine?'

She leaned over me and held me in her arms while I had a little weep. 'I checked up on Leo, now that we know his real name is Leontes Kokorakis. His wife is divorcing him for physical and emotional abuse. He hurt you because he could. It's how he treats women. If you are angry, be angry at him. He will get what he deserves.' She called him a name in Greek that had not entered my limited lexicon of swear words, but I thought I might remember it.

I wiped my eyes with my hands. 'Thank you, Delphine.'

'You're welcome.' She disappeared into the bathroom, adding bubbles I suspected, and some of the local bath salts to ease muscle pain. I'd bought them for post-gardening fatigue, little knowing I'd need them for this.

Alex came back with soup and bread on a tray. He placed it on my lap and stood back. I reached out to take his hand. 'I'm sorry, I didn't mean to snap at you.'

He grinned. 'I think you British have a saying, yes? To know somebody warts and all? If this is your worst wart, then all is good.' He kissed me on the top of my head.

I tried not to eat the soup *too* quickly, but it was Eleni's and so good. So was the bath, and getting into clean clothes, and sitting out in the garden as I had been told. I'd turned into a bloody invalid.

Delphine went home, promising to see me soon, and Alex sprawled out beside me on the bench, lifting his face to the sun.

I felt weepy again, which definitely wasn't me. Must be delayed shock, said my rational brain. The rest of me said it was because nobody had ever hurt me physically before. I'd never had these sorts of injuries, and it hurt everything. My sense of who I was and what my life was like, and it made me horrified on behalf of women who suffered like this all the time. I harboured a tiny worm of fear about Alex, too. Clearly I was the sort of woman who picked abusers. Will had bullied me relentlessly for years, and Leo thought it was fine to beat me. What if Alex was the same? What if I attracted abusers? What if I had brought all this on myself?

'Tell me what you're thinking,' said Alex, twisting slightly so he could look at me.

I shook my head. 'Nothing really, I was just drifting off,' I said, but I couldn't meet his eyes.

He laughed and picked up my hand, which was clenched so tightly I'd made nail marks in my palm. He unfurled my hand and kissed it. Then he read my mind.

'I will never hurt you, Anna. I have never hit or abused anybody in my whole life. I have always been the geeky, skinny kid in the corner. I love computers, I love boats and now I love you. I am a simple man. If you can give me your love, I will love you back and we can have a nice time together and see what the future brings. Simple. Okay?'

Would I ever stop crying? 'Yes. Yes that would be wonderful. That's what I want too. Thank you.'

I could feel his eyes still on me. 'You know, you should not be too hard on yourself,' he said. 'I don't know anyone who could have been through the last two days and not be upset. It was frightening and dangerous.' He squeezed my hand. 'What kind of a person would you be if you could just laugh it off, hey?'

'Braver, that's what I would be. But I guess I'm like you. I want a quiet, happy life.'

'Then let's try to do that.'

He leaned across and kissed me so tenderly on the lips I nearly went off weeping again. Time to focus and get some advice. 'I want to tell Nikos that I don't want to run his businesses, Alex. I'll sell it all once I inherit it anyway. I can't work out what to say though. How not to insult him, or sound ungrateful. But he needs to know, I can't just pretend I'm going to take the business over, can I?'

He folded his arms across his chest and looked up into the old fig tree. 'I wondered what you planned on doing with the fortune you will inherit. I can't see you running a building company, it's true.'

'So how do I say that to Nikos?'

He slid an arm around the back of my neck and drew me to him. 'You will know what to say when you speak to him. You have the ability to see people clearly, Anna. Trust in yourself to do the right thing.'

I welled up again. 'I don't though. Look how rubbish I was at seeing through Leo.'

This time, I was saved by Aunt Irini, who happened to be passing by the back gate at exactly the right time to catch us in the garden.

'Anna,' she said, dashing up the path and plonking a kiss on my cheek. 'Are you all right? This nice young man has been telling me all that happened. He is taking good care of you? I have brought you honey cakes. Here,' she said and pulled a small paper bag out of her large one, dropping it into my lap. 'And, if it is all right, I have made lamb stew and have too much for myself. Could I bring you some for your meal? It would please me to do this for you. Oh God above,' she said, noticing my bruises, 'what did that monster do to you? I was having dinner with my son last night and knew nothing. If I had been here...' She spat on the ground and uttered a curse that made no sense in translation but had something to do with goats and blood.

She made me laugh. 'Aunt Irini, it's good to see you. I have no doubt that you would have seen him off, but don't worry, the police are out looking for him. Would you like some tea?'

Luckily, she looked at the state I was in, and took herself off home.

We were still sitting quietly in the last of the afternoon sunshine before the sun disappeared behind the mountain when she returned with an enormous casserole dish from which came a wonderful smell of roast lamb and herbs. 'It will be fine sitting on the counter until you need it, then in the oven for about forty minutes and it will be good.' She took it into the kitchen and placed it on top of the stove.

She was gone for at least ten minutes and finally I craned my neck to see what she was doing in there. 'Are you okay, Aunt Irini?' I asked.

'Come and see,' she said.

I struggled to my feet and followed her back inside. In my living room she had placed several pieces of her own painted pottery, and three family photographs. One was the photograph she had shared with me already, but the other two were different. An old, old picture of a young couple looking serious on their wedding day. 'Nyssa and Andreas?' I asked and she smiled. And another old one which was full of people at a celebration. In it, after careful looking, I found my parents as teenagers, holding hands. 'Whose birthday was it?' I asked.

'It was your mother's sixteenth birthday, and all the family gathered. It was just before your father...' She looked at my tired eyes and shrugged. 'I will tell you who everybody is another time. Now, rest.'

'Thank you. Thank you for the photos and for the beautiful ceramics.'

'Pah, somebody has to have them when I'm gone, and my daughter isn't interested if it doesn't come from IKEA, and Stavros is a priest, so what can he own? I wanted to give you back your family history.' She bustled off through the back door.

'She's a remarkable woman,' said Alex, locking the back door and placing a shiny new key on the table.

I hadn't even noticed the door had been fixed. 'When did you have that done?'

'I did it myself. Irini visited the ironmonger shop for me this morning and Delphine arrived and looked after you while I collected my tools and some spare wood. I did it while you were asleep. Though how you slept through banging and an electric screwdriver, I don't know.' He grinned. 'Stay where you are, I'll light the lamps and we can have a fire and later we can eat and watch a film. Will that suit you, madam?'

It did.

'I'm glad. Then as soon as we sort out your family, and the Leo problem, maybe we can spend more time together without you being in danger of death?' He whistled as he went off to clean out the grate.

They are rare, Alex's type of man. He had an optimism that was hard to quench, and I didn't want to be the one who quenched it. He actually liked me the way I was. Rare, as I said.

The sun had disappeared so I followed him inside, glad to be able to lock the door against intruders. I had never felt unsafe until now, but until Leo was behind bars, I didn't think I could relax. Turned out I was right not to, he hadn't finished with me yet.

25

Early next morning, after a restless night's sleep, we were both awake and snuggled down under the duvet.

'Do you need to get back to your boat today? Tell me the truth.'

'I do. I have a job that must be finished before I can get her into the water. Will you be okay on your own if I go and do it?'

'Of course, I've got the hairdresser coming, don't forget, and Irini is next door, and Delphine up the road. I'm not going to be lonely.'

'Great, I'll not be too long, but you keep your phone on all the time, okay?' He dashed into the shower and whistled a tune through his teeth.

Where on earth did he get the energy to whistle? I still felt like I had been hit by a bus. I had far deeper bruises than those on my body, and I needed more sleep. Much more sleep. I curled up again, and had almost drifted off, when:

'I am done,' said Alex, appearing at the foot of the bed fully dressed.

I clambered out of bed and wrapped my arms around him, burying my head in the middle of his chest. I was able to breathe more easily when I was holding him. I sighed and melted in further, until Alex lifted up my chin so he could see my eyes. 'Will you be all right? I can cancel if you need me to stay. Just say.'

'I'm okay. I need to ring home and book my flights. Trying to right a family feud is going to be a challenge for all of us but I want to bring them back together, Alex. They have spent the best years of their lives apart on the whim of a cruel father, and they're getting old.'

'You're giving them back their family.'

'Well, I'm going to try. I haven't attempted to contact my uncle Stephanos though. For all that Leo told me, I think he is the one financing Leo to take over Nikos' empire. More lies, I expect. I'll talk about that with Nikos and Delphine later.' I took a step back from him and held both his hands. 'I've worked out what I want to say to Nikos, and if he agrees, then he will have put right the wrongs that he did to my friends, and we can go forward with a better plan than me taking over a business I don't want. Because I can always say no, can't I?'

Alex gave a thoughtful nod. 'You are going to blackmail him while you have the power?'

I grinned at him. 'Exactly!' It sounded easy when I said it to Alex, but inside I was worrying that I could split my family apart again before we even got to know each other. I had to pray that the tug of family and of blood would be stronger than Nikos' Cretan pride.

Alex kissed me and set my toes tingling, and I made him promise to return quickly even though I wasn't sure I was up to much exercise. Having him hold me while I slept was worth a huge amount. Sex we could catch up on later.

I was up and ready for the promised hairdresser when she arrived carrying a huge nylon bag. She set up in my kitchen and opened her bag out on the table. I'd never seen so much makeup and hair product outside a beauty department. Her Greek was fast and colloquial, and I found it hard to follow, but eventually she chopped several inches off my hair, layering over the bald bits so that a sort of extended fringe covered the gaps, and did the same layering at the back, although the bump was shrinking already. I liked it, it was a sort of shaggy bob. It suited my hair and my face. She did my eyebrows too, and spent ages showing me how to camouflage the bruising on my neck. I felt quite spoilt and really enjoyed myself. It was good to lavish a bit of attention on simple things that made me feel better.

Once she had gone, I brought up my saved flight information and booked onto a flight leaving Chania the following day. I didn't want to be here any longer with Leo on the loose, and I was worried about Dad.

Mum and I needed a chat, too.

I played with the phone for a while, working out what I wanted to say. In the end, I told Mum that I knew the full story of Dad's past, and wanted to come home and talk to her and Dad about it. I didn't want to give any more details over the phone.

She was frightened, angry and upset, all at the same time. A feat my mother could achieve without breaking a sweat. 'Are you trying to kill me? How can I look your father in the eye again? He will think I have betrayed him. You have betrayed him!'

'Mum, it will be all right, I promise. It's time to bring this to an end, before it's too late to put it right.'

'It's buried too deep. Your father cannot forgive his brother. You don't understand.' Her voice rose from anxious to shrill.

'I understand fine. Listen,' I said to incoherent muttering at the end of the line, 'I've met Delphine, Nikos' wife and I'm helping her with a design project. I've also met Nikos and been to their house. They're our family, Mum.'

She choked. 'What? How? How did you even meet him? What have you been doing over there? How? Oh, God in heaven, this has all happened since you left Will. It's a nightmare. I want my nice daughter back, not this...'

'This what?' My hackles rose. She always did this to me.

'No, nothing, I meant nothing. It is a shock, that's all.'

I took a deep breath and tried for a reasonable tone. 'Look, let's not talk on the phone, it's always difficult, and there is so much I need to tell you. I'll see you at about one in the morning on Thursday. You don't need to wait up, I've got my key.' Somewhere. 'And, Mum? Give my love to Dad. I am looking forward to seeing you, you do know that, don't you?'

She was sniffling. 'Of course, and we love you very much. We will see you soon, darling. Bye.' I heard her sob as she put the phone down.

Aarggh. I felt upset too.

While I was in the getting-things-done mood, I rang Delphine and asked if I could come up and talk to them before flying home to Manchester. She was delighted that I was feeling better, and asked me to come at twelve, when Nikos would be home. That left me a couple of hours to marshal my arguments, and then I would put my plan to Nikos and see what he said. No pressure.

I walked to the house slowly. The sun on my face was easing my worries, and the paracetamol was easing my soreness.

Delphine greeted me warmly. 'You look fantastic,' she said as she let me into the study. 'Your hair really suits you and I can hardly see the bruises. Did you enjoy it this morning?'

'I did. Thank you so much, Delphine. I feel much better too after a couple of nights' sleep.'

We sat opposite each other on the sofas, as we had done just a few days before, only this time it felt very different. This time I knew what I needed to ask, and I had my uncle at a disadvantage. He needed me more than I needed him. 'Thank you for agreeing to see me, Uncle, I know you're busy.'

'Not too busy for you, Anna. What do you need?' asked Nikos, pouring coffee from a pot.

I had to pitch it right. 'Well, it has been forty years since you have seen or spoken to my father, your own brother. I knew nothing of my history, of you, of Delphine, of your business, until a few short weeks ago. The revelations came thick and fast when I finally started to get people to talk to me, and I discovered my father did have a family after all.' I took a sip of coffee. It was good and strong. I tried to be delicate, but it felt urgent. 'Isn't it time, Uncle, that you broke this feud, moved on and welcomed your family back home? Surely the grip of your father has lessened over the years?'

Nikos sighed and took a gulp of coffee. 'Straight to the point, I see. Anna, I know what you are saying is true. It has weighed on my mind for years. But...'

'But it was too hard to even try?'

'Not that, but I thought they would both be settled, with families and businesses. What good would it do to bring it all back up again? The pain and the shock of that time. It was too much to bear. I didn't want to bring it all back again.'

Delphine interrupted: 'But when we found out that you had come to the island, and were living in Nyssa's old house, that was when we realised that we did have a family, after all.' She squeezed Nikos' hand. 'And it was a wonderful thing, was it not, Niko?'

'Was it, Uncle Niko? Wonderful?' I watched as his eyes looked at the ceiling for help.

'Not at first, no. I was frightened that you had come to disrupt everything. That you would bring trouble to my home.'

Oh God. 'And I did bring trouble, but I didn't mean to. I'm so sorry about Leo.'

'He was the one I should have been frightened of, not you, it is true. But he is also my nephew, just as you are my niece, and now I have signed over everything to you, and he is on the run from the police. You see, you have brought trouble, even if you didn't mean to.'

He was right about that. 'Yes, I want to put that right. That is why I'm here. I'm going back to England tomorrow to see my parents. My father is ill, and I need to see him.'

'Ill? What is the matter with him?' asked Delphine.

'I'm not sure yet, but if he can travel, my aim is to bring them both back to Crete, at least for a holiday, before it's too late.'

Nikos' eyes filled up. 'You would do this?'

'I want to. It's time.'

He smiled. 'I can see you have your grandmother's spirit.'

'That's not all I want to do. I'm very unsure about Stephanos. From what Leo let slip the other night, he is probably the driving force behind Leo's attack on you. But he does deserve the chance to explain himself at least. So, I'd like to contact him once I'm back from England.'

'This may...' he added a phrase in English, '... this may "open a can of worms" as you would say.'

'I know. I won't do anything without your full knowledge. I want to make this old wound better, not inflame it. Leo initially told me his father had refused to allow him to come to Crete, and then cut him off because he came anyway. But then he said the other night, halfway through trying to strangle me, that his father had promised him your business. Lies, lies and yet more lies, I think.'

'Excuse me interrupting again,' said Delphine, 'but this is a huge task.' She laughed gently. 'You are dealing with enormous Cretan egos, Anna. It will be hard for Nikos to say he is sorry, and harder still for the brothers to accept his apology.'

'I know that, but what if Dad is seriously ill? What if he dies without ever setting foot in his homeland again? How can that be better than at least trying?'

Nikos inclined his head again. 'If you wish to do this, I would be forever in your debt.' He used a starched handkerchief to dab at his eyes.

'I really do want to do it. Thank you.' I drank more coffee, and sorted my thoughts. 'There is one more thing I want to ask. It's to do with what happened in Paleochora.' I rushed on before he could interrupt. 'Delphine and I have been helping Mr and Mrs Andreanakis with their new home, but Constantinos Papadikis still has nothing.'

Delphine sighed. 'I am looking for a position for him in one of the restaurants here, perhaps.'

'I may have a better idea, if you will hear me out. Will you set him up to run a not-for-profit café again? Like he did before? One where all the profits go into creating new chefs and waiting staff? One that will offer training for unemployed people?' I gave Nikos a moment to let this sink in. 'Think of it as a chance for you to give back to your people.'

He turned to look at Delphine, and I could almost see the cogs shifting as he worked out the best angle for him.

I added, 'You could set up the charity in your name. That would be a legacy worth leaving.'

Delphine laughed. 'She is quite brilliant, Niko. Of course you should set up a charity to help the unemployed. It will solve the problem of Constantinos. I will run the charity for you, and then we will pass it on to Anna when we are too old to do it anymore.' Her eyes shone. 'It is the right thing to do. You said you would help him. This way we all win. Say yes, Niko, say yes.'

He was silent for a few moments, and I held my breath. This was almost as important to me as getting the brothers back together. In many ways more important, because it would start Nikos on the road to doing good with his money, not just making ever more profit.

Finally, he sighed. 'I agree. It will be a fitting tribute to me, and good for the town. Delphie, will you get it started? I would like to meet the young man. He has made a good impression on you, Anna.'

'He has. He is one of the most passionate and compassionate young people I have ever met. He is a good man who will work hard for the town.'

Nikos looked at me with his hooded black eyes and gave a wry smile. 'I think I will be apologising to a lot of people now that you are here to change my life.'

'And mine,' said Delphine, smiling widely. 'At last I can do something useful. I am excited.'

Nikos shuffled forward on the sofa, ready to get up. 'If that is all, I have a meeting with the Chania police. I expect them to tell me what they have been doing to arrest my nephew.' He patted me on the arm. 'It is good to have you in the family, Anna. I can see that we will have many interesting debates in the future. Let me know what happens with your father. I am sorry that he is ill.'

He walked to the window and indicated the old house down the drive. 'I have lived in this big house for many years. I built it so that I didn't have to live in the house where I was born any longer. After my mother left us, I couldn't go back inside, although your grandfather lived there until he died. Perhaps, one day, it may be opened up once more, and your family might live there?' He crossed to the door, shouted for his driver and waved goodbye.

Once he had gone, Delphine and I let out sighs of relief.

'I am amazed that you got him to agree to all that,' she said. 'You really have brought magic with you.'

'I don't know about that,' I said. 'But I knew that this would be his most vulnerable moment, so I thought I'd exploit it as much as I could.'

She just gaped at me, and in seconds we were both giggling. 'Brave girl,' she said. 'I usually just shout at him until he gives in.'

I felt a bit shaky to be honest, and a bit giddy, but I was beginning to understand that Nikos acted mainly out of fear, not cruelty. 'He thinks that the only way to live is to be tougher, meaner and harder than everybody else, Delphine. I'm hoping that he will come to understand that there are better ways to live.' I had held onto the final demand, saving it for another day, but I thought it would be useful to give Delphine a clue. 'This may sound ridiculous, but I want Nikos to give up the whole business in the future, and I'd like your support.'

Her smiled dropped. 'How would we live?'

I almost leapt off the chair. 'Sell it! Sell the whole lot as going concerns to local business people. It will bring in millions, and Nikos won't have to work all the time and you'll have some time together. And Leo won't be able to get his hands on any of it!'

Her face closed up. 'Give up everything? It would be like dying to him. Doing a good deed that will make him look good is one thing, becoming a retired old man? I don't think that would ever work. You don't know him like I do. Give up this crazy idea, Anna.'

'Look, I know I'm pushing hard, but I truly believe it will be better for us all. I can't cope with Leo coming after me again, and you know that's what will happen. He won't just give up!' I knew

I'd pushed her too far and too quickly, but at least she could see I was scared. Selling made so much more sense than giving a total amateur a huge business, and sorted out the inheritance problem in one go. It was logical. But I'd been impatient and upset her.

I tried again. 'So let's do one step at a time. First, we put right the wrongs of the past, then we talk about how to change the future. There is no rush. Can we at least agree on that?'

'I will help all that I can. I have become used to a...' – she waved a hand around – 'a certain level of comfort, but you are right, we could live comfortably on the proceeds of the sale of the businesses. Persuading Nikos to sell is a different matter. This is his life. His life, Anna. It will be a terrible disappointment to him. But, as you say, there is no rush to suggest this. He is only sixty-two.'

Delphine stood, so I did, too.

'Now,' she said, 'I am going to drive over the mountain to make sure that the decorators are starting work on Mrs Andreanakis' new house. I'll pick her up on the way so she can see what has been done. What do you have planned?' She walked me to the door.

'I'm going to pack, and then I have a few calls to make before I fly home.' I kissed her on the cheek. 'Thanks for your support with Uncle Nikos. It is quite exciting, isn't it?'

'Yes. Well some of it is, but take care. I would not mention selling the business to him just yet. He would be so angry. I will work on him a little. Come round for a quiet dinner with that very attractive man when you get back. And possibly your parents will come too?'

'Maybe,' I said. I waved and walked back down the hill. Wouldn't that be a wonderful end to a mad month? My Mum and Dad back home and the family back together.

I kept my excitement inside until I got into the house, and then did a little jig around the kitchen. I hadn't achieved all that I wanted, but I'd made a good start. In the bathroom mirror, a different woman looked out. The sun, and the makeup to be fair, had begun to do its work on my pasty skin, and I'd changed my hair, and I was in love. I wasn't even worried about running into Will when I went home, either. Not much, anyway. I'd released my inner lioness, and she wasn't going back in her cage.

Bursting with excitement, and desperate to tell someone, I went round to Aunt Irini's and found her scrubbing the step. Did people still do that? They did in Crete.

'Anna, how wonderful to see you. Are you well?' Irini struggled to her feet and wrung out the cloth in a bucket of water. 'Have you had lunch? I have newly made cheese pies, and Stavros is also...' She looked down the street. 'Here he is now! Son, we have another guest for lunch.'

Stavros gave me a kiss on each cheek, and Irini led me inside, and I was suddenly in the family. My Greek was more fluent after all the practice so they could relax a bit, and I didn't get lost so often mid-sentence. We had a perfect lunch of hot pies and spring greens that had come straight off the mountain that morning according to Irini, even though she had probably bought them from the market like everybody else. She made me smile.

Stavros said, 'There has been much happening, Anna. Are you able to tell us about it?'

'The excitement has reached you then?'

'Police, violent attacks, we have heard it all. Mother was so pleased that you are safe, and so am I.'

'Thank you. Yes, it seems I was a gullible fool, but it's going to be okay now. I hope.'

They both looked at me expectantly.

Once I started telling the story it all came tumbling out, to tears and laughter and expressions of incredulity from them both. We had to have a drink from Irini's best bottle of raki when I'd finally finished in order to celebrate my great victory.

'You have done so well, Anna,' she said. 'You have achieved justice for those who were wronged, and set your uncle on a better path.'

'I was frightened for most of the morning, to be honest. I'm not really cut out for bullying people.'

Stavros snorted through his vast beard. 'Nonsense, you are a Kokorakis to the core. Now that you know a little of your history, remind me to tell you about your grandmother during the war sometime.' He twinkled a grin. 'No, you come from a long line of brave women. Adventure is part of you. It is in your soul. It just needed to be freed.' He tilted his glass at me, drank it down in one, and allowed his mother to fill it back up.

I laughed and downed my own glass, coughing slightly as it caught the back of my throat. 'Tell me now, please,' I said, 'I'd love to know more about Nyssa.'

He laughed too. 'I will then tell you a little.' He folded his hands across his stomach, ready for telling a story. 'Nyssa lived in the mountains as a girl, and her family kept Messara horses, the only breed native to Crete. They are small, hardy creatures, perfect for the mountains and the weather.'

'She was wild as a girl, always going off on her horse,' added Irini.

'Anyway, when war came, many horses were sent secretly to Albania to save them from the Germans, who wanted them for carrying equipment, and also for their meat. Nyssa would not let hers go, she hid him near an old shepherd's hut far up the mountain, and that is how she became a courier for the resistance when she was only fourteen.' He raised both shaggy eyebrows at me.

'Wow, really? It must have been so dangerous, and she was just a girl.'

Irini spluttered raki into her glass. 'Dangerous? She would sneak all over the island on that horse, watching the Germans, taking information from one mountain camp to another in all weathers, facing enemies at every turn. She was essential to the resistance.' Irini drew herself up proudly. 'She was a heroine to us all.' She glanced at Stavros. 'Sorry, son, you tell it.'

He put a hand over hers, and smiled fondly. 'You are right, Mama, she was, and she was brilliant at what she did until she was caught one night by a German soldier and he shot her horse.' He looked grave.

'What happened? Was she captured?' I asked, desperate to know more.

Irini interrupted again: 'No! She killed him. Killed him with her little knife.' She made slashing gestures at the table. 'And he deserved to die for what his kind did to our country.' She topped up the glasses. 'Yiamas!'

I think Irini was a little worse for wear.

'So that is what your grandmother did in the war, Anna. You see, her brave spirit has carried on.'

Stav toasted me, I toasted him, and I stared often at the photograph of Nyssa on the kitchen wall, as she stood surrounded by family and friends. She was a tough, brave, totally uncompromising fighter. Oh, and she killed someone when she was a child. What a family. It certainly explained why she had the strength to walk away from my grandfather. 'I wish she had lived a little longer, I would have loved to have been able to talk to her as I can to you.'

'She did at least come to know you when you were a little girl,' said Irini, 'and she loved you from the start.'

'And you will tell me the rest of her story when I come back from the UK?'

'Of course. There is much to tell,' said Irini.

I laughed a lot that afternoon, and it did me so much good. I'd learnt so much about my family in a few short days. I'd achieved part of the mission I'd set myself. Now I was going to see it through by getting my family back here.

I waddled off home, definitely tiddly, and slept for two hours on the sofa. When I woke up I was cold and it was getting dark, so I scraped out the fire and lit a new one, and made mountain tea. The little grey cat was perched on my windowsill again. So I let her in to sit near the fire while I drank tea and felt calmer than I had for a while. Yes, Leo was still out there somewhere, but I had to get on with my life. It felt different having a family other than my parents, but it was a good feeling.

There was, however, no time to relax. I headed upstairs and sorted out the guest room, which had been acting as the store-room for Mrs Andreanakis' soft furnishings. I didn't have a proper loft, more a four-foot high space that I could crawl around in so I loaded it up with her stuff, and found the new bedding I'd bought. I cleaned the room of residual bathroom dust and vacuumed. Once I had the bed made up, I added hangers to the wardrobe and the downstairs table lamp was installed on a little table next to the bed; the room looked cosy and comfortable. I just hoped that there may be need for it by the weekend.

Finally, I packed a case of clothes suitable for Manchester at the end of April. Jumpers, jeans and a waterproof jacket, basically.

Then I waited in the living room for Alex to get home, and take me out to dinner. We had a lot to talk about.

26

I actually enjoyed the drive from Kissamos to the airport on Thursday, even though there were lorries everywhere and I missed the airport turn-off on my first attempt. I'd had to promise Alex to keep in touch, which wasn't hard, and Irini was more excited than I was and came out to wave me off. I double-checked that the car was locked and left it in the long-stay car park, having made it promise not to get stolen. Then I prepared for a very long day where I planned to sleep as much as possible.

The taxi finally dropped me outside the restaurant in Manchester at almost two the following morning. There was a light on in the front bedroom, and Mum arrived at the side door before I needed to find my key. She was wrapped in the fluffy dressing gown I'd bought her for Christmas and stood with her arms open to hug me as I got to the door. Behind her stood Dad, on the bottom step of the stairs, his normally luxuriant dark hair sticking out at odd angles. He was so grey-looking and so small, I could hardly recognise the vibrant, strong man I'd left behind only two months before.

'It's so good to see you, darling,' Mum said into my shoulder, and almost squeezed the breath out of me, but I couldn't take my eyes off my father, who looked awful. 'Come on, upstairs,' she said. 'Let's get you a drink and into bed. I've put you a hot water bottle in already to warm it up.'

I dragged my case up the narrow stairs and dropped it in my old bedroom. They'd redecorated! Sneaky pair. I checked myself out in the mirror, and fixed my silk scarf more firmly round my neck. The hair looked fine, considering.

We sat round the kitchen table while Mum made me cocoa, not that I'd need it to send me to sleep, I could have done that standing up. Over the steam I snatched glances at my dad, and watched her eyes sliding away from his. He was really ill, that was obvious, and they hadn't told me how ill. Now wasn't the time to discuss it, though, as we all needed to sleep. So I chatted to them about Grandmother's house, and how lovely it now was, and how I'd met Aunt Irini and the members of the expat society who had become friends.

After a scant wash and climbing into a toasty, soft bed, I sent a little prayer up to the god I didn't believe in that Dad was going to be okay.

My family don't rise early. Their working day begins after nine, and I woke to the sound of the shower through the thin wall. I lay there for a while, examining the tasteful décor, until with a sickening thump I recognised the hand of my ex-husband. I'd bet anything all of this had been his idea. Even the bed linen, in tasteful beige and khaki, was his style. The style he'd forced on me for years.

There was a knock on the door, and in came my mother with a mug of tea.

'Oh, you angel,' I said, shuffling up against the headboard.

'Drink this while your father is in the shower,' she said, whispering and glancing at the wall.

'What's the matter with him, Mum? He looks so ill.'

She sighed and took my hand. 'Prostate cancer, the doctor says.'

'Mum! Why didn't you tell me?' I was aghast. 'All the times we've spoken. How could you keep this from me? Oh God, how serious is it?' I wobbled the mug back onto the bedside table. Tears prickled in the corners of my eyes but I dashed them away. 'Tell me, please.'

'Stage Three.'

'But that means it's spread...'

'Oh, he has a good chance if the drugs and radiotherapy work. The success rate is high, I've heard.' She sighed. 'It was your father who wouldn't let me tell you, of course.'

'Of course, my dear father tells me nothing important, as usual.' I couldn't stop the bitterness and instantly felt guilty. This was hardly the time. 'Sorry, go on.'

'He was diagnosed just before you left, and had an operation the following week. We didn't want to ruin your adventure for you. You do understand?'

'Operation?' He'd had an operation, and no one told me. And then I remembered all the phone calls I'd not answered from Will. 'Oh. Did Will try to tell me?'

Mum wouldn't look at me. 'I turned to him. Of course I did,' she defended herself. 'He's been wonderful, Anna.' She wiped a tear away. 'It's been so dreadful, especially the chemotherapy which has hit your father so hard. William has taken us to the hospital on many occasions. Wonderful...' She trailed off.

I couldn't stop the tears then. I seemed to have done nothing but cry for weeks. What kind of a daughter was I that my own father didn't feel able to tell me he was seriously ill? And why didn't my mother open her bloody loyal mouth? And why hadn't I given Will a chance to tell me?

'Oh, Mum, I'm so sorry I wasn't here. I didn't answer Will's calls. I thought he would just try to get me to go back with him. I could easily have stayed at home for another couple of months. I've been so selfish, haven't I?'

Dad appeared at the door, dressed and with his hair thinner but smartly combed. His face was still drawn, but he looked better. I leapt out of bed and wrapped my arms around him. 'Dad, I didn't know. I'm so sorry I wasn't here for you.'

He shrugged, his usual response to my emotional outbursts, and patted me on the back. 'Anna, you are here now, and I would rather see you when I am up and about, than on the days when I am ill. I will have more than two weeks now, to feel better, until the next one. Come, have breakfast with me before I go to work.'

'You're still working in the restaurant, now? Why?'

He patted my arm again. 'Not working, just supervising. My new chef has taken on the cooking.' He took the stairs slowly.

New chef? I turned back to look at Mum, still sitting on the bed. 'Yes, all is changed here.' She waved a hand in such a gesture of futility I panicked. 'What treatment is he on at the moment?'

'He's on the chemo, then the radiotherapy to follow. Then, who knows? We look forward, not backwards. Come on, breakfast.' She struggled to her feet and gave me another shock. My mother was the most active, lively, young fifty-six-year-old I knew. Now, she looked ten years older, worn down by all her worries about Dad, and of course, me.

I had a quick shower, checked out my bruises, which were coming along nicely, and pulled on jeans, a long-sleeved T-shirt and a cotton polo-neck jumper. Manchester in April was cold and wet, so it was easy to hide the bruises. I didn't want Mum to see any evidence of exactly what my 'adventures' had entailed.

Downstairs, in the old kitchen where so much food had been prepared for so many people, many of whom had become family friends over the years, I was amazed. There was a definite sprucing up in evidence, and a lot more stainless steel. In the corner, where our little breakfast table had always been, there was a larger table with six chairs. Fussing around placing eggs and toast on the table was a tall, fair-haired, skinny man in a chef's whites and hat. He was not in any way Greek.

'Anna,' said Dad, 'meet Michael, our new chef.'

Michael hurried over and stuck out his hand. 'Pleased to meet you, Anna,' he said in the soft tones of North Lancashire.

'Pleased to meet you too,' I said. 'You're not Greek then, Michael?' He looked about twenty-five. Only just out of acne, really.

'No, Preston for my sins, but I was sous chef at Manouso's for five years, so I've done my training, and your dad keeps me on my toes.'

He skipped off and brought a pot of coffee over. 'Please, take a seat and enjoy your brekkie, I'm just going to prep some veg. Give me a shout if you need anything.' Michael stood over at the new steel prep table and got chopping.

If it wasn't for the fact that I was, as usual, totally starving, I'd have run into a small corner and sobbed. Never had I felt so ripped away from all that I had taken for granted. My strong parents were small and diminished, my dad wasn't cooking in his beloved restaurant. He might die. Dad might die. There was a child in charge, and my mum and dad were just doing what he said. How could this have happened in a few weeks?

'Oi, dreamer,' said Mum, 'where have you gone off to? Come on, eat. You need food after that long journey.'

I ate eggs and toast and fruit and drank coffee, all on automatic pilot. While I'd been faffing about decorating and playing Mother Teresa, the two most important people in my world were suffering. Despite what they say, the Catholics don't have the monopoly on guilt, it's built into the Cretan psyche, too, and it was fermenting, churning. The world of Leo and the Kokorakises seemed very far away. How could I force my poorly dad to face up to his past? I sipped coffee and spread jam on a bit of toast. On the other hand, if I didn't ask him now, I might never get the chance to put it all right. I chewed but couldn't taste anything.

Dad stood up, carefully. 'Let's go and check out the front, Anna. Tell me what you think of the changes.'

I followed him into the restaurant. It looked great, too. Michael had persuaded the parents to ditch the tired old Greek posters, and change the checked tablecloths and cutlery. It looked good, and much more modern. 'I like it. It will attract younger customers, I'm sure.'

He brushed imaginary crumbs from a table and sniffed. 'It's not my style, but yes, Michael has made such a difference, and allowed us to keep going through all this. But now...'

'Now?'

'Well, it is time we sold the restaurant so me and your mother have a little time for ourselves. We are just staying on until Michael has found his feet, and then we will sign the papers.'

'Oh, Dad.' Sell the restaurant? Sell my home? 'I can't imagine you not being here.' And I couldn't. It was the only family home I remembered; we'd lived there since I was a baby. 'But perhaps it's for the best.' Perhaps it was meant to be.

'How are you doing?'

'Oh, you know. It's hell for a while, then it's better for a while. But it goes on forever, it seems.'

'How can I help?'

'Just having you here is wonderful.' He took my hand. 'I have never told you how proud I am of you, Anna, for all the things you have achieved. When you think that I came here as a boy from Crete, with little hope... well, we haven't done too badly, have we?'

I gave him a hug. 'No, Dad, we've done pretty well. You've done pretty well.'

Mum came through at that moment and we had a family hug. It must have been almost thirty years since our little family had held each other like that. And even longer since we had all cried together.

I went back up to my room and unpacked a few things, then put on my flat boots, coat and rearranged my scarf. It was time to have a walk through my old neighbourhood, clear my head, and decide how best to approach my father. Mum had been sneaking worried glances at me all morning, hoping I wouldn't just blurt it out. I wouldn't do that. There had to be a way to do it without hurting him.

Promising not to be gone long, I set out along Wilmslow Road then turned off and walked along Mauldeth Road to the little park, where I sat for a while and watched small children playing and their mums chatting or scrolling down their phones. I used to come here a lot for a bit of peace when things got too much at home. My small group of girlfriends had used the park as our private hanging out space. We used to get really annoyed when local boys tried to share it. Happy days. I wondered briefly what they were all doing now.

Life felt very normal back in Manchester. It had been so easy when I'd lived here. I knew the rules, knew how to behave, knew that mad people would not be coming after me, knew that the only man who mattered was my husband, knew that sadness walked with me. Thank God I'd run away. I let out a shaky laugh. Yes, these last few weeks had been terrifying, but I felt alive, properly myself. I had been brave. I could do things all by myself, and I was not intimidated by thugs.

I pulled myself up off the bench and set off to walk down Burton Road, past the red-brick terraces and the blossom trees in full bloom. Spring had come to Manchester. I did a circuit and popped into the bank for some cash, and then I switched my phone on and waited for a British network to take over from my Greek one. Unsurprisingly, there was a missed call from Will, so I plucked up courage and rang him. Better out here on the street than at home, although I did pop down a side street to get away from the ever-present noise of road traffic. I'd become used to the relative quiet of my little street in Kissamos.

'Hi, Will, it's me.'

'At last, you deign to call me.'

Frosty at best. 'Look, I'm so sorry I didn't respond to your calls. I foolishly expected my parents to tell me what was happening back here. Daft, eh?'

'They didn't want to worry you. I thought it would come better from me.'

'Did you?' I couldn't hold onto my temper any longer. 'So, as usual, you decide what's best for me, and for them? You're not part of my family anymore. Nothing's changed for you, has it, Will?'

'Darling, I have no idea what you're talking about. You must be tired after your long trip. Let me take you to lunch so we can have a proper chat. I'll pick you up at, say, one o'clock? We could go to The Lime Tree down the road, that's always good value and I know you love their desserts...'

It sounds pathetic, but tears of frustration prickled at the corners of my eyes. He always did this. Just took over my life. I may well even have stamped my foot, although I had learnt finally, through sheer bad experience, the best way to manage Will Hunter. 'Stop it, Will! We are *divorced*. We're not planning a date. I have no intention of ever seeing you again. Go and find some other innocent girl to manipulate. You leave my parents alone, and you leave me alone, otherwise I'll get my lawyer back onto you again. Got it?' I didn't wait for a reply. I blocked his number.

Having calmed down from that little episode, I rang Alex, who was hard at work on the underbelly of his boat, which he promised was almost ready to go back in the water. At which point he said we could go out for a little sail, just the two of us. I could hear the heat in his voice over the crackly line. I couldn't wait to get back to Crete. At the end of the call, he said, 'Bye, love you.' And my heart gave a wallop. He still loved me.

Dad was upstairs printing out the day's specials menus in the little office, and Mum was making coffee when I got back. Mum and I went and sat in the living room, clasping hot mugs.

'Are you going to talk to him?' she whispered.

'Yes, I need to. Have you said anything?'

She shook her head and gave a shrug at the same time. I understood. It was a tough one to broach, especially with him.

Dad walked into the room and sat in his usual chair. He drank down some coffee but pulled a face. 'I can't taste anything with this stupid chemo,' he grumbled. 'Everything tastes disgusting.'

I laughed, but gently. 'It must be awful, Dad. What you need is a bit of sunshine, and some warmth on those bones.'

He jerked away from the china mug, put it down carefully on the table and glared at Mum. 'You, what have you said?'

'She hasn't said anything, for goodness' sake. Look, Dad, I'm living in your mother's house, in your home town, on Crete, your island, and you haven't asked a single question. You must want to know about what I've been doing?'

'So, tell me then. What have you been doing?' He folded his arms across his chest.

'Dad, don't get angry, but I've met Uncle Nikos and talked to him. I've met Mum's relatives and talked to them. I know about what happened.'

He looked shocked for a moment, but then he grunted. 'What was the point of finding out? It upsets your mother and means nothing to me.'

'Rubbish, it means so much to you that you couldn't even tell me about your own family. I'm not a kid anymore, Dad; I know what this long silence has all been about. And it's time it was over. Please come back with me and stay for a while. It's time.' I reached across and took his hand, but he pulled it back and scrubbed hard at his face.

'You don't understand. There is a feud that can never be...'

'*Was*, there *was* a feud. Forty years ago you were banished. Not yesterday. Your father died fifteen years ago, your poor mother two years ago, and you never got to see them before they died. Why? Because of a cruel, stupid decision taken by your father when you were just a boy. He's gone now, Dad. Let's put it right.'

He jerked again. 'But what of Nikos? He has never tried to make amends. Never contacted us, even when your mother took you there. He took it all from me.' The bitterness, almost anguish, was too much for him to bear, but I had to push on.

'Oh, Dad, I've talked to Nikos, and he is so sorry for what happened. He wants to see you too. Really. He wants to apologise. He would love you to come home. Can't you just move on, and give him a chance to put things right? He owes it to you, and he wants to do this.'

Dad stared at the shelf of Cretan pottery over the sideboard. I realised with a pang that this was Aunt Irini's pottery, and that Mum and I had brought it back from our trips many years before.

Mum said, 'Think, Theo. It broke your mother's heart when Andreas made that terrible decision. She never spoke to him again.'

'And,' I added, grateful for her point, 'Nikos has built another house for himself. He couldn't go back into the old family home, after it happened. He isn't proud of what he did. He feels your loss terribly,' I said. 'And, Dad, you're not getting any younger, and Nikos needs to make amends. Please let him apologise.'

Dad put down his coffee, leaned forward and rested his hands on his knees. 'I cannot simply "move on", Anna, as you say. And what about Stephanos, banished to America at sixteen years of age?' He let out a sigh, almost a sob. 'We lost everything, Anna. You don't understand how hard it was. And Nikos, he could have said no to our father, but he didn't.' He wiped his eyes on the cuff of his shirt. 'You have no idea what it has been like, not to see my homeland for all these years. Andreas ripped out our hearts.' He banged on the table with a closed fist and got to his feet.

Mum got up too, and put her arms around him. She spoke softly in Greek, so quietly I could hardly make out a word, but Dad reluctantly sat down again.

'Tell me about him, about Nikos,' he said.

So I did. I told him about Delphine and the oil and wine business and the huge building business, Nikos' new charity, and the big house.

'All so good for him, I get it,' Dad grumbled. 'I've heard enough now.'

'But you haven't, Dad, you haven't heard it all.' Now or never. 'Nikos has made me heir to his business empire.' I watched his face, waiting for the explosion.

'Mother of God,' he said, hitting one fist into his other palm. 'Then there is justice. We will get it all. Justice that he has no children to love and take on his name. I am glad, glad that his name will die out when he dies, and God willing it will be soon.'

'Theo!' shouted Mum. 'He's your brother. Don't wish him dead, not when death hovers over this family already!'

You see, you can take the girl out of a village in Crete and bring her to a sophisticated country like the UK and she can run a successful modern business, but deep down, she still has the superstitions of an old Greek woman. 'Mother! What an awful thing to say! Death isn't hovering anywhere, thank you very much. Dad will get better. It's the chemo making him feel awful.'

They stood next to each other, staring down at me. I don't usually shout at them. 'For God's sake, sit down, the pair of you. There's more.'

When they were back in their seats and we had drunk some of the coffee and calmed down a bit, I explained about Leo and his takeover bid. Obviously I said nothing about him hurting me.

'So, I will contact Stephanos, too, but for all I know, he put Leo up to it. But I want him to come back to the island, too. I think you all need to sort this out between you before it's too late. Stephanos has three sons, and grandchildren, Dad.'

Mum took a deep breath. 'Theo, I have stayed away from my family for all these years because of you, because I love you and I am your wife, but now I am begging you. Please let us go home. Now is the time. We are selling up the restaurant. What is there to keep us here in the cold and the wet?'

'Just come for a holiday,' I begged. 'Come back with me next week.'

He reared again. 'Pah, don't be stupid. I am in the middle of chemo. How can I fly away? How could I get insurance to cover me?'

He'd got me there. But only for a moment. 'You know what? Stuff it. Fly without insurance. If you come for two weeks, you'll be back in plenty of time for your next injection. Or, better still, I'll get Delphine to arrange for you to have the chemo at the hospital in Chania. Then you can stay longer.'

'You could do that?' asked Mum, eyes wide.

'She could. The Kokorakises are one of the most powerful families on the island, Mum. I'm sure she can arrange to transfer treatment to Crete for a while.' She could certainly afford to do it privately, I thought. She could probably afford a private jet, too, but we wouldn't need that, I hoped.

Dad looked between us, at his wife's shining face, and my earnest one, and gave the tiniest shrug. 'Let me alone, both of you, I need to rest. I'll speak with you at dinner.' He struggled back up and shuffled off to the bedroom, where he closed the door and I heard the sound of a bedspring creak as he climbed in.

'We have exhausted him,' said Mum.

'It's a lot for him to take in, but I could see it in his eyes, like I can see it in yours. He wants to go home.'

'He feels he is near the end.' She held up a hand to stop me from interrupting. 'I know what you say, but that is how he feels.'

I took her hand. 'You'll be surprised at how healing the sun will be for him. You know, Aunt Irini will be delighted to see you. I can just imagine the pair of you chatting away in her lovely garden. Oh, Mum, please get him to say yes, you really need to do this.'

'She is your second great cousin, Anna, not my mother's sister.'

'I know that, though how you remember it all, I have no idea. It's easier just to call her Aunt, and she doesn't mind.'

She chuckled. 'I haven't seen her since I took you so many years ago. We talk on the phone, but how I long for the sun, and going home again, but it has all been a dream. Until now. It smells completely different over there, you know, with the wild flowers and the herbs. Oh, and the markets, the churches, the festivals, the flowers. I miss it all so much.'

'I know, Mum,' I said gently, 'I live there now.'

'And we would be all together in Crete. It would be a dream come true.' Her eyes shone with tears.

'And I can help you to find a house, and decorate it for you.' I told her about the Andreanakises and the fire, and how Delphine had taken over sorting it out for them.

'So Nikos is not as good as you have painted him.'

'No, he's a businessman before everything else. It's where he gets his self-respect from. But I'm getting him to see things a little differently, I hope. I seem to be getting through to him, anyway. He agreed to set up the charity in his name to help unemployed youngsters, so that's a step forward for him. Ideally, I'd like him to take the decision to sell it all before I have to inherit anything because I'll sell it anyway. There's no way I'm running a huge business like that. I haven't got it in me. But I'm going to get there slowly. I don't want to alienate him.'

'And, of course, you have a cousin claiming his share?'

'Not just one cousin. There are two more brothers in America, too, also sons of Stephanos, and who knows what they might want?' I shrugged. 'You know, Mum, I don't want any of Nikos' businesses. I want to be a designer and live in my little house and be happy, but I'm not letting Leo get his greedy hands on any of it. And he'll harass me for the rest of my life if I don't get rid of it.'

She squeezed my hand. 'It used to be guns, when old

Andreas was alive. That's how the family made their fortune. He would smuggle them in from Morocco and Turkey, and sell them to the resistance. Your grandmother helped him. She was quite famous for her work in the resistance. That money of Nikos' has always been dirty. That's what I used to tell your father when the anger threatened to eat him up. We don't need dirty money, I would say. We have each other, and we have you, and we have a good life here.' She smiled at me, sadly. 'But it isn't home, is it?'

'No, it isn't home.'

Knowing that we would have to wait for Dad to reappear before I could do any more, I persuaded Mum to go shopping with me in Manchester for some new summer clothes, and we had a great girly afternoon buying sandals, tops, a new swimming costume, several skirts and some more cropped jeans. I could see that I would need to add hold baggage for the return journey, especially as I intended to take back mature Cheddar cheese and boxes of proper tea bags. Enough of that Lipton stuff.

We piled back into the flat, lugging bags of shopping and giggling about the cost, to find Dad sitting on the old sofa in the living room, a glass of something red in his hand. He looked up and gave Mum the warmest smile. 'It's good to see you looking happy again, Galena. We have been so sad recently.'

Then he looked at me with a very different expression. My heart thumped. I stood in the doorway.

'When you left us I didn't think your mother would ever recover. Our only child, who couldn't even give us a grandchild to love, leaving her husband and going off on some adventure, to the one place I could never agree to.' He wiped his eyes. 'And then, illness. Cancer.' He spat the word out. 'And I thought it was all over for us. I thought she would die of a broken heart, and I? Well, I will just die of this.' He thumped his stomach.

Mum dropped her bags on the floor and collapsed down beside him. 'Theo, please, don't do this to yourself.' She kissed his hands.

I stood there gasping like a fish on dry land. How could he talk to me like that? Like I'd hurt them on purpose? 'Is that what you think? That I wouldn't have children to spite you?' I dropped to my knees in front of him and held onto his other hand. 'Dad, I want children, of course I do, but it wasn't in the plan.'

Their faces showed only confusion.

'Will's plan: "There must be no interruption to our rise and rise". Children would have meant mess, confusion and me having to take time off work and there was no room for that in the plan. So I wasn't allowed. In the same way I wasn't allowed to wear red or curl my hair, or eat proper food or have friends of my own. My life wasn't real, Dad. It was all a show to stroke his ego. Do you see? That's why I left him. He was strangling me slowly.' With a tasteful taupe silk scarf.

Dad lifted his teary eyes to mine. 'Why did you never say that he was cruel?'

Mum blew her nose on a tissue. I felt bad to burst the bubble of wonderfulness in which she placed Will, but it was time. I was far enough away from it all to see what had really been happening. 'I was so young, only twenty, and how could I know how a marriage should work? We had lovely things, cars, holidays, articles in the national magazines. But no real love, no fun, just control and behaving myself. I was a nervous wreck half the time, trying to please him. But I don't want any of that now. I've found what I needed. I'm happy. I have friends, I'm finding work, and maybe, love. Come back with me. I think it's what you need, too.' I could only stare at him and wait.

Eventually, as dusk began to fall and my knees were about to give out, he gave the smallest nod. 'Perhaps you are right.

Perhaps it is time.' He turned to Mum. 'I have been cruel to keep you away from your family all this time.'

To me he said, 'So, let's go and see my brother and see what he has to say after all these years.'

It was more than I could have hoped for. We were going home. I longed for Alex, for my house and my new family and finally getting rid of Will and his influence on my mother. I leapt up and swiped tears away. Enough of that, I had work to do. 'I have phone calls to make. Thank you, Papa,' I said and leaned down to kiss the top of his head.

27

Of course, nothing is ever as simple as 'why don't you come back with me now?', is it?

I went downstairs before six that evening and the restaurant was just preparing to open. Michael, the chef, had the rest of the staff in the kitchen with him and was going over the menu in detail. He was young, but he was definitely in charge, and the way he talked about the food explained why Dad had wanted the restaurant to go to him. I ordered us a simple meal of chicken souvlaki, chips and salad, and a carafe of red wine to have upstairs in the little kitchen in the flat.

Once the parents were settled in front of the TV for the evening news, I rang Delphine and explained what we needed. I had Dad's medicines in front of me and sent a photo of each of them over the phone, then asked her to alert the local hospital to see if there was anything we should do. She was quite excited and didn't seem fazed by the request. I'd ring our local hospital in the morning, and convince them that Dad would be all right to travel. I hoped he was.

Over dinner, Dad was quiet but calm. He seemed to have accepted that he was about to do something momentous. But

Mum couldn't hide her excitement, and kept reaching across to grab my hand. Made drinking my wine decidedly dangerous.

Then I had a thought. 'I don't suppose either of you has an up-to-date passport?' I asked. Blank faces greeted me.

'I've never been anywhere,' said Dad. 'I did get a British passport when we took out citizenship about forty years ago. Only used it once.'

'And mine ran out years ago,' added Mum.

I reached for a pen and paper, and started a list. 'First thing tomorrow, we go to the post office and get photos. Then we'll go to the passport office in Liverpool and wait for them to be processed.'

'You can do that?' said Mum.

'Yes, I did it when I first went abroad with Will,' I said, 'when I was at uni. Don't you remember? It was the most boring day of my life, but I got it, so don't worry, I'll do the same tomorrow. Then I promise I'll contact the hospital and check it out with them.' I didn't expect for a moment that they'd be happy, but as Dad had said, he may die anyway, so why wait?

'Now, you two, I need you to think about what you need to do in terms of packing and who you need to tell that you're going away. Over there it's warm during the day now, but cool at night, and soon it will be summer! We'll sort out plane tickets when we've got your passports sorted. Easy.'

'You'll need some better clothes, Theo,' said Mum. 'We can't have your rich brother thinking we are the poor relations, can we?'

He rolled his eyes.

I laughed. 'We could all go together tomorrow. Photos first, so we can complete the forms before we go. Drop the passport applications off and then go shopping in Liverpool. It'll be much more fun than sitting in the passport office, waiting.'

Dad shrugged and wiggled his feet. 'I suppose I do need summer shoes,' he said.

'Shoes?' scoffed Mum. 'And the rest. You need a whole new set of clothes. And I will take no arguments.' Her eyes lit up.

Shopping is the main way Mum and I come together. You could say that it's our natural talent. That's why I like doing it for a living. It's my happy place.

'If we can sort it all out over the weekend, how would you feel about flying on Monday?' I asked. 'That way I can use my booked seat and just add yours on.'

I think Dad was in dull acceptance mode, he simply raised a hand in defeat. I couldn't imagine what was running through his head.

'Yes, that will be fine, won't it, Theo? We're going home,' Mum said. And it did indeed feel like that.

Next morning there was no lying in bed late. I could hear them chattering away in their bedroom, and by the time I emerged they were fully dressed and Mum was on the phone, booking them both in at the local hairdresser.

Dad gave me a rueful look. 'Why am I going to a hairdresser? What is wrong with Luigi's where I have gone all my life?'

'Humour her, Dad. You look very smart anyway.'

'This is for the passport photos, she says. I feel like I am going to a wedding.'

Mum looked dressed for an occasion, too, in full makeup. 'You look great,' I said.

'Humph, I looked at our old passport photos, and I'm damned if I'm going to look like a convict on this one. Right, breakfast and then hair, and then down to the post office.' She looked at Dad. 'You, bring the credit card. We need new suitcases, and you need shoes and trousers and shirts and underwear.'

I couldn't help but laugh. Marks and Spencer would get a hammering today. 'Don't tire him out, Mum.'

'I won't, but I don't want us to look like the poor relatives either. There is no need for us to be ashamed of our lives.'

'Too right, you're both brilliant, and it's good to see you enjoying yourself, even if Dad looks like he's being tortured.'

He actually laughed. 'Come on, family,' he said, 'let's eat and get going.'

Once they were done at the hairdresser's, and we had the photos and the forms filled in, thanks to a fantastically helpful woman in the post office, I drove us in Dad's old Volvo over to Liverpool. The man behind the counter at the passport office told us that we may as well go away for the rest of the day, so we did our clothes and suitcase shopping. Well, Mum and I did. As soon as he had chosen a couple of pairs of shoes, Mum settled Dad into a pub that was showing Formula One racing and he was happy with a beer, a pie and the newspaper.

We didn't mess about; I learnt all I know about shopping from my mum. The first pass is where you look at everything once, then you have a cup of tea, and think about whether you have something similar already (ouch), and only then do you go back and get what you need. Fail-safe, and stops my usual impulse-buying issue. I bought a suitcase as well; there was just too much stuff to get into my little bag.

Finally, we got back to the passport office just before closing time and retrieved two shiny passports. We were all set to go. I was amazed we'd managed it.

We were all quiet on the way home. It was just over an hour

from Liverpool but we were slow in the Friday night traffic and Dad dozed off in the back. Mum was looking at the new passports and thinking. She rubbed her knuckles backwards and forwards across her teeth. Dead giveaway. 'What is it?' I asked quietly.

'Are we doing the right thing, Anna? Your father is so ill, and to go back, now. What if it is dangerous?'

'It's not dangerous for goodness' sake. It's not the Wild West. The hospital in Chania is first rate. Nikos needs to make amends, Dad needs to go home. You need to go home. I need to go home. End of.'

She looked at me. 'You feel like Crete is your home?'

'I'm beginning to. Look, Mum, you have to accept that it is over between me and Will. I'm not going back to him. I've, well, I've met someone.'

She tutted. 'That didn't take you long. Who?'

'It's been almost two years! I'm hardly out every night partying. No, this is a Swedish man called Alex, and he is one of the kindest people I know. It's early days, but, I have a good feeling.' I could hardly wait to get back to him.

'Oh, well, I shall look forward to meeting him then,' said Mum, folding her arms.

And not much else was said for the rest of the journey.

As my sulking mother disappeared up the stairs with a pile of bags, Dad stopped me at the door. 'I'm glad you have found somebody, Anna. I could never have said, but I didn't like Will from the start. Too cold. So I really am looking forward to meeting this man. I'm just sorry he isn't a nice Greek boy.' He grinned at me and picked up the last two bags, leaving me with the suitcases.

Later, Dad disappeared down into the kitchens to talk to Michael about looking after the restaurant for several weeks. He was gone for some time, and I could only imagine the list of instructions he had for the poor guy. I think he may have talked about the final agreement to sell, as well. It was time. Time for us to go home.

28

Touching down onto Cretan soil was a moment I won't forget. I could see the pair of them, hanging sideways to watch the plane flying in over the city. We'd had to wait in Athens airport for a couple of hours for the transfer, and they'd enjoyed having coffee and cheese pies at a little concession in the foyer. It wasn't home, but they were closer. I'd paid extra for the parents to sit up front on the Chania connection, but because of the late booking I was several rows behind them. As I'd expected, Dad had slept through most of the journey, but Mum woke him and ordered drinks and fussed around until he was what she considered presentable. I was amazed he let her get away with it.

Waiting for our bags, Dad kept glancing around as if he was expecting people from his boyhood to spring out and know immediately who he was. They were both excited, and I could see, nervous. I got a trolley and pushed my way into a good spot to grab the cases.

'It won't be long now,' I said. 'I'll leave you at the entrance, pick up the car and come back to get you. I hope I can get all the luggage in my little car.'

We stood for a moment at the top of the steps outside the airport. It was full evening now but some birds still sang and the scent of spring flowers came from well-tended beds. And it was a warm wind blowing, not a cold gale.

Good little Fiat was where I had left it, covered in a thin layer of red dust but otherwise unscathed. I had to squash Mum in the back with half the luggage as it wouldn't all fit in the boot, but it was finally all in and we set off for home.

I could feel Dad trembling next to me. He was muttering under his breath. Was he crying? 'Dad, are you okay?'

'I don't know. It's been so long.' He clutched at his chest.

'Breathe, Dad.'

Mum snaked a hand over the seat and held onto his shoulder. 'It will be fine, love,' she said. 'We're just going to stay at Anna's. That's all there is to think about for tonight. You must be very tired, and you don't need to think about anything else for now. Okay?'

'Okay, you're right, I'm getting all upset. But, as you both say, the feud is over, and my brother wants to see me. I never thought this day would come.' He gave a shaky laugh. 'Look at me, the big man, crying like a baby.'

'Yes, get a grip, Father,' I said, and patted his knee. 'Let's do this one step at a time.'

My main concern was that my house would be in one piece when I got back and that there had been no unwanted visits from Leo. It appeared the police had not been able to apprehend him in the week, according to Delphine. It was another worry to add to my list.

The main road from the airport skirts Chania, and runs through the lower end of the mountains. I could feel them pulling at me, Lefki Ora, the White Mountains, and I knew they would feel it too, but Dad had lapsed into a brooding silence and

Mum was twisting in her seat trying to remember landmarks in the dark.

The approach to Kissamos isn't spectacular; in fact, the road just gets a little more populated until you find yourself amongst shops, tavernas and restaurants, many of which were still closed at this time of the year. Dad perked up, though, as we got towards the centre of town.

'Could we stop and see?' he asked, almost fearful.

So instead of going straight home, I took them down the little streets towards the museum and into the heart of the town. I stopped and let them get out for a wander. It was quite busy for a Monday, the tavernas and cafés were full of people eating and drinking now that Lent was over.

'Tzanakaki Square,' said Dad. 'I spent a lot of my teenage years hanging around here with my friends.' He took Mum's hand and they turned in a slow circle, taking it all in. 'It's where I met you,' he said to her. 'You were sitting on the wall with your friends, flirting with all the boys except me. I was so jealous.'

'I did it on purpose,' purred my mother and gave him a very serious kiss.

'Enough already, you two. I know, how about a drink before we go home? That bar is open. I'll bet you're hungry too.' I led them to a table outside the little bar and they ordered a drink, and I watched the tension seeping out of my father's shoulders. A small smile played around his mouth.

He caught my eye. 'I'm home.'

We had coffee and raki and olives and shared a few small plates of food and let the bustle of the town flow around us. There were families with children chatting and eating, early season tourists trying to interpret street signs and choose a menu, and shop workers finally closed for the night enjoying a drink on their way home. Young people rode past on motorbikes and scooters wearing no helmets, girls straddled over the engines, hair blowing behind them. Elderly ladies, all in black, shuffled past, chatting and grinning their toothless grins. All was well. My own tension eased to the point where I realised that my shoulders and neck had turned into an iron bar over the past few days.

Mum still had her eyes on stalks, but Dad was calmer after several shots of raki and a little food. He was still grey, though, and I was worried about making him ill with all the excitement. Then I reminded myself he was sixty, not a hundred and sixty. I worried until the owner of Dimitri's Taverna, which was on the opposite corner to where we sat, came hesitantly across the road.

'Excuse me,' he said, 'but are you Theo?'

Dad just stared at him.

The man slapped his chest. 'Dimitri! Your best friend! How could you forget me?'

Dad stood up and his mouth dropped open. 'Dimitri?' was all he managed before he was enveloped in a bear hug. 'I...'

'You have been gone so long...' Dimitri pulled up short and looked around him. 'How? Why are you back?' He dropped his voice to a whisper. 'Is your brother...?'

'No,' said Dad through tears, 'not dead, but it is over, I can come home.'

It was almost midnight when I dragged them away. Once Dad and Dimitri started to talk, the years fell away, back to when they were two young men on the brink of their adult lives. We were introduced to Dimitri's wife, both of his children, one of whom had to be pulled out of the kitchen, and we had to promise to go back the following night to eat before we were

246

allowed to leave. Odd that their lives hadn't turned out all that differently, really. Both of them had gone into the food trade.

'Okay, back in the car, the pair of you,' I said. 'So much for an early night!'

I probably shouldn't have driven the last few hundred yards home after two glasses of raki, but I didn't care. Dad had thrown off the depression that was dogging him, and Mum was still weeping at every opportunity, but with delight, not sadness. And me? I was completely exhausted and longing for my bed. Operation Bring Them Home had done me in.

We drew up outside the house, and got out. I tried to be as quiet as I could, but not much got past Irini, even in the middle of the night. As soon as my parents were out of the car, and we'd begun unloading the luggage into the living room, she came out of her house like a woman half her age, wrapped in a huge dressing gown, and that led to another half hour of talking and hugging and weeping.

I lugged the suitcases upstairs and made sure the bedroom and bathroom were ready for them. I eyed the still unopened pot of terracotta bathroom paint. 'I'll get to you soon, do not fear,' I told it. Finally, I gently escorted my Aunt Irini out, and suggested she join us for a late breakfast the next morning.

Once she had gone, I saw that my parents had no energy left at all. They'd been going on adrenaline, but it only gets you so far. Sleep was needed. 'Welcome to my home, Mum and Dad. It is your home, too, for as long as you want to stay. Don't act like guests. You'll find everything you need in the cupboards. I think you need to go to bed now, and please don't wake me up in the morning!'

Mum beamed at me. 'It's beautiful, Anna, what you have done with Nyssa's house. Thank you for doing this. Thank you.' She turned to Dad. 'Come on, bedtime.' Then she gave me a hug and I felt closer to her than I ever had.

Dad didn't speak, he just climbed the narrow stairs after her and they found their room. They spent a few minutes in the bathroom, then all was quiet. I rubbed my face. Hell's teeth, but this was a mad experiment. I debated texting Alex, and Delphine, but decided they would be asleep, and that was where I should also be.

I'd done the first part in reconciling the brothers. Two of them were at least on the same island. Tomorrow I would tackle the third, and arrange for Dad and Nikos to meet. Oh, joy.

29

I woke to the sunlight beating down on my face as usual, and stretched. The sound of traffic and people's voices came and went through the open window as they headed into town for the Tuesday market, which reminded me that I was now feeding three, and would need to shop soon. I slipped out of bed and listened at the guest bedroom doorway; all was quiet, so I took the opportunity to shower and choose what I would wear. I used my new makeup and tied a little cotton scarf around my neck to make sure the bruises, which were turning green and yellow, were hidden. Nice. Then I styled my hair as best I could and sprayed it with half a can of hairspray to hold it. Done. This was going to be a big day for all of us, especially Dad and Nikos, and I didn't want any unnecessary distractions like bald patches getting in the way.

Of course, one of the stairs creaked loudly as I crept down them so it was too late to worry about waking them up. It was the work of a few moments to make a list for market and down a welcome coffee. And I had another few moments to contemplate what the day might bring, like news that Leo was in custody. I picked up my phone. Could I risk a call to the police station with the parents upstairs? No, the officer had said they would inform me of any news, so I should wait. So, instead, I rang Delphine and told her about the night before and how wonderful it was for Dad to have met an old friend in the town on his first night here. Then we made arrangements to go up to the house for lunch.

'Oh,' said Delphine, 'also I have arranged for the family doctor to come to your house at nine on Thursday to see Theo. Will that be all right? The English hospital has sent on his details as you requested.'

'That's wonderful, thank you so much for doing that. I'll feel better if I know he's okay. See you later.'

I then managed a quick call to Alex, who was delighted that I was back, and a bit concerned about meeting my parents so soon into their trip. Nevertheless, I warned him not to make plans for that evening, as we had promised to go back to Dimitri's Taverna, and I'd love him to join us. He laughed and said he could tell there was no point in arguing. Good man.

Throwing open the back door to let the light in, the grey cat, who was lounging in the morning sun on top of the adjoining wall, raised her head and miaowed at me. Over the wall, Irini was hoeing round her courgette and salad plants. I cast a quick worried glance at my tiny plot but they looked fine. Amazingly, as I'd abandoned them for almost a week.

'Kalimera,' she said, and put down the hoe. 'Don't worry, I have watered your plants and taken out the weeds.' She came across to the wall, and beamed at me. 'Thank you for giving me back my cousin, and for bringing your father home.' She put a hand to my cheek. 'You'll see, the sun will make him well again. Are they still asleep?'

'I think so, they're very tired. Thanks, Aunt Irini, for looking after the place for me. I didn't know for sure I'd be bringing them back with me, but here we are, and we're meeting Nikos and Delphine at lunchtime.' My worries about the meeting must have shown on my face.

'Don't worry, they are brothers. They will find a way through to each other, and they have their wives with them to hold onto them if the emotions run high.' She made a little gesture, waving her hand about. 'Cretan men, they go up, they go down. It's hard to keep them even!' She laughed loudly, and as if on cue, Mum came pottering out into the garden.

'Oh, you've made the house so lovely, darling,' she said, 'and look at your little garden.' She gave me a kiss and leaned across the wall to kiss her cousin. 'Kalimera, Irini, are you well?'

Irini said she was well, thank you, and I got a word in while I still could. 'Will you join us for breakfast?' I asked and she beamed again. I didn't think I was going to have much difficulty with my mother about moving back home.

I left them chatting and made my way back into the kitchen to lay another setting at the table. I could hear the shower running, so Dad was up too. I found stale bread which would be fine toasted, honey, yogurt, some fruit that wasn't too soft and some Mizithra cheese. I boiled some eggs. A feast.

Dad came downstairs and stood in the living room, looking at everything. I knew he was picking up and looking at the photos Irini had given to me, and the ones I had found in Nyssa's folder, which were piled on the dresser. He wandered into the kitchen and gave me a kiss on the cheek. That was a first. 'Thank you for making me come, Anna,' he said. 'This is a beautiful home.'

He'd never said that about our designer house in Alderley Edge, and he was right. That was never a home.

Dad sat at the table in the kitchen, so I called the ladies in and we had a noisy, chatty breakfast.

Once they were full of food and coffee, and Dad looked

better than he had for a week, Irini invited them round to her house. She'd invited Stavros along to meet his aunt and uncle. At least I thought they would be called aunt and uncle. Family relationships are quite difficult, I find, to fathom.

I left them to it and went off to the market to stock up on fresh food and to stretch my legs. On the way I called in at Maria's. It felt like months since I was last there, although it had been lovely to have her over for dinner. And then things had gone completely pear-shaped, and I hadn't seen her since. The taverna was packed, as it always was on a market day, so I struggled past the shopping bags and plonked myself at the bar. As soon as she noticed me, Maria rushed around to the front of the bar and hugged me, quite ferociously.

'Welcome back, my friend! It's a miracle, Anna. He's given me the taverna. It's mine!' And she danced me around the tiny space between the tables and the bar. 'I know it was you who persuaded him, and I cannot thank you enough. Your money is no good in here anymore, isn't that right, Spiros?'

Spiros came through from the kitchen and jerked his head at me. It wasn't a smile, but better than his usual scowl. He went back to cooking. 'I'd still throw him out,' I whispered, and she laughed.

'Maybe, but he has been very, shall we say, grateful since Kokorakis changed his mind.'

'Ooh, how nice. I may have news myself on that score...'

Maria's dark eyes became huge.

'But I haven't got time to tell you about that at the moment, as more has happened. Maria, I've brought my parents back with me, and I think they may come back to live here. It's exciting.' And with that I hopped off the stool and went off to the market, leaving an intrigued Maria behind.

When I got home, the parents had returned and were sitting quietly in the garden. Dad was dressed in a check shirt, stone-coloured chinos and his brown deck shoes. He looked relaxed and not as grey after a good sleep. Mum looked equally good in a summer dress and cardigan. 'You two have scrubbed up well,' I said. 'Give me an hour or so to sort out the food in the kitchen and then we'll set off.' I knelt down in front of them and took a hand in each of mine. 'It'll be okay, you know. He'll be as worried about this as you are. More, probably. Just stay calm, and see how the afternoon goes.'

We walked slowly up the hill, and I let them reminisce about places they recognised. Dad was quiet as we approached the gates, and Mum's mouth dropped open. Dad looked once at the big house, and then walked across to stand outside the empty villa that had been his childhood home. Mum held his hand.

'Come on, we can have a proper look later,' I said, conscious that the housekeeper, Eleni, was waiting at the open door. In the entrance hall Nikos stood, formally dressed in one of the beautifully-cut dark suits that he favoured, Delphine at his side in grey silk. Without even trying, they had out-styled us all.

'Welcome, my brother, to my home,' said Nikos, and held out his arms.

Dad was shaking to maintain some self-control, but he managed it. He stayed where he was for a moment, then walked forward and offered his hand. 'Niko, you look well.'

'Better than you, I fear,' was the reply. He grasped Dad's hand and held onto it.

Dad snorted. 'You always were a tactless bastard.'

And Nikos gave a loud belly laugh. 'And you always saw through me.'

They continued to stare at each other. I wasn't actually breathing at this point, and had unconsciously grabbed my mother's hand, like a five-year-old. Please let them be okay, was all I could think.

Delphine stepped in. 'Welcome, Galena, Theo, and Anna too, of course. Welcome, please come into the sitting room.' She took my mother's arm and we went with her, leaving the two men facing each other in the hall. 'Come along, you two,' she said over her shoulder, 'let's get to know each other a little better.'

Her request broke the stalemate and they followed us, much to my relief. I didn't want them going off and having private conversations where Nikos could tell Dad about Leo's behaviour before I did. Mum would have a fit. I needed to whitewash it a little.

Delphine seated us on the grey velvet sofa, and she sat opposite with her husband. Eleni came in and took aperitif orders. I went straight for wine, no messing about. It was just like getting ready to pitch to a new client, I was a bundle of nerves and ready to improvise. I'd do anything to make it go smoothly. The huge picture window was bare of curtains, I noticed, and with it came the fantastic light and view down to the ocean.

'So, Theo,' said Nikos, 'tell me about your life. I have met your beautiful daughter, and I can see she gets her looks from her mother.'

Dad snorted again. 'Your sense of humour hasn't changed, has it? Well, once I found somewhere to live, I trained to be a chef, brought Galena over from Crete, and we made our life running the restaurant.' He gestured to the room. 'Clearly, we have not done as well as you.'

Nikos made his own gesture. 'This? This means nothing, as I have come to realise too late in my life. Family is the most important thing, and I...' He stopped. 'Well, I let you go, and for that I can never forgive myself.' He moved forward to the edge of his seat. 'Do you ever think you will be able to forgive me, Theo?'

We all looked at Dad, who wasn't smiling. He was silent, looking down at his hands folded in his lap. When he spoke, it was slowly, gravely. 'I have held hatred in my heart for almost my whole life. Hatred for you, hatred for my father, and hatred for all that being banished from my home took away from me.'

He raised his eyes and looked at his brother. 'But now, after speaking with my daughter, I understand that you are not an evil man, but that you were weak in front of our father, and I was weak too, or I would have come back and fought you for my place here. My pride was stronger than my sense. So, maybe we are as bad as each other. Maybe, there could be something shared between us, especially as you have tried to steal Anna away from us, with all your promises to her.' He said the last sentence with a twinkle in his eye.

'Nobody's stealing me from anybody,' I piped up, 'I want you all in my life. If I'm going to inherit Uncle Nikos' business, then I intend to use the profits to do good. And anyway, it won't be for years yet, will it? So we have all the time in the world to get to know each other. To be a family.' Get me, the peacemaker.

Delphine stood. 'And what better way to do that than over food? Come through to the dining room.'

Mum's face was a picture as she followed Delphine, holding tightly onto Dad's hand. I could see her trying not to cry but also open-mouthed as she took in the grandeur of the marble floors and the ridiculously long table. At least Delphine had had the sensitivity to place us all around one end of it. The food came and we did small talk, Delphine keeping the chat going while I kept a close eye on the men.

'I'm not going to fall over, Anna,' said Dad at one point. 'You don't have to keep checking on me. I'm fine.' Admonished, I relaxed a little and had another glass of wine, thinking that I needed to go steady and keep it all running smoothly.

'This food is delightful, Delphine,' Mum said. 'Greek but modern, more nouvelle cuisine than hearty. It's so good.'

Delphine beamed at her. 'Thank you, Galena. Eleni, my housekeeper, she trained in Paris. She will be honoured that you like it.'

I really would have to spend some time with Eleni if I wanted to refine my cooking. I was anticipating dessert, if it was half as good as the main courses, I'd be in heaven.

Dad was pretty quiet. I guessed he had a lot of thinking to do now that he was back at home and there was no feud and his estranged brother was sitting next to him. It would have shaken his whole world view. And, of course, he was selling the restaurant, the one solid foundation for his life in England. I didn't dare ask him how he was again, so I joined in the chit-chat about weather, and curtains, and who they were going to see while they were over here.

After lunch, Nikos asked Dad if he would like to see the old villa, and off they went, just the two of them, to see Dad's childhood home. I was desperate to go too, but I could wait. If they could survive time on their own, they could begin to heal. Please don't tell Dad about Leo, I urged Nikos' retreating back. Not yet.

Once we were on our own, Mum couldn't stop herself from gushing over. 'Oh thank you, Anna, for bringing us back. It's been too long. And thank you, Delphine, for helping us to manage this meeting. Theo is a good man, but this long separation has made him bitter and old before his time.' She faltered. 'And this illness, well, who knows what might happen? So this has come at the right time, and I'm so grateful.' All the tears she'd been holding onto took that moment to spill over, and I was happy for Delphine to take her off to sort herself out.

I looked out of the large window, down the drive to the villa and wondered what they were up to in there. I really wanted to see if Nikos had emptied it, or left it as it was fifteen years ago when their father had died.

Delphine came in and stood behind my shoulder. 'No shooting. That must be a good sign, no?'

I laughed. 'It's gone better than I thought it would, that's true. Do you think we can do this? Bring the family back together after all this time?'

She smiled at me. 'As you said, we have time. Oh, by the way, the decorators are working on the Andreanakis house, and all is going well. We should go over and see progress next week some time.'

'I'd like that, it'll bring a bit of normality back into my life, and I can get rid of the bags of her stuff that are currently in my loft.'

'I have also begun to look for somewhere for Constantinos, as we promised. I think this will be a great thing that we can do. Thank you for making it happen.'

'The English phrase is "strike while the iron is hot",' I said. 'Nikos would probably turn me down now that he's thinking straight.'

She said, 'Maybe, or maybe you are who he has been waiting for. Look, they are returning, and still talking.'

'Mum said they were very close as boys growing up. It was the betrayal that broke Dad.'

'And have you contacted the youngest brother yet?'

'No, not had a chance yet.'

'Well, you need to know that he is here on the island. The police rang to say that he landed this morning. I think he may be looking for his son, too.'

'How hard can it be to catch an American, out of season, on

an island?' I asked, exasperated. 'I need to know we're safe, Delphine, especially now.'

'I know, but don't worry, Nikos has made sure the police are following Stephanos. I think your suspicion that Stephanos is in league with his son to take over Nikos' business is correct. It would be better if you didn't make contact with him until we are sure. If his lawyers contact Nikos, then we will know.'

Don't worry? I sat back down in a daze, and remembered little of the next hour or so. Dad and Nikos came back, and when we got up to leave, there was definitely a bit more warmth in their goodbyes. We promised to meet up later in the week, but I was glad to get away. I'd pushed Leo to the back of my mind, but now he was back in there, and I was frightened now that I had my parents staying with me.

We strolled back home and I suggested an afternoon nap if they were to be fit for a long night at Dimitri's. I knew they wanted to chat too, and there were few spots for privacy in my house.

'Be good. I'm off to see a friend, but I'll be back in time to take you out for yet more food and wine!' I placed the spare keys on the dresser. 'Just lock up if you want to go out anywhere.'

I was worried stiff. In fact, I locked the front door behind me as I left and walked the half-mile along the beach to the boat-yard deep in thought. It would have been completely naïve to imagine that Leo's bid for the business would go away just because Nikos and I had said no. After all, Stephanos and his sons had as much claim to it as I did in law, even if Nikos didn't want them to inherit.

It would be so much easier to rip up the agreement with Nikos and allow Leo to take over, wouldn't it? I stopped and contemplated the ocean. But that would mean he would be here, in my town, forever, and I couldn't bear that. Liar, abuser. A man

I couldn't trust. And I didn't think for a moment that he had any good intentions as far as supporting the local community was concerned. No, I had to fight, again. I wanted that business and all its wealth to do something marvellous. And I needed a bit of Swedish courage to help me fight for it.

30

I'd not seen Alex's boat, and I had no idea what it would look like. I did know it was called *Runaway*. There were several boats on stilts in the yard in various stages of repair but I had no trouble identifying Alex's. It was the one where he was standing on a ladder in a pair of tatty shorts and a faded T-shirt painting in the name along the shiny wooden hull. It was a fabulous-looking boat, like a 1920s pleasure cruiser, but with sails. I got up close behind him, and said, cheesily, 'Permission to come aboard, Captain?' He nearly fell off his ladder.

'Anna? I thought we were meeting later?' But he must have seen something in my eyes, because he clambered down and took me in his arms. 'What has happened?' He held me for a short while. At least it felt like a short while, it could have been a week and still over too soon. He released me and said, 'Come with me.'

I followed him up the ladder and onto the deck. It had blonde wood flooring and a dining table fixed to the deck. In the main cabin were long sofas along the sides, another dining table and the pilot's chair at the front with a proper wheel to steer by.

Inside, the wood panelling was mahogany, which gleamed in the soft afternoon sunlight. 'It's beautiful, Alex.'

He smiled and took me on a tour, showing me the very well-appointed guest rooms and the tiny staff quarters. 'So I live in luxury in the master suite during the winter, and then slum it with the crew below decks in the summer. Tough life.' He filled a kettle and said, 'Coffee, tea, something stronger?'

I voted for tea and looked around the galley as he boiled a kettle. Everything had a place that would keep it safe in bad weather. The appliances were ultra-modern and sleek. I'd enjoy cooking in it, I thought. I tried to learn the sailing terms for what was on board while Alex made the drinks, although there was no way I could call a toilet a 'head' without giggling.

I hadn't given his offer to cook for him over the summer a second thought, for obvious near-death experience reasons, but this was a gorgeous kitchen on a wonderful boat. I might have to think again. It would be another adventure. I could always design in the winter months.

Alex led me into the master suite, which was like a miniature hotel suite but with little round windows. I perched on the bed and looked around while sipping tea and I could feel questions, fears and tears all fighting to get out.

Alex looked at my contorted face and said, 'Want to spill it all?'

We lay back together on the king-size bed, propped against pillows, sipping tea and, suffice it to say that it took an hour or so to tell the wonderful story of my parents coming home and meeting Nikos, and then to worry him with the news of Leo and his father. Alex listened as he always did, without interrupting, and with full concentration. When I'd finished, and calmed down, he kissed the palms of my hands, and then kissed away the tears on my cheeks and finally he found my mouth. He unzipped my dress and folded it over the chair, and then gave the rest of me his full attention, too.

It was after six when I woke from the best kind of sleep, and I had to get home for the parents. I needed a shower and another change of clothes. 'Do you want to come back with me now?' I asked his ear.

He laughed. 'No, that would be a real giveaway. You look so beautiful, Anna, lying there so peacefully.' He curled a lock of my hair around his finger and traced his cool hand down my body.

'That'll be the dusk, I look better in the dark.'

He laughed and kissed me deeply. 'Take a compliment properly.'

'Stop, now, or I'll never get away.' I struggled out from under him, found the bathroom, washed a little mascara off my face and made myself presentable. 'Alex, could you pick us up at eight? That's if you don't mind driving? I don't trust myself at the moment not to have a drink. I seem to need it.'

'Of course, do you need a lift now?'

'No, I'll enjoy the walk. At least I will when I find my shoes.' I scrabbled under the bed, and there they were. I was reluctant to leave, but eager to get home. I didn't want the aged ones to think I'd abandoned them forever.

I left him lying on the bed, all lean and brown and gorgeous, clambered carefully down the ladder and sang on the way home. It may even have been Whitney Houston.

I arrived back to find my parents enjoying a glass of wine on the bench in the back garden. The sun had just disappeared over the top of the mountain, and the temperature was dropping. I had a close look at Dad, and he looked so much better. So did

Mum. They both looked rested and calm. The sleep had clearly done them good. Then I had that horrible thought that nobody wants to have regarding their own parents, that they too had been having sex in the afternoon. Meh. 'Well, you two are looking good,' I said, glad the dusk was hiding the flush of give-away pink on my cheeks. 'I could do with a quick shower and a change of clothes. Alex will come and collect us at eight o'clock.'

'That's very nice of him,' said Mum, getting up and following me into the kitchen. 'Tell me,' she said quietly, 'is he kind to you?'

'Oh, Mum, he's gentle and brave and kind. And he lives on this amazing yacht in the bay. I'll get him to take us out on it soon.'

She took my hand. 'I only ever wanted you to be happy, you know. I didn't realise that you were unhappy. I was too busy to notice, and Will was always so charming.'

'It's okay. Really. That time's behind us. Let's look forward to the future. Dad looks better,' I said, changing the subject.

'He is, more like his old self, but we must remember he is ill, and not tire him out.' She called Dad inside to sit on the sofa, and I found them a local news channel on the laptop so that they could catch up on what was happening in town. Thinking about it, sex probably hadn't been on the menu at all, not with Dad so ill. It was wishful thinking, I suppose, that he was magically healed just from coming to Crete.

Upstairs, I had a long shower, and felt that parts of me were healing. The main part was the part Will had damaged, that I had thought was irreparably broken, but wasn't. And the other was the part that had made running away the only option. I hadn't realised at the time that I was running home. Running *to* the rest of my life, not away. Yes, it had been a bumpy landing, but it would all work out, I was sure. I checked out the bruises on my ribs and neck and they were finally healing too.

When Alex knocked on the door just before eight I had to fight my mother to get there first. She stood right behind my shoulder and peered over it. He, naturally, looked wonderful in his blue linen shirt that was the same colour as his eyes. I kissed him lightly on the lips and drew him into the room, where I caught Mum and Dad exchanging a glance.

Holding his hand, I said, 'Galena and Theo, this is Alex Johannsen. He's from Sweden.'

Dad was first to shake his hand, and Mum smiled up at him, quite shyly for her. They were a bit stuck for words. Another first. Dad took control.

'So, Anna tells us you live on a boat, Alex,' he said, inviting Alex to sit next to him on the sofa, and I sent up a silent thank you.

'Mum, why don't you pop up and get yours and Dad's jackets? You'll need them later.'

She indicated that I was to follow her up the stairs, so I did, reluctantly into their bedroom. 'What?'

'He's so old! I had no idea he would be old! Are you sure, Anna? Are you sure?' she whispered.

She was so sincere I couldn't take offence. 'Mother, leave me, and him, alone. He's forty-three, and that's only eight years older than me.'

She sniffed. 'I suppose he has a proper job, not just messing about in a boat.'

I wasn't prepared to have that conversation. 'Leave it. I'll tell you more later. For now, be nice, and let's have some fun with Dimitri. Come on.'

She followed me out of the room tutting, and I grinned. It would do her good not to know everything straight away.

～

Dimitri had done us proud. Somehow, during the course of the day, he had rounded up four of Dad's old friends from school, and one of Mum's. The inside of the taverna was decorated with balloons and candles, and there was a feast of food laid out on a table at the side of the room. In the corner a local band played a mix of classic Cretan folk music as well as a more modern repertoire which sounded quite odd on a bouzouki, even though it got feet tapping.

There was eating, dancing, drinking and so much talking I thought my ears would burst. I was introduced to far more people than I could ever remember, and so was Alex. I did manage to check that he was all right at one point during the evening, but otherwise he sat in the corner, and let the rest of us get on with having fun. I was pulled onto the dance floor by Dimitri and made to dance to a tune I had last heard when I was eight years old. Mum and Dad were already on their feet swaying and stamping. My heart almost burst with happiness to see my parents back where they belonged. And, there was no way the cool Swede was allowed to sit it out, so I dragged him up and we all made complete fools of ourselves. It was a brilliant, ecstatic night.

Mum signalled that Dad had had enough just before midnight, and it still took half an hour to say our goodbyes. I was glad that we had asked Alex to drive us home. Dad had gone white and was very quiet. He was exhausted again.

Once home they went straight up to bed. I took them water and checked that Dad was okay, but within minutes of him getting into bed, he was asleep. 'I hope it wasn't too much for him,' I whispered to Mum outside the door.

'He was so happy tonight,' she said, 'if he has to die, let it be now.'

Sometimes, my mother would test the patience of a saint. 'Don't say that. He's getting better; you just have to look at him.'

She didn't answer, just brushed past me into the bathroom. 'Night,' she said through the door as I made my way downstairs.

Alex stood up and held me. 'Well, that was a very good night,' he murmured into my hair, 'and an exceptional afternoon. I'm going to go home, as I have work to do tomorrow and you need to focus on your parents for the next few days.'

'Hmm… My mother certainly needs some refocusing, that's true. Can we get together soon though?'

He did this thing that he had done once before, that I realised was all Alex. He kissed me on my forehead, then on each eyelid, then on my mouth. It felt like a blessing, somehow, and I went all melty again. He did that to me all too easily, I was discovering.

'Call me, or just drop by, you know where I am.' He gave me another, lingering kiss, picked up his car keys and slipped out into the darkness.

I lay in bed later, unable to sleep, too full of food and wine and all that had happened to me since I set foot on this island. Bad and good, terrifying and beautiful. It was never boring here.

I hadn't really had time to process the fact that Leo and his father were still here causing trouble no doubt. Having time, on that dark, quiet night to think, I couldn't imagine that Leo was about to let all his efforts go to waste. All they needed was to get me and Nikos into a room and force us to sign it all away. They could blackmail Nikos with the tax office, and I wasn't going to fight them in the courts. I'd had enough of that. I shuddered. We wouldn't be safe until Leo was in prison for assault or back in America with his father.

31

I did sleep eventually, thank goodness. Next morning, all was quiet next door, so I got dressed and went down to think about breakfast. The parents would emerge at some point, but we had no plans for the day, so there was no rush. I opened the back door and gave my little plants some water. I was going to have to arrange a water collection and sprinkler system for the summer. I expected that the nice man in the garden centre would help me.

What I didn't expect was a hammering at the front door. It made me jump, and when I got back inside the house, two large men standing outside the door made the whole room go dark. My heart pounded. What now?

Every instinct told me to hide, but I opened the door and saw a man who was the spitting image of my dad, but several centimetres taller. Could it be? 'Uncle Stephanos?' My voice quivered. I still wasn't ready to see strange men at my door. I held onto the door so they couldn't get in, just in case, and scanned the street for any sign of Leo.

The man was polite and spoke with a strong American

accent. 'Hello, yes, you must be Anna, I'm Stephanos Kokorakis.' He held out his hand, which I shook. 'May I come in?'

I looked past him to the dour man behind him. The gold-rimmed glasses and black eyes made him look like an extra from a war film, and I recoiled from him instantly.

Stephanos noticed my hesitation. 'This is my lawyer, Laskaris.'

Mr Laskaris gazed at me, eyes cold and unblinking. I reluctantly opened the door wider just as my father came down the stairs behind me.

'What's happening?' he asked, then his eyes widened and he took in a sharp breath.

'Stephie?' Dad stopped on the last stair, which put him eye to eye with his taller sibling.

I motioned them inside. No point doing this on the street. Laskaris came in and stood by the cold fireplace until I sat him in the armchair. I didn't want him lurking. Stephanos stood at the door for a moment longer, before my father stepped forward and embraced his younger brother.

'Stephie. I never thought...' He swiped at tears with his fist, overcome with emotion.

Stephanos pushed him away, quite gently, and surveyed my house like he owned it. I wasn't sure what was going on, but it didn't feel like happy families. I was terrified. If he was here, was Leo here too? Or had he got to Nikos already?

Stephanos stood in front of the fireplace, hands clasped behind his back. 'We will have plenty of time to get to know each other, Theo. I never expected to see you again. We are as strangers after all this time.'

'Not strangers, brothers,' said Dad, sitting on the sofa. 'Brothers separated through no fault of their own.' He leaned forward, resting his arms on his knees and looked up at Stephanos. 'But it does not have to be that way anymore. I have spoken to Nikos, and he is sorry for what he did. Do you hear me? Sorry.' He patted the seat. 'Come and sit next to me. Let's talk.'

A look of contempt slid across Stephanos' features. 'There's a time for talking.' He gestured at the lawyer, who opened the briefcase on his lap and pulled out several sheets of typed paper. 'But it sure isn't now.' He made another gesture and in through the open back door came Leo, who lounged against the door jamb, smirking and smoking one of his foul cigarettes.

I gasped in horror. The police really hadn't caught him. He was here, at my door, again. My legs turned liquid and I had to lean against the wall.

'Hi there. See you've met my dad.' He looked at my father, who sat open-mouthed on the sofa. 'And you must be Anna's father. The café owner. Full of surprises, aren't you, Anna?'

'You're not welcome here, Leo.' I pulled the scarf from my neck and showed my uncle the bruises. 'This is what he did to me last time he was here. Your son. He almost strangled me.' I turned back to Leo, all my pent-up anger turning my voice hard. 'Get out. I'm calling the police.' I made a grab for my phone, which was on the dresser, but Leo caught my arm before I could reach it. He squeezed my arm so tightly I gasped with pain. 'Ow! You're hurting me. Let go!'

Dad jumped to his feet. 'Get your hands off my daughter! Get out of this house. We're calling the police.' Two red spots appeared on his cheeks and I could hear his ragged breathing. He's not a tall man, my dad, but he's got a loud voice and has a way of intimidating people when he needs to. I didn't expect shouting to work this time, though, and I was terrified that Leo would hurt him.

'Dad,' I said, 'it's okay, sit back down.' I squared up to Stephanos as best I could with my arm twisted behind my back and my legs wobbling. 'Tell him to let me go, please.'

There was no response. I couldn't believe he'd let Leo hurt me. 'I'm not going to sign anything, so you can just take it away. How dare you come into my house and hurt me?' I glared at Laskaris, who sat calmly, holding papers and a pen. 'Go through Nikos' lawyers if you want to contest the will, but I won't sign. Go on, leave.'

It took all my self-control not to look up towards the bedroom, where Mum must be listening. Please let her have phoned the police. I gradually managed to pull my arm back down until it was at least by my side and not so painful, even if I was still held tight.

Stephanos and Laskaris looked at Leo, from which I understood that it was his job to make me say yes. I didn't like the fact that he seemed to be enjoying the role so much. Leo pulled me back towards the chair where the lawyer sat but I fought against him. 'This will never stand up in court, you know,' I shouted, trying not to let my voice shake too much. 'If this isn't duress, I don't know what is. This isn't legal. You can't *make* me sign anything.'

I tried to throw Leo's hand off my arm, but he wouldn't let go. He had a crazy expression on his face. Desperation, I thought.

Stephanos took control. 'Let us sit at your table. Allow me to explain the terms to you. At that point you may change your mind. Excuse my son, he can be overenthusiastic.'

Leo pushed me overenthusiastically through into the kitchen and onto a chair under the window. He sat next to me. The lawyer, fast on his feet, slid in on the other side so I couldn't escape. Dad also moved fast and sat opposite me. I gave him a look of gratitude. I was still quite frightened, more of this uncle who had Leo under such tight control than of Leo.

'Now, Anna,' said Stephanos. 'Laskaris is showing you the papers we would like you to sign. They will guarantee you a cash payment of twenty-five per cent of the total value of the estate on the death of your Uncle Nikos. It will be a considerable sum. You will sign the document, which will not come into effect until after your uncle dies, passing the businesses over to my son, Leo. You may, of course, keep any legacies et cetera made specifically to you.'

His eyes bored into me. I knew he was merely assessing the worthiness of the opposition. However, if I caved in at the thought of several million euros immediately, then it would save me and him a huge amount of legal work. A small part of me was tempted. My dad was ill, I didn't want the business. If I signed, it would all stop, and I'd still end up with more cash than I could ever have dreamed of.

I raised my eyes towards my father and he gave me the smallest of smiles and a subtle shake of the head. The rich American wasn't going to get it all his own way as far as he was concerned. I couldn't imagine what Dad was thinking about this first meeting with his younger brother, but I could see that my grandfather's worst traits had skipped to the youngest of the three. He was cruel, hard and all about the business.

'If you sign the document,' Stephanos continued, 'Nikos need never know of this agreement. He can live the rest of his life safe in the knowledge that you will inherit, and you can relax, knowing that you won't have to worry about the business aspects. It's a fair offer.'

Leo, who had been silent but bursting with tension, finally let go of my arm and banged on the table. 'Come on, Anna! You don't want all that hassle. Give it to me. I have as much right as you to inherit.' He rattled the papers and threw the pen at me. 'Sign the damn things.'

I kept both hands firmly clasped, mostly to stop them shaking. 'You can't make me do this. As I said before, take it through the courts.' I needed a better argument. 'Leo, Nikos could easily live another twenty or more years. He might not retire for another ten. You can't hang about doing nothing for all that time. Go and do something else. Go back to America.'

Dad said, 'My daughter will not sign your documents. I suggest you leave and I will inform my brother that you wish to challenge his intentions through the courts.' He pushed back his chair and stood up. 'I think that is all we have to say. Please leave.'

I tried to stand as well, but didn't get far. Laskaris, silent until now, hissed in my ear, 'It would be wise for you to sit and listen, Miss Georgiou, we are not finished yet.'

'Not finished with what?' came a gravelly voice from the front door. Uncle Nikos stood there, with his driver, Panos, standing behind him, looking menacing in his dark suit.

At that moment Mum came running down the stairs and into the kitchen, where she clung onto Dad. 'At last! Come in, Niko,' she said over her shoulder. 'I think you might want to hear what's going on. This person,' she spat the words at Leo, 'this person has attacked my daughter, bruised her neck and is now holding her captive. He tried to strangle her, Niko.' She then faced up to Stephanos, who also stood. 'And this man, this is your brother, apparently. You should be ashamed to come into my daughter's house like this. Ashamed.'

I have to hand it to her, my mother can do venom like Cruella de Vil.

Nikos stood next to Dad in the kitchen doorway. We were all standing by this time, crowded round my pine table. 'Theo,' he said, 'could you take your wife into the other room, please?' He moved into the small space they reluctantly vacated.

Mum and Dad backed into the living room, just far enough to give Nikos some room. They were both staring at me. I could feel them giving me strength.

'Niko,' snarled his younger brother, not bothering to disguise his disgust. 'Surprise, surprise. So here you are, top of the heap,

272

king of all you survey. You've done pretty well for yourself, haven't you? But of course you have, you had the best start in the world. It was all handed to you on a plate.'

'I was ready to apologise to you for that, Stephie. I made a terrible mistake when I was young. I can never make it up to you. I am sorry. I mean it. But you have done well in America. You have a fine family and a good business. Why come here to cause trouble? I can leave my business to whomever I please.'

'But it should be mine,' he retorted. 'What's the point in giving it to her? It's like throwing it all away on a whim. I'm just trying to get her to see sense. This is an agreement between me and this girl. It has nothing to do with you.'

Nikos spread his hands wide. 'And you use your thuggish son to achieve that aim by attempting to strangle my niece?' His eyes widened. 'Stephie, I had hoped for so much from our first meeting. It would have been over food, and drinks, and not this, whatever it is. Intimidation, threats, assault. You do things differently in America, hey?' He changed tack. 'What exactly did you want her to sign?' Nikos gestured to his companion. 'My assistant would be very interested to see the papers you have with you.'

Panos leant forward to take them from the table.

So did Leo. But I was closest. I grabbed them up, pressed them close to my chest and said, 'No. Just get out. I'm not signing anything.' I was close to tears. This wasn't the reunion I'd planned. Nothing like it. Stephanos gave off hate, in waves. I was so grateful to Nikos for taking control. He was used to the gladiatorial arenas of big business. I just wanted it all to stop.

'I think Anna has some rights, Stephano,' said Nikos again, refusing to lose his temper. 'It's hard to believe that we three brothers are in the same room for the first time in forty years and yet we are still at each other's throats.'

Dad pushed back into the kitchen. 'He's not my brother,

Niko. No longer. No brother of mine would allow his son to hurt my daughter, and approve of it. Stephie, you were the youngest and the brightest of us, but something bad has happened to you.'

Nikos said, 'That is true. You are your father's son, Stephano, but you're not our brother.' He reached across the table and took the papers from me, passing them to Panos before Leo could react. 'We will study these papers and decide what action to take. You' – he stared hard at Leo – 'you are not welcome here. You will never be welcome in Kissamos. Forget starting a business here.'

Nikos cocked his head at Stephanos. 'Accept it. There is nothing here for you. You have lost. It's better for you if you go home.' He stood back from the table, taking Dad with him so there was room for the men to pass. 'The sooner you leave the better, because when the police catch up with Leo here, they will arrest him for assault, and attempted murder, and in Crete that means a long prison sentence.'

'Which he deserves,' added Dad.

Stephanos boiled with rage. 'This is not over. You can't intimidate me with your threats. I'm not just going to go away and leave it. You owe me, Niko, and one way or another I'm going to get what I'm owed. I'll do whatever it takes.' He pushed past Nikos, shoving him hard against the cupboards and stormed out through the front door, closely followed by Laskaris and lastly Leo, who spared me a murderous glance as he followed his father to their car.

I collapsed back onto the chair and tried to calm my heart. What a family. Mum shuffled in next to me and held onto me, while Nikos scanned the documents.

'He made you a good offer, Anna, I think you might have been tempted?'

I let out a nervous laugh. 'I've never met a man so horrible.

No wonder Leo is a nasty piece of work. No, I'd never have agreed to his terms. It was a damn cheek anyway to start negotiating on the terms of a will before you're even dead!'

He smiled. 'Before I'm even ill, in fact.'

'Sorry, that didn't come out right. At least they've gone. Thank you for coming when you did. I was frightened that I wouldn't be able to hold out much longer. Oh, and thank you for bringing Panos. That made Leo think twice.'

Panos smiled and went back outside to guard the car, or whatever he got up to.

And now we had some talking to do.

32

The heat and anger disappeared out of the house on the breeze that blew a promise of the heat of summer through the open doors.

Dad, more grey-faced than I would have liked, said, 'I think you need to tell me what exactly has been going on, Anna.'

Mum pushed herself out of the chair. 'Well, I think I need to make us all a pot of coffee and we can just calm down a bit. I don't know about the rest of you, but I was terrified that awful boy was going to hurt Anna again. Look at her poor, poor neck! She could have died!'

I sighed. I couldn't put it off any longer. I pushed myself to my feet, even though all of me felt bruised, not just the new ones on my left arm. 'I suppose so. Will you stay, Uncle Niko, and help me tell the story?'

'I will. I need to make a call first, to let Delphine know what has happened, and to tell the police Leo is here in Kissamos.'

He wandered out into the spring sunshine and I helped Mum make coffee, and plate up the cakes we liked for breakfast. Little shivers kept running across my skin as my brain and body tried to work through the whole mess, and I tried to work out how to say what I needed to say to my parents.

Once Nikos returned, we told the story between us, but I didn't give details of the short relationship between me and Leo. They didn't need to know that. Mum moaned and cursed and generally overreacted her way through the telling, especially when it came to the assault. I couldn't blame her for being furious, it had been outrageous behaviour, and the more I thought about it, the angrier I became too. All over again. He nearly killed me.

By the time Nikos and I had finished, we had drunk the coffee, had another refill and finished off the pastries. Mum's coffee was stronger than I make it and I could feel the butterfly sensation and shakiness as it hit my system, and that combined with two paracetamol was giving me lots of messages, most of which said 'go to sleep'.

'And so,' said Nikos, 'I have changed my will and made Anna my heir.' He reached across and took my hand. 'I am happy to say that she has accepted, although she is already making me spend it.' He smiled at me.

Mum drained the dregs of her coffee and told Dad he had to rest.

'I will,' he said. 'But I can't stop thinking about Stephanos, and why he went so wrong. He was right in one thing, though, we really are strangers.' He got up, patted Nikos on the shoulder and went back up the stairs, followed by Mum, harassing him into bed for a nap.

'And you haven't had your medication,' she muttered on the stairs, 'all this excitement can't be good for you.'

Left on our own, I fought down the panicky sensation in the pit of my stomach and told Nikos what I'd been thinking about since the last time we had met. 'I have to say something to you, and I need you to listen and not get angry.'

He played with an unlit cigarette, tapping it onto the pack and flipping it over and over.

'You can smoke it if you like, the door is open.'

He lit up and took a deep inhalation. 'Thank you. Go on.'

I still hate smoking, hate it, but there is a time and a place, and he would need this one. 'I don't *want* to inherit your business. I only agreed to sign the document to help you.'

'What do you mean?'

'Stephanos will not just go away. If he can't get what he wants, he'll find a way. He'll alert the taxman, and have your books checked for irregularities. He's had Leo spying on you for months, looking for weaknesses. He'll find a way to get what he wants. It's about revenge, with him, not good sense. He will be haunting you for years, and so will Leo and I don't think I can cope with that. He scares me.'

Nikos let out a plume of smoke, nodding slowly. 'And you have a plan to solve this problem?'

Yipes. The crux of the matter. 'I think I do. How about selling the whole thing as a going concern? Now, or soon, and then retiring early? Get rid of the problem.'

To his credit, Nikos didn't react immediately. He took another drag on his cigarette and pushed smoke out through his teeth, peering at me under his heavy lids. 'And why should I do that? To give in to him?'

'No, you'll be making sure he never gets his hands on what is yours!' I took a moment to organise my thoughts. 'This is difficult to put into words. You see, I have no children, so I have no heirs either. I have no idea about managing a business like yours. I don't want anything to do with building houses, which, as far as I know, brings you in the bulk of your income.' I put my hand on his arm. 'Once you did pass on, I would just sell it all anyway. I want to live simply. I don't want all that responsibility or to be in fear of takeovers, like you have been. Or in fear for my life, as I have been. I can't live like that.'

'You would leave me with nothing?'

'No! Far from it. You would have a huge amount of money in the bank! Think about what you and Delphine could do with that. You've agreed to open a charitable foundation to help the young unemployed. Make that your task for the next few years. Use your money for good. Grow your status as a philanthropist, not a businessman. Make that your legacy to Crete. Otherwise, what use is money growing ever larger in a bank account when you already have all that you could ever want?'

He didn't look at me, or move for at least five minutes. I had no idea what he was thinking and could feel myself starting to fidget. 'You could hold onto the oil and wine businesses to keep you busy,' I tried.

Nikos stubbed out his cigarette on the edge of his plate, and stood up. 'I must go. I will think about what you have said, and talk about it with Delphine. Thank you for being honest, although it is a great disappointment to me. I thought I had found an heir for my business, perhaps I have not.' He gave me a sad smile. 'But at least I have an heir.'

I walked him to the front door, and he waved at Panos. He turned and gave me a kiss on the cheek and a hug. 'You are a remarkable person, Anna Georgiou. It is many years since I met someone who isn't frightened of me.'

As soon as I had closed the door, Mum clattered down the stairs. She also gave me a hug. 'So proud of you, darling.'

'Mum, were you listening to our private conversation?'

'Heard every word. It'll be a miracle if it works, but according to Irini, the tax people are after him anyway and he knows it, so the sooner he packs it all up, pays his taxes properly and does something good for the community, the better. Otherwise, he'll probably spend his last few years in prison.'

I was amazed. She'd picked up all this useful information in a couple of days. 'You don't like him much, do you?'

'Never did. Cruel, quick to put people down, and when he just went along with his father's evil wishes, well, I lost all respect for him. But you, you have seen a different man. He's in your debt now, and that's a good position to be in. I hope he will see sense.'

'So do I. I don't think my American uncle and cousin are going to hang about until he dies of old age, are they?'

'No, I can only think that their initial discussions with Nikos' lawyers didn't go so well, and that's why they thought they could put pressure on you, my brave girl.'

'Well, if there's any justice in the world, they'll be charged with assault and intimidation. At least Leo should be.'

'They may end up being deported.'

'Yes! Perfect.' I wanted them gone, forever, from my island. Not that I thought it would be that easy.

I piled plates and cups into the sink and ran water. 'Help me dry the dishes.' I passed her a tea towel. There was comfort in doing something simple. 'Is Dad asleep?'

'Yes, I made him get back into bed. I'm worried that by overdoing things he may set himself back. But, he's been more alive these last few days than he has been in a long time.' She found the cupboard and piled up the dry plates and cups. 'You have changed so much in these few months. I never saw that Will was holding you down, holding you back even, until now. You belong here I think, among the Cretan people.'

I carried on wiping down the worktops, emotions too close to the surface to speak. We finished the cleaning in silence.

'So, is this Alex "the one"?' she asked, doing air quotes.

I glanced at her. 'Yes, I think he is.'

She gave me a sly grin. 'Then perhaps, grandchildren may happen, eh?'

'I hope so, I really do.' I scrubbed at my eyes. Typical of my mother to have come through a dangerous situation, only to focus on the possibility of grandchildren. But then, why not? What had happened was so far out of our normal experience, it didn't compute. Grandchildren, so much longed for, did.

I knew I wasn't going to be able to settle the restlessness in my head if I stayed home. So when in doubt, shop. 'Shall we go out for a walk round town? The shops will still be open.'

Her eyes sparkled. 'Let's do it. I'll leave a note for your father in case he wakes up.' She shot upstairs to get ready and I locked the back door and tested the windows. I left the spare key for Dad on the table, so that I could lock the front door, too, without imprisoning him. It would be a while until I felt safe in my house. I wished the police would do their job.

I checked my phone and remembered that Delphine had arranged for her doctor to come to the house on Thursday morning to check on Dad. So I wrote that on the note for Dad as well. I texted her back, and gave her a summary of what I'd said to Nikos. It would give her a bit of forewarning. I had no idea what would happen once he got home, but at least she was prepared. Then I texted Alex and copied and pasted the same message to him, but with kisses.

That done, I dug out my bag and shoes, and put on a bit of makeup and off we set. I was in dire need of a few mindless shopping hours, pootling around the market.

33

We had a few quiet days where I didn't hear from Nikos, although I doubted he had forgotten me. Delphine's doctor came as promised, and whisked Dad off in a private ambulance to the hospital in Chania, almost giving Mum a heart attack, but he was returned the next day, looking and feeling better. He took to taking short walks into town, and renewing his old friendships, reading the newspaper in the café and chatting with the other men. He loved it. Mum spent time with Irini, visiting relatives and catching up. I avoided such excursions where possible, except for chauffeuring them to places in the car. I enjoyed the peace and seeing them so happy. I didn't see Alex for those few days, it was enough to enjoy their company.

There was still the niggling worry that Leo had not yet been arrested though. Crete is a big island, but I was surprised at his ability to hide. He did spend months tramping over the hills spying and he could easily survive up in the mountains for the summer if he chose to. I had a hope that he might have gone already, off with his father to plot their revenge from Athens. I still locked the house carefully and stayed alert. He wouldn't leave me alone, especially at night.

I took time out one afternoon to contact Cassia and Tinos, as Nikos and Delphine had agreed that I would be the one to break the good news about the new project. I arranged to meet them at Maria's taverna for a drink. Cassia had been intrigued on the phone but I gave nothing away until we were seated outside on the deck, looking out at the sea, and having to wear sunglasses against the glare reflected off the waves. In the distance, huge tankers plied their wares slowly across the bay. Summer was definitely on its way.

'So, what do you have to tell us, Anna?' asked Tinos, sipping beer from the bottle.

I didn't know quite where to begin. I told them my parents had come back for a holiday the week before, which explained my absence from Greek class, and then broke the family connection to the Kokorakis family. 'Don't worry, I won't develop bad landlord tendencies,' I said to their shocked faces.

Cassia got the first word in. 'You are Mr K's niece?' she spluttered. 'No!' She caught her twin's eye and they laughed in amazement. 'Well, I never suspected that. You have a saying in English, I think, "chalk and cheese". Is that right?'

'Too right. But he is my uncle and he and my dad have spoken for the first time in forty years, so all is good.' I didn't tell them about Leo and his father. It was all a bit raw.

'In fact, I have been working on Uncle Nikos over the last couple of weeks, to get him to put right what he did wrong. You know how Delphine and I have been helping the Andreanakises to buy a new house? Well, she and Nikos also want to help you, Tino. To make amends.'

Tinos looked out to sea, long fringe blowing back in the breeze. 'I don't want help from that man,' he said and the stubborn set of his jaw made me believe him.

However, the stubborn set of mine meant there was no way I was giving up. 'Just listen. They are setting up a charitable foundation, to offer help to unemployed local people, and they want you to run it. A training school for chefs and waiters that will have a café and possibly a restaurant or a bakery? Oh, I don't know, or anything else you think might be needed. Cassia, you could offer legal advice there, free, for example.'

Tinos didn't speak. He sucked on his beer.

Cassia jumped in. At least she was showing some excitement. 'Tino, get off your high horse and listen. You would be able to do what you have always wanted to do, free from worries about money, helping people get back to work. It could be fantastic!'

'With his money? His dirty money?' He shook his fringe aside as it blew into his eyes again.

She rolled her eyes. 'The money's not dirty, Tino. It's just money. Kokorakis' practices are dirty, sometimes, it's true, but this is a good thing he wants to do. Think about it.'

I burst in. 'Use it to do good, Tino. Please don't give up this chance because you're hurting.' Honestly, I'd never thought he would turn it down. It was his dream. Men, always letting pride make stupid decisions for them.

Cassia said, 'So, to be clear. This is Kokorakis trying to make us forget all that he has done to us?'

'No, not forget, make amends. He's fully aware of what he's done. Delphine has seen to that. Things are changing up there.'

Maria came out to see if we wanted anything else, and stopped halfway through a sentence when she sensed the mood. 'I can come back, sorry,' she said.

'No, stay. Maria, you can hear this too. Kokorakis wants to set up a charitable foundation for Tinos to run, teaching young people how to cook, and how to run a restaurant. The unemployed will benefit from this. They will be able to get jobs.'

'I don't want his dirty money,' said Tinos again.

Maria stuffed a cloth into her apron pocket and cocked her head to one side. 'So, you don't want to use his money, I understand that. But I think you're not in a position to refuse, are you? You either go back to Athens, with your tail between your legs, having achieved nothing, or you use this money to do good here on the island, and by God we need it.' She gave a huge shrug. 'Don't throw the donkey out because it brays at night.'

She may not have said exactly that, but some of these Greek proverbs really are beyond my ability to translate.

Cassia nudged her brother, who was holding onto his sore arm and had drifted away. Revisiting the night of the fire, I expected. 'Let it go,' she said. 'Let's take his money and do what we have always wanted. I'll make sure the legal paperwork is fair, and I'll help you. It could be wonderful, Tino.'

'It could,' said Maria. 'Come on, make the old bastard pay for once. You could make a beautiful school for cooking.'

Tinos looked up at her, and gave her an equally large shrug back. 'Okay, okay. You got me. I have to move on. I have to forget. But I don't have to like him, do I?' He held his hands up and batted his sister away before she could hug him, or speak. 'Stop it. Stop talking at me now, you three witches. Anna, what would I have to do?'

Phew.

'Nothing yet. Delphine will contact you when she has found some premises for you to look at. It will be her you deal with, not Nikos, so don't worry, although he does want to meet you. Thank you for saying yes. It's going to be wonderful. I think he can finally put right the wrongs that he did to you. Thanks for letting him do it.'

Maria put her hand on my shoulder and addressed the others. 'You must know that Anna has done all this, and she made Kokorakis give me the lease to the taverna, too, so I am not out on the street. This is all mine now.' She did a twirl on the deck. 'She has done so much since she came here to change how things are. How they have always been. Let us celebrate that.' And with that, out came the raki, and we toasted the future.

The call for us to go up to the big house came on the following Saturday. I realised that my parents had been on the island for almost a week and we hadn't had a conversation about the future yet. I should have realised that Delphine would have something planned.

We arrived just after two in the afternoon, on a glorious day with a pale-blue sky and the smell of wild flowers in the air. We walked up the hill, and Dad was happy to get a little exercise. The sun had begun to tan his skin, and he was tolerating food better. Mum looked great too; she was happier than I had seen her for a long time. I must have been blind not to have noticed that the restaurant had become not just too much for them, but something they didn't want to do anymore. Dad's illness had given them the perfect excuse to find a new owner. I briefly hoped Michael was enjoying himself back in wet old Manchester.

But then I wondered how difficult it is to give up what you know, especially if it has been giving you a good living for so many years? That was a question we would face that afternoon.

Delphine met us on the drive and led us, not into the big house, but over to the villa, where the doors were open and the curtains drawn back. 'Welcome,' she said, and gave us all hugs. 'I thought you should see your old home as it could be, Theo, not wearing shrouds as it was last week. Come in.'

She'd been working hard. The rooms were bright and sunny. She must have had a cleaning company in, as everywhere sparkled. She led us through each room downstairs, and I watched my dad seeing it all again, and thinking of his mother and father. It was so long since anyone had lived there. Sad, really.

The old furniture was still in place, but Delphine had put new cushions and throws on the sofas, and tablecloths on the tables and had the wood polished until it shone. It was fascinating for me. It was still a traditional Cretan house, with framed photographs of relatives I didn't know on the walls, a huge dresser decked with china in the dining room, and in the kitchen, three small barrels standing one on top of the other in a corner. They looked like they had been there forever. Nikos was standing in front of the barrels, waiting for us and holding a tray of small glasses.

'Anna, you may not know our tradition,' he said, 'but when a Cretan child is born, his parents put aside a barrel of wine, usually their own wine, and save it to drink when that child turns eighteen, then twenty-one, when they marry, or have a baby. On many, many occasions. This' – he indicated the middle barrel – 'is Theo's barrel. Do you remember, Theo?'

Dad spread his hands wide. 'Of course I remember. We drank it at my eighteenth birthday. It was like nectar.'

'Then we should drink today, for today I have my family back and we are at home.' He poured us all a small glass and toasted Dad with a hearty, 'Yiamas!'

It tasted like port, and was absolutely delicious. 'Wow, Dad, you're a good vintage,' I said, and he laughed.

'Yiamas to you all,' Dad said, and we had to down the second glass in one. It was certainly warming.

'And now,' said Nikos, 'we should try my wine, which is even older, and even better.' So we did.

I may be biased, but Dad's was nicer, and I couldn't help

looking at the third barrel, and thinking how sad it was that Stephanos would never get to drink his own barrel of wine.

Delphine led us through into the dining room, which was set for lunch, and I admired some very old plates and bowls full to the brim with food.

'They were Nyssa's pride and joy,' said Delphine, 'and it's right that we are using them again.'

As usual, the housekeeper, Eleni, was on hand to serve us and we tucked into another excellent meal. I really was going to have to get cookery lessons from her.

At the end of the meal, during which I kept stealing glances at Nikos to try to gauge his mood, he called us to order. I'd been discussing the Andreanakis house with Mum and Delphine, but we soon quietened down. Nikos stood up and cleared his throat.

'I have not set foot in this house since our father died fifteen years ago. Our mother did not come home at all once Theo and Stephanos left. Father broke her heart forever. I know that you, Galena, had some contact with her when Anna was very young, and it must have been a comfort to her to know that you were doing well and had a child of your own to love.' He smiled sadly at Delphine. 'We have never been so lucky. But when Anna came to the island, it changed everything. In a few short weeks our lives have completely altered, and it is down to her.'

He put a hand out to stop me from interrupting. 'No, I know that Leo and his father coming here were not your doing, and I'm not talking about that nonsense. It was a horrible time. I meant that you have made me look at myself, and what I have become.'

I didn't dare look at the others. Would he do what I'd suggested?

'When my father died, I had little in my life except work. I found Delphine, but it was too late, I had become entranced by my own ability to make money. And I was cruel, I know that now. Of course, I made the excuse that it was just business as I had somebody beaten up or took back their home when they couldn't pay up. I never allowed myself to feel anything, it was easier that way.' He looked at Delphine and his eyes filled with tears. 'Why you stayed with me, I will never know. But I am grateful. Life without you would be like a death for me.' He took a sip of wine and rubbed his brow.

'So, today I have come to a decision. Theo, Galena, come home. Take this house, it is yours.'

Dad stood up to face his elder brother. 'You mean this?'

Nikos grinned at him. 'Please, come back.'

Dad turned to Mum, took her hand and asked her, 'Do you want this? Would you live here with me?'

'Of course I would, you old fool,' she said. 'Haven't I wanted this for half my life? We can come home. We can live in our own town with our own people, in your family home. Of course I want to! Thank you, Niko, I appreciate what you have done for us.' She dipped her head at him.

'Then we will accept,' said Dad. 'Thank you.' He raised his glass and we had a toast. I stole a glance at Delphine, who was looking straight at me. She winked.

Mum's smile was so wide it almost made me cry, and I may have had a little weep when Dad sat down and kissed my mother and they held onto each other like teenagers. They were coming here to live, with me. It was more than I could have hoped for.

'And I have more news for you,' said Delphine. 'The chief of police rang Nikos this morning. Leo was arrested early today on board a container ship bound for Italy. His father is back in Athens and will be charged, too. So you are safe!'

I didn't know what to say. A huge and heavy weight lifted from me. I'd hardly realised I was carrying it around until it was gone. 'Will Leo go to prison?'

Nikos said, 'He will if you are prepared to testify against him. The police have the photographs, and we can get the officer and doctor to support you.' He stared intently at me.

I didn't hesitate. 'Of course I'll go to court. He needs to be punished, and so does his father. Sorry, I know Stephanos is your brother, but you can't go around behaving like he does, can you?' I was feeling breathless at the thought of going into court and facing them again, but I had to toughen up if I was going to get justice. 'Yes, I'll do it.'

'Good. Good,' said Nikos, 'then we will make sure that justice is done. Now you can put him out of your mind for several months, and enjoy yourself, can't you?'

'Yes, I think I can,' I replied, and laughed with them all.

We had another walk around the house after lunch, Mum peering into all the rooms, and me planning décor in my head. Even Nikos was relaxed and smiling. It was a happy afternoon.

Delphine asked Panos to drive us home, as Dad was reeling, and not from the drink he had consumed, he was in shock. 'I don't know if I can cope,' he said, and sat quietly on a sofa until the car came round to the front of the villa.

Nikos took me off into a corner. 'I am thinking about what you said, Anna. You are right. Delphine and I could live simply and I wouldn't have to be in fear for my future all the time if I sold to the vultures who are gathering.' He gave me a dry kiss on the cheek. 'I will think some more.'

'Thank you, for all of this, and for bringing my father back to his home.'

'I didn't do it, you did. I should have done it years ago. How I have wasted all our lives through this nonsense. And Stephie, little Stephie. I have to blame myself for what he has become.' He shook his head and led me out to the car.

'That's not true, Uncle. Your father made him that way, not

you.' I clambered into the car after my parents, noting Mum's concerned face.

⁓

'Off for a nap with you, Theo,' she said as soon as we got in the house. 'We have some thinking and planning to do, and I want you clear-headed.'

Dad dutifully climbed the stairs. 'I need to lie down,' he said, and I heard him get into bed.

Mum took my hand as soon as we were alone. 'I don't know what you did to change Nikos but well done. You've given us a whole new future to look forward to, and your father actually listened to you. A miracle,' she said, laughing quietly.

I laughed too, but with relief. 'I'm really hoping that Nikos agrees to sell, and steps away from the business. It's running those huge businesses that has made him a hard man, but it's right that he should pay for what he's done.'

Her eyes widened.

'Don't worry, he's already agreed to most of what I asked him to do. Who knows, he may give up the business after all. Especially to avoid the taxman.'

She laughed, then looked more serious. 'And what about this Leo, your cousin? You haven't told me all about him, have you?' She wasn't stupid, my mum.

'We had a brief fling. Really, that's all it was. I knew straight away that there was something wrong about him. I knew I couldn't trust him, but it was difficult to put my finger on exactly what was wrong about him.' I rubbed my neck. 'Then I found out what he was really like. I'm already dreading having to face them both in court, but I'll get through it, because you'll be with me, won't you? But let's not think about them now, let's do more important stuff.'

We settled down on the sofa then, me with my laptop and Mum with a notepad and pen.

'So,' she said, 'what did you have to do first when you moved out here?'

The afternoon wore on, and we enjoyed plotting and planning together, but I had a small ache somewhere in the region of my heart. 'Mum, I want to go and see Alex, and tell him what's happened. I haven't seen him for days. Will you and Dad be all right on your own tonight? There's plenty of food if you can stuff anymore in, and you can watch a film if you like, although I guess you have a lot to talk about, too.'

'We'll be fine. In fact, it will be easier if we are on our own so I can talk freely to him. For a start, we'll need to ring Michael and accept his offer. I have so much to arrange.' She threw her pen into the air and caught it. 'You know, darling, I can't tell you how happy I will be to turn my back on that dingy flat and the sheer slog of running that restaurant. I never thought this could ever happen. It was just a dream.' She started to cry, and waved me off. 'Go and see your man, we'll be fine.'

Elation is the most fleeting emotion, but one of the very best. I strode out along the prom feeling light, as if only willpower could stop me from flying away into the endless blue of the sky. I was giddy with it, the feeling that life would be good. That the world was full of possibilities. Why did I have to be a designer all year round? Couldn't I do that over the winter months? Could I cook on a boat? Could I be with Alex all the time?

When I got to the boatyard, I was horrified to see that the yacht had gone from its dry dock. Then I stopped panicking and walked a little further to the marina, where the yacht was tied up against a jetty, and Alex was working on the deck wearing his usual tatty cut-off denims and an ancient T-shirt. He looked gorgeous, and my heart leapt in a way it never had.

He wiped his hands on a rag and gave me the most beautiful smile. Never had a summer cooking on a yacht looked more inviting.

THE END

ACKNOWLEDGEMENTS

It takes many minds to make a book but firstly I'd like to thank Betsy Reavley at Bloodhound Books for supporting me in a complete change of genre from crime mysteries to novels more rooted in relationships, and to the team at Bloodhound who make it all happen. Also thanks go to my very early readers, Liz Pinfield and Cathy White for suggestions and comments which helped strengthen the story. It was great to work with Ian Skewis as my editor; he helped me make a better, tighter book. Finally, thanks to Stuart Steadman and those close friends who always encourage me to get on with it, rather than just sit and talk about it.

Printed in Great Britain
by Amazon

50982075R00180